THE ATTACHÉ

OR SAM SLICK IN ENGLAND

THE ATTACHÉ

OR SAM SLICK IN ENGLAND

Thomas Chandler Haliburton

Duplex libelli dos est; quod risum movet,
Et quod prudenti vitam consilio monet.

NONSUCH

First published 1844
Copyright © in this edition 2005
Nonsuch Publishing Ltd

Nonsuch Publishing Limited
The Mill, Brimscombe Port, Stroud, Gloucestershire, GL5 2QG
www.nonsuch-publishing.com

Distributed in Canada by Vanwell Publishing

British Library Cataloguing in Publication Data.
A catalogue record for this book is available from the British Library.

ISBN 1-84588-049-8

Typesetting and origination by Nonsuch Publishing Limited
Printed in Great Britain by Oaklands Book Services Limited

CONTENTS

INTRODUCTION TO THE MODERN EDITION

Sam's a cute man Gineral ... It's generally allowed a man
must rise airly in the morning' to catch him asleep, I can tell
you.

Sam Slick, the Yankee observer who turned his keen eye and sharp wit on
the life of colonial Nova Scotia, and who was to become one of the most
popular literary characters in nineteenth-century English literature, was
first introduced in the pages of *The Novascotian* in 1835. The character
and his observations rapidly became a hit with the general public and *The
Clockmaker, or the Sayings and Doings of Sam Slick*, a collection of sketches
from *The Novascotian*, was published in 1837 in London and quickly
followed by two more volumes in 1838 and 1840.

The author of these stories, Thomas Chandler Haliburton, was born
in Windsor, Nova Scotia in 1796. Haliburton came from a distinguished
'Blue Blood' family, and he followed his father and grandfather into law,
being called to the bar in 1819 and establishing a successful law practice
in Annapolis Royal, Nova Scotia's old capital, in 1820. As well as law,
he had a profound interest in the rather turbulent politics of the time
and from 1826-1829 he served as a member of the provincial House of
Assembly. On his father's death in 1829 Haliburton was appointed to his
vacant seat in Court of Common Pleas for the Middle Division of Nova
Scotia and in 1841 was elevated to the Supreme Court of Nova Scotia.
Outside his judicial role, Haliburton was also an active businessman. He
was president of the Windsor Agricultural Society, a major investor in a

gypsum mine and president of a joint stock company which owned the
Avon River Bridge in Windsor.

Haliburton's career as an author was launched in 1823 with the
publication of the historical work *General Description of Nova Scotia*,
followed in 1829 by the two volume *Historical and Statistical Account of
Nova Scotia*. In total he was to write four histories, as well as a number of
political pamphlets and a book on colonial policy in Canada, *The Bubbles
of Canada*, published in 1839. However, it was to be his fictional works, in
particular the Sam Slick novels, which were to be his enduring legacy to
Canadian and world literature. The character of Sam Slick was developed
as a means to express Haliburton's more liberal politics without offending
the Anglican conservative ruling elite, which dominated Canadian politics
at this time. As a member of this elite, Haliburton was unable to openly
express his progressive views without repercussions, and so he used the
character of Slick as his mouthpiece.

After the success of the three volumes of *The Clockmaker*, not only
in Canada, but in America and Britain, the demand for more Sam Slick
stories led Haliburton to send his character to England, in the role
of attaché in an American diplomatic mission to the British imperial
government. Haliburton himself had close links to England. Both his
paternal and maternal grandparents were English immigrants and on
a visit to his stepmother's relations in Henley-on-Thames in 1816
Haliburton met and married his first wife, Louisa Neville, who was the
daughter of a captain in the 19th Light Dragoons. In April 1838, when
he took his second volume of *The Clockmaker* to England for publication,
he actively sought government patronage which would allow him to
move to England. Finally, in 1856, when he was forced to retire from
the Supreme Court on the grounds of ill health, Haliburton chose to
leave Nova Scotia and move to England permanently. He married Sarah
Harriet Williams, an English widow, and settled in Islesworth, becoming
MP for Launceston, North Cornwall, for six years.

Despite his fondness for Britain, Haliburton does not allow this to
stop his character from satirising its traditions and politics. Slick, the
Episcopalian preacher Joshua Hopewell and the previously unnamed
narrator, Squire Thomas Poker, Esq., all have their chance to comment on
a wide range of subjects, from Britain's colonial policy to girls' boarding
schools. Interestingly, in *The Attaché* the author uses the character of

Hopewell to express his more conservative views and reservations about the democratic movement that was developing in America.

Although after the publication of *The Attaché* Haliburton announced his retirement of the character, due to popular demand and financial considerations after problems with his gypsum business, the character was resurrected for two final series again set in Nova Scotia, *Sam Slick's Wise Saws and Modern Instances*, published in 1853, and *Nature and Human Nature*, published in 1855. In 1858 the University of Oxford recognised Haliburton's contribution to literature when he became the first colonial writer to be awarded an honorary degree in literature by this university.

In the mid-nineteenth century Thomas Chandler Haliburton's work rivalled Dickens in popularity and he was the only colonial writer to achieve an international reputation during that time. Haliburton's fame continues to the present day and Sam Slick is rightly considered to be one of the great classic Canadian literary figures of all times.

VOLUME I

VOLUME 1

I

THE OLD AND THE NEW WORLD

THE first series of this work had scarcely issued from the press, when I was compelled to return to Nova Scotia, on urgent private affairs. I was fortunately not detained long, and arrived again at Liverpool after an absence of three months. To my surprise, I found Mr. Slick at the Liner's Hotel. He was evidently out of spirits, and even the excitement of my unexpected return did not wholly dissipate his gloom. My fears were at first awakened for the safety of my excellent friend Mr. Hopewell, but I was delighted to find that he was in good health, and in no way the cause of Mr. Slick's anxiety. I pushed my enquiries no further, but left it to him to disclose, as I knew he would in due time, the source of his grief. His outer man was no less changed than his countenance. He wore a dress-coat and pantaloons, a gaudy-figured silk waistcoat, black satin stock, and Parisian hat. A large diamond brooch decorated his bosom, and a heavy gold chain, suspended over his waistcoat, secured his watch; while one of very delicate texture and exquisite workmanship supported an eye-glass. To complete the metamorphos, he had cultivated a very military moustache, and an imperial of the most approved size finished the picture. I was astonished and grieved beyond measure to find that three short months had effected such a total change in him. He had set up for a man of fashion, and in his failure had made himself, what he in his happier days would have called "a caution to sinners." His plain unpretending attire, frank rough manners, and sound practical good sense, had heretofore always disarmed criticism, and rendered his peculiarities, if not attractive, at least inoffensive and amusing; in as much as altogether they constituted a very original and a very striking character. He had now rendered himself ridiculous. It is impossible to express the pain with which I contemplated this awkward, over-dressed, vulgar caricature; and the difficulty with which I recognised my old friend the Clockmaker in dandy Slick. Dress, however, can be put on or laid aside with ease, but fortunately a man's train of thinking is not so readily changed. It was a source of great satisfaction to me, therefore, to find, as soon as he began to converse, that, with the exception of a very great increase of personal vanity, he was still himself.

"Well, I am glad to see you again, too, Squire," he said, "it railly makes me feel kinder all-overish to shake hands along with you onct more; and won't Minister feel hand-over-foot in a twitteration when he hears you've come back. Poor dear old critter, he loves you like a son; he says you are the only man that has done us justice, and that though you rub us pretty hard sometimes, you touch up the blue noses, and the British, too, every mite and mossel as much, and that it is all done good-natured, and no spite or prejudice in it nother. There is no abuse in your books, he says. Yes, I am glad to see you, 'cause now I *have* got some one to talk to, that *has* got some sense, and *can* understand me, for the English don't actilly know nothin' out of their own diggins. There is a great contrast atween the Old and the New World, ain't there? I was talking to John Russel the other day about it."

"Who is *he*?" I said; "is he a skipper of one of the liners?"

"Lord love you, no; he is the great noble—Lord Russel—the leadin' Whig statesman. It's only about a week ago I dined with him to Norfolk's—no, it warn't to Norfolk's, it was to Normanby's."

"Is that the way," I again asked, "that you speak of those persons?"

"Isn't it the way they speak to each other?" said he; "doesn't Wellington say, 'Stanley, shall I take wine with you?' and if *they* do, why shouldn't I? It mayn't be proper for a common Britisher to say so, because they ain't equal; but it's proper for us, for we *are*, that's a fact; and if it wa'n't boastin', superior too, (and look at here, who are these big bugs now, and what was they originally?) for we have natur's nobility. Lord, I wish you could hear Steverman talk of them and their ceremonies."

"Don't you follow Steverman's example, my good friend," I said; "he has rendered himself very ridiculous by assuming this familiar tone. It is very bad taste to talk that way, and no such absurd ceremony exists of creating peers, as I understand he says there is; that is a mere invention of his to gratify democratic prejudice. Speak of them and to them as you see well-bred people in this country do, neither obsequiously nor familiarly, but in a manner that shows you respect both them and yourself."

"Come, I like that talk," said Mr. Slick; "I'm a candid man, I am indeed, and manners is a thing I rather pride my self on. I ha'n't had no great schoolin' that way in airly days, but movin' in high life, as I do, I want to sustain the honour of our great nation abroad; and if there is a wrong figur' I'm for spitten' on the slate, rubbin' it out and puttin' in a right one. I'll ask Minister what he thinks of it, for he is a book; but you, ('xcuse me, Squire, no offence I hope, for I don't mean none,) but you are nothin' but a colonist you see, and don't know everything. But, as I was a sayin', there is a nation sight of difference too, ain't there, atween an old and a new country? but come, let's go into the coffee-room, and sit down, and talk, for sitten' is just as cheap as standin' in a general way."

This spacious apartment was on the right hand of the entrance hall, furnished and fitted in the usual manner. Immediately behind it was the bar-room, which communicated with it in one corner by an open window, and with the hall by a similar aperture. In this corner sat or stood the bar-maid for the purpose of receiving and communicating orders.

"Look at that gall," said Mr. Slick, 'ain't she a smasher? What a tall, well-made, handsome piece of furniture she is, ain't she? Look at her hair, ain't it neat? and her clothes fit so well, and are so nice, and her cap so white, and her complexion so clear, and she looks so good-natured, and smiles so sweet, it does one good to look at her. She is a whole team and a horse to spare, that gall,—that's a fact. I go and call for two or three glasses of brandy-cocktail more than I want every day, just for the sake of talking to her. She always says, 'What will you be pleased to have, sir?' 'Somethin',' says I, 'that I can't have,' lookin' at her pretty mouth about the wickedest; well, she laughs, for she knows what I mean; and says, 'P'r'aps you will have a glass of bitters, sir?' and she goes and gets it. Well, this goes on three or four times a day, every time the identical same tune, only with variations.

"About an hour afore you come in I was there agin. 'What will you be pleased to have, sir?' says she agin, laughin'. 'Somethin' I can't get,' says I, a laughin' too, and a smackin' of my lips and a lettin' off sparks from my eyes like a blacksmith's chimney. 'You can't tell that till you try,' says she;

'but you can have your bitters at any rate,' and she drawed a glass and gave it to me. It tan'te so bad that, is it? Well, now she has seed you before, and knows you very well; go to her and see how nicely she will courtshy, how pretty she will smile, and how lady-like she will say, 'How do do, sir? I hope you are quite well, sir; have you just arrived?—Here, chambermaid, show this gentleman to No. 200.—Sorry, sir, we are so full, but to-morrow we will move you into a better room.—Thomas, take up this gentleman's luggage;" and then she'd courtshy agin, and smile handsome. Don't that look well now? do you want anything better nor that, eh? if you do, you are hard to please, that's all. But stop a bit, don't be in such an everlastin' almighty hurry; think afore you speak; go there agin—set her a smilin' once more, and look close. It's only skin deep—just on the surface, like a cat's paw on the water, it's nothin' but a rimple like, and no more; then look closer still and you will desearn the color of it.

"I see you laugh at the color of a smile, but still watch and you'll see it. Look now, don't you see the color of the shilling there, it's white, and cold, and silvery,—*it's a bought smile*, and a bought smile, like an artificial flower, has no sweetness in it. There is no natur—it's a cheat—it's a pretty cheat—it don't ryle you none, but still it's a cheat. It's like whipt cream; open your mouth wide, take it all in, and shut your lips down on it tight, and it's nothin'—it's only a mouthful of moonshine; yes, it's a pretty cheat, that's a fact. This ain't confined to the women nother. Petticoats have smiles and courtshys, and the trowsers bows and scrapes, and my-lords for you, there ain't no great difference that way; so send for the landlord. 'Lardner,' says you, 'Sir,' says he, and he makes you a cold, low, deep, formal bow, as much as to say, 'Speak, Lord, for thy sarvent is a dog.' 'I want to go to church to-morrow,' says you; 'what church do you recommend?' Well, he eyes you all over, careful, afore he answers, so as not to back up a wrong tree. He sees you are from t'other side of the water; he guesses, therefore, you can't be a church-man, and must be a radical: and them that calculate that way miss a figure as often as not, I can tell you. So he takes his cue to please you. 'St. Luke's, sir, is a fine church, and plenty of room, for there ain't no congregation; M'Neil's church has no congregation, nother, in a manner; you can only call it a well-dressed mob,—but it has no room; for folks go there to hear politics.' 'Why what is he?' says you. 'Oh, a church man,' says he, with a long face as if he was the devil. 'No,' says you, 'I don't mean that; but what is his politics?' 'Oh, sir, I am sorry to say, violent—, 'Yes; but what are they?' 'Oh,' says he, lookin' awful shocked, 'tory, sir.' 'Oh, then,' says you, 'he's just the boy that will suit me, for I am tory too, to the back-bone.' Lardner seems whamble-cropt, scratches his head, looks as if he was delivered of a mistake, bows, and walks off, a sayin' to himself—'Well, if that don't pass, I swear; who'd a thought that cursed long-backed, long-necked, punkin-headed colonist was a churchman and a tory? The ugly devil is worse than he looks, d—n him.'

"Arter takin' these two samples out of the bulk, now go to Halifax, Nova Scotia, and streak it off to Windsor, hot foot. First stage is Bedford Basin. Poor, dear old Marm Bedford, the moment she sets eyes on you, is out to meet you in less than half no time. Oh, look at the colour of that smile. It's a good wholesome reddish-colour, fresh and warm from the heart, and it's more than skin-deep, too, for there is a laugh walking arm-in-arm with it, lock and lock, that fetches her sides up with a hitch at every jolt of it. Then that hand ain't a ghost's hand, I can tell you, it's good solid flesh and blood, and it gives you a shake that says, 'I'm in rail, right down airnest.' 'Oh, Squire, is that you?—well, I am glad to see you; you are welcome home agin:—we was most afeered you was goin' to leave us; folks made so much of you t'other side of the water. Well, travellin' agrees with you—it does indeed—you look quite hearty agin.'

"'But, come,' says you, 'sit down, my old friend, and tell me the news, for I have seen nobody yet; I only landed two hours ago. 'Well,' she'll say, 'the Admiral's daughter's married, and the Commissioner's daughter is married:' and then, shuttin' the door, 'they do say Miss A. is to be married to Colonel B. and the widow X. to lawyer V. but I don't believe the last, for she is too good for him: he's a low, radical fellow, that, and she has too much good sense to take such a creature as him.' 'What bishop was that I saw here just now?' says you. 'A Westindgy bishop,' says she; 'he left half-an-hour ago, with a pair of hosses, two servants, three pounds of butter, a dozen of fresh eggs, and a basket of blue berries.' But Miss M., what do you think, Squire? she has given Captain Tufthunt the mitten, she has indeed, upon my word!—fact, I assure you. Ain't it curious, Squire, weddin's is never out of women's heads. They never think of nothin' else. A young gall is always thinkin' of her own; as soon as she is married, she is a match makin' for her companions, and when she is a little grain older, her darter's weddin' is uppermost agin. Oh, it takes great study to know a woman,—how cunnin' they are! Ask a young gall the news, she'll tell you of all the deaths in the place, to make you think she don't trouble herself about marriages Ask an old woman, she'll tell you of all the marriages to make you think she is takin' an interest in the world that she ain't. They sartainly do beat all, do women. Well, then, Marm will jump up all of a sudden, and say, 'But, dear me, while I am a sitten' here a talkin', there is no orders for your lunch; what will you have, Squire.' 'What you can't get anywhere in first chop style,' says you, 'but in Nova Scotia, and never here in perfection but at your house—a broiled chicken and blue-nose potatoes.' 'Ah!' says she, puttin' up her finger and lookin' arch, 'now you are makin' fun of us, Squire?' 'Upon my soul I am not,' says you, and you may safely swear to that too, I can tell you; for that house has a broiled chicken and a potatoe for a man that's in a hurry to move on, that may stump the world. Well, then you'll light a cigar, and stroll out to look about the location, for you know every tree, and stone, and brook, and hill, about there, as well as you know beans, and they will talk to the heart as plain as if they was gifted with gab. Oh, home is home, however homely, I can tell you. And as you go out, you see faces in the bar-room you know, and it's 'Oh, Squire, how are you?—Welcome home agin,—glad to see you once more; how have you had your health in a general way?—Saw your folks driven out yesterday—they are all well to home.'

"They don't take their hats off, them chaps, for they ain't dependants, like tenants here: most of them farmers are as well off as you be, and some on 'em better; but they jist up and give you a shake of the daddle, and ain't a bit the less pleased; your books have made 'em better known, I can tell you. They are kinder proud of 'em, that's a fact. Then the moment your back is turned, what's their talk?—why it's, 'Well it's kinder nateral to see him back here again among us, ain't it; he is lookin' well, but he is broken a good deal, too; he don't look so cheerful as he used to did, and don't you mind, as he grows older, he looks more like his father, too?' 'I've heered a good many people remark it,' says they.—'Where on airth,' says one, 'did he get all them queer stories he has sot down in his books, and them Yankee words, don't it beat all natur?' 'Get them,' says another; 'why he is a sociable kind of man, and as he travels round the circuits, he happens on a purpose, accidentally like, with folks, and sets 'em a talkin', or makes an excuse to light a cigar, goes in, sets down and hears all and sees all. I mind,

I drove him to Liverpool, to court there onct, and on our way we stopt at
Sawaway village. Well, I stays out to mind the horse, and what does he do
but goes in, and scrapes acquaintance with Marm,—for if there is a man
and a woman in the room, petticoats is sartain to carry the day with him.
Well, when I come back, there was him and Marm a standin' up by the
mantel-piece, as thick as two thieves, a chattin' away as if they had knowed
each other for ever a'most. When she come out, says she, 'Who on airth is
that man? he is the most sociable man I ever seed.' 'That,' says I, 'why it's
Lawyer Poker.' 'Poker!' says she, in great fright, and a rasin' of her voice,
'which Poker, for there is two of that name, one that lives to Halifax, and
one that lives to Windsor; which is it?' says she, 'tell me this minnit.' 'Why,'
says I, 'him that wrote the "Clockmaker."' 'What, Sam Slick?' says she, and
she screamed out at the tip eend of her tongue, 'Oh, my goodies! if I had
knowed that I wouldn't have gone into the room on no account. They say,
though he appears to take no notice, nothin' never escapes him; he hears
everything, and sees everything, and has his eye in every cubby-hole. Oh,
dear, dear, here I am with the oldest gownd on I have, with two buttons off
behind, and my hair not curled, and me a talkin' away as if he was only a
common man! It will be all down in the next book, see if it ain't. Lord love
you, what made you bring him here,—I am frighten to death; oh, dear! oh,
dear! only think of this old gownd!'—That's the way he gets them stories,
he gets them in travellin'.'

"Oh, Squire, there's a vast difference atween a thick peopled and a thin
peopled country. Here you may go in and out of a bar-room or coffee-
room a thousand times and no one will even ax who you are. They don't
know, and they don't want to know. Well then, Squire, just as you are a
leaven of Bedford-house to progress to Windsor, out runs black Jim, (you
recollect Jim that has been there so long, don't you?) a grinnin' from ear
to ear like a catamount, and opens carriage door. 'Grad to see you back,
massa; miss you a travellin' shocking bad, sar. I like your society werry
much, you werry good company, sar.' You give him a look as much as to
say, 'What do you mean, you black rascal?' and then laugh, 'cause you
know he tried to be civil, and you give him a shilling, and then Jim
shows you two rods of ivory, such as they never seed in this country, in
all their born days. Oh, yes, smile for smile, heart for heart, kindness for
kindness, welcome for welcome—give me old Nova Scotia yet;—there
ain't nothin' like it here."

There was much truth in the observations of Mr. Slick, but at the same time they are not free from error. Strangers can never expect to be received in any country with the same cordiality friends and old patrons are; and even where the disposition exists, if crowds travel, there is but little time that can be spared for congratulations. In the main, however, the contrast he has drawn is correct, and every colonist, at least, must feel, that this sort of civility is more sincere and less mercenary in the *new* than in the *old world*.

II

THE BOARDING-SCHOOLS

WHILE strolling about the neighbourhood of the town this afternoon, we passed what Colonel Slick would have called "several little detachments of young ladies," belonging to a boarding-school, each detachment having at its head an officer of the establishment. Youth, innocence, and beauty, have always great attractions for me; I like young people, I delight in talking to them. There is a joyousness and buoyancy about them, and they are so full of life and hope, it revives my drooping spirits, it awakens agreeable recollections, and makes me feel, for the time at least, that I am young myself. "Look at those beautiful creatures," I said, "Mr. Slick. They seem as happy as birds just escaped from a cage."

"Yes," said he, "and what a cussed shame it is to put 'em into a cage at all. In the West Indgies, in old times, every plantation had a cage for the little niggers, a great large enormous room, and all the little darkies was put in there and spoon-fed with meal-vittals by some old granny, and they were as fat as chickens and as lively as crickets, (you never see such happy little imps of darkness since you was born,) and their mothers was sent off to the fields to work. It saved labor and saved time, and labor and time is money, and it warn't a bad contrivance. Well, old Bunton, Joe Sturge, and such sort of cattle of the Abolition breed, when they heerd of this, went a roarin' and a bellowin' about all over England, like cows that had lost their calves, about the horrid cruelty of these nigger coops.

"Now, these boardin'-schools for gals here is a hundred thousand times wuss than the nurseries was. Mothers send their children here 'cause they are too lazy to tend 'em, or too ignorant to teach 'em themselves, or 'cause they want 'em out o' the way that they may go into company, and not be kept to home by kickin', squeelin', gabblin' brats; and what do they larn here? why, nothin' that they had ought to, and everything that they had ought not to. They don't love their parents, 'cause they haint got that care, and that fondlin', and protection, and that habit that breeds love. Love won't grow in cold ground, I can tell you. It must be sheltered from the frost, and protected from the storm, and watered with tears, and warmed with the heat of the heart, and the soil be kept free from weeds; and it must have support to lean on, and be tended with care day and night, or it pines, grows yaller, fades away, and dies. It's a tender plant is love, or else I don't know human natur, that's all. Well, the parents don't love them nother. *Mothers can get weaned as well as babies.* The same causes almost makes folks love their children, that makes their children love them. Who ever liked another man's flower-garden as well as his own? Did you ever see one that did, for I never did? He haint tended it, he haint watched its growth, he haint seed the flowers bud, unfold, and bloom. *They haint growed up under his eye and hand, he taint attached to them, and don't care who plucks 'em.*

"And then who can teach religion but a mother? Religion is a thing of the affections. Lord! parsons may preach, and clerks may make 'sponses forever, but they won't reach the little heart of a little child. All *I* got, I got from mother, for father was so almighty impatient; if I made the leastest mistake in the world in readin' the Bible, he used to fall to and swear like a trooper, and that spiled all. Minister was always kind and gentle, but he was old, and old age seems so far off from a child, that it listens with awe, scary like, and runs away screamin' with delight as soon as it's over, and forgets all. Oh! It's an onnatural thing to tear a poor little gal away from home, and from all she knows and loves, and shove her into a house of strangers, and race off and leave her. Oh! what a sight of little chords it must stretch, so that they are never no good arterwards, or else snap 'em right short off. How it must harden the heart and tread down all the young sproutin' feelin's, so that they can never grow up and ripen.

"Why, a gall ought be nothin' but a lump of affection, as a Mother Carey's chicken is nothin' but a lump of fat; not that she has to love so much, but to endure so much; not that she has to bill and coo all day, for they plaguy soon get tired of that; but that she has to give up time and give up inclination, and alter her likes and alter her dislikes, and do everythin' and bear everythin', and all for affection. She ought to love, so that duty is a pleasure, *for where there is no love there will be no duty done right.* You wouldn't hear of so many runaway matches if it warn't for them cussed boardin'-schools, I know. A young chap sees one of these angeliferous galls a goin' a walkin', and enquires who she is and what she is. He hears she has a great forten', and he knows she has great beauty—splendid gall she is, too. She has been taught to stand strait and walk strait, like a drill-sarjeant. She knows how to get into a carriage and show no legs, and to get out o' one as much onlike a bear and as much like a lady as possible, never starn fust, but like a diver, head fust. She can stand in fust, second, or third position to church, and hold her book and her elbous graceful,—very important church lessons them too, much more than the lessons parsons reads. Then she knows a little tiny prayer-book makes a big hand look hugeaceous, and a big one makes it look small; and, besides, she knows all about smiles, the smile to set with or walk with, the smile to talk with, the smile o' surprise, the smile scorny, and the smile piteous. She is a most accomplished gal, that's a fact, how can it be otherwise in natur? Aint she at a female seminary, where, though the mistress don't know nothin', she can teach everythin', 'cause it's a fashionable school, and very aristocratic and very dear. It must be good, it costs so much; and you can't get nothin' good without a good price, that's a fact.

"Well, forten hunter watches and watches till he attracts attention, and the moment she looks at him his eye tells her he loves her. Creation, man! you might as well walk over a desert of gunpowder, shod with steel soles and flint heels, as to tell that to a gal for the fust time, whose heart her school-mistress and her mother had both made her feel was empty, and that all her education went to write on a paper and put in its window 'Lodgin's to let here for a single man.' She is all in a conflustugation in a minute—a lover!—a real lover too, not a school boy, but an elegant young man, just such a one as she had heered tell of in novels. How romantic aint it? and yet, Squire, how nateral too, for this poor desarted gal to think like a fool fust, and act like a fool arterwards, aint it? She knows she warn't made to grow alone, and that like a vine she ought to have sunthin' to twine round for support; and when she sees this man, the little tendrils of her heart incline right that way at oncet.

"But then love never runs smooth. How in the world are they ever to meet, seein' that there is a great high brick wall atween them, and she is

shot up most o' the time? Ah! there is the rub. Do you know, dear? There
is but one safe way, loveliest of women, only one,—run away. Run away!
That's an awful word, it frightens her 'most to death; she goes right off to
bed and cries like anything, and that clears her head and she thinks it all
over, for it won't do to take such a step as that without considerin', will
it? 'Let me see,' says she, suppose I do go, what do I leave? A cold, formal,
perlite mistress, horrid pitikelar, and horrid vexed when men admire her
boarders more than her, a taunten or a todyin' assistant, and a whole
regement of dancin' masters, musick masters, and French masters. Lessons,
lessons, lessons, all for the head and nothin' for the heart; hard work and a
prison-house, with nothin' to see but feller prisoners a pinin' through the
bars like me. And what do I run *for*? Why, an ardent, passionate, red-hot
lover, that is to love me all my life, and more and more every day of my
life, and who will shoot himself or drown himself if I don't, for he can't
live without me, and who has glorious plans of happiness, and is sure of
success in the world, and all that. It taint racin' off from father and mother
nother, for they ain't here; an' besides, I am sure and sartain they will be
reconciled in a minute, when they hear what a splendid match I have
made, and what a dear beautiful man I have married.' It is done.

  "Ah! where was old marm then, that the little thing could have raced
back and nestled in her bosom, and throwd her arms round her neck, and
put her face away back to her ears to hide her blushes? and say 'dear ma',
I am in love;' and that she agin could press her up to her heart, and kiss
her, and cry with her, and kind o' give way at fust, so as not to snub her
too short at oncet, for fear of rearin', or kickin', or backin', or sulkin',
but gentle, little by little, jist by degrees get her all right agin. Oh! where
was mother's eye when fortin'-hunter was a scalin' the brick wall, that it
might see the hawk that was a threatenin' of her chicken; and where
was old father with his gun to scare him off, or to wing him so he could
do no harm? Why, mother was a dancin' at Almack's, and father was a
huntin'; then it sarves 'em right, the poacher has been into the presarve
and snared the bird, and I don't pity 'em one mossel.

  "Well, time runs away as well as lovers. In nine days puppies and
bridegrooms begin to get their eyes open in a general way. It taint so easy
for brides, they are longer about it; but they do see at last, and when they
do, it's about the clearest. So, one fine day, poor little miss begins to open
her peepers, and the fust thing she disarns is a tired, lyin' lover—promises

broke that never was meant to be kept,—hopes as false as vows, and a mess of her own makin', that's pretty considerable tarnation all over. Oh! how she sobs, and cries, and guesses she was wrong, and repents; and then she writes home, and begs pardon, and, child-like, says she will never do so again. Poor crittur, it's one o' them kind o' things that can't be done agin,—oncet done, done for ever; yes, she begs pardon, but father won't forgive, for he has been larfed at; mother won't forgive, 'cause she has to forgive herself fust, and that she can't do; and both won't forgive, for it's settin' a bad example. All doors behind the poor little wretch are closed, and there is but one open before her, and that looks into a churchyard. They are nice little places to stroll in, is buryin'-grounds, when you aint nothin' to do but read varses on tomb-stones; but it taint every one likes to go there to sleep with the silent folks that's onder ground, I can tell you. It looks plaguy like her home that's prepared for her though, for there is a little spot on the cheek, and a little pain in the side, and a little backin' cough, and an eye sometimes watery, and sometimes hectic bright, and the sperits is all gone. Well, I've seed them signs so often, I know as well what follows, as if it was rain arter three white frosts, melancholy—consumption—a broken heart, and the grave.—*This is the fruit of a boardin'-school; beautiful fruit, aint it? It ripened afore its time, and dropt of the tree airly. The core was eaten by a worm, and that worm was bred in a boardin' school.*

"Lord, what a world this is! We have to think in harness as well as draw in harness. We talk of this government being free, and that government being free, but fashion makes slaves of us all. If we don't obey we aint civilised. You must think with the world, or go out of the world. Now, in the high life I've been movin' in lately, we must swear by Shakspeare whether we have a taste for plays or not,—swaller it in a lump, like a bolus, obscene parts and all, or we have no soul. We must go into fits if Milton is spoke of, though we can't read it if we was to die for it, or we have no tastes; such is high life, and high life governs low life.

"Every Englishman and every American that goes to the Continent must admire Paris, its tawdry theatres, its nasty filthy parks, its rude people, its cheaten tradesmen; its horrid formal parties, its affected politicians, its bombastical braggin' officers and all. If they don't they are vulgar wretches that don't know nothin', and can't tell a fricaseed cat from a stewed frog. Let 'em travel on and they darsn't say what they think of

them horrid, stupid, oncomfortable, gamblin' Garman waterin? places
nother. Oh, no! fashion says you can't.

"It's just so with these cussed boardin' schools; you must swear by 'em,
or folks will open their eyes and say, 'Where was you raird, young man?
Does your mothor know you are out?' Oh, dear! how many gals they
have ruined, how many folks they have fooled, and how many families
they have capsised, so they never was righted agin. It taint no easy matter,
I can tell you, for folks of small forten to rig a gal out for one o' these
seminaries that have the sign 'man-traps set here,' stuck over the door. It
costs a considerable of a sum, which, in middlin' life is a little forten like.
Well, half the time a gal is allowed to run wild 'till she is fourteen years
old, or thereabouts, browsin' here and browsin' there, and jumpin' out of
this pastur' into that pastur' like mad. Then she is run down and catched:
a bearin' rein put on her to make her carry up her head well; a large bit
put atween her teeth to give her a good mouth, a cer-single belt strapt
tight round her waist to give her a good figur', and a dancin'-master hired
to give her her paces, and off she is sent to a boardin'-school to get the
finishin' touch. There she is kept for three, or four, or five years, as the
case may be, till she has larnt what she ought to have knowed at ten. Her
edication is then slicked off complete; a manty-maker gets her up well,
and she is sent back to home with the Tower stamp on her, 'edicated at
a boardin'-school.' She astonishes the natives round about where the old
folks live, and makes 'em stare agin, she is so improved. She plays beautiful
on the piano, two pieces, they were crack pieces, larned onder the eye
and ear of the master; but there is a secret nobody knows but her, she
can't play nothin' else. She sings two or three songs, the last lessons larnt
to school, and the last she ever will larn. She has two or three beautiful
drawin's, but there is a secret here, too; the master finished 'em and she
can't do another. She speaks French beautiful, but its fortunate she aint
in France now, so that secret is safe. She is a very agreeable gal, and talks
very pleasantly, for she has seen the world.

She was to London for a few weeks; saw the last play, and knows a
great deal about the theatre. She has been to the opera oncet, and has seen
Celeste and Fanny Estler, and heard La Blache and Grisi, and is a judge of
dancin' and singin'. She saw the Queen a horseback in the Park, and is a
judge of ridin'; and was at a party at Lady Syllabub's, and knows London
life. This varnish lasts a whole year. The two new pieces wear out, and

the songs get old, and the drawin's everybody has seed, and the London millinery wants renewin', and the Queen has another Princess, and there is another singer at the Opera, and all is gone but the credit, 'she was edicated at a boardin' school.'

"But that aint the wust nother, she is never no good arterwards. If she has a great forten, it aint so much matter, for rich folks can do what they please; but if she aint, why a head oncet turned like a stifle-joint oncet put out in a horse, it aint never quite right agin. It will take a sudden twist agin when you least expect it. A taste for dress—a taste for company—a taste for expense, and a taste for beaux was larnt to boardin'-school, and larnt so well it's never forgot. A taste for no housekeepin', for no domestic affairs, and for no anythin' good or useful, was larnt to boardin'-school too, and these two tastes bein' kind o' rudiments, never wear out and grow rusty.

"Well, when Miss comes home, when old father and old marm go to lay down the law, she won't take it from 'em, and then 'there is the devil to pay and no pitch hot.' She has been away three years, maybe five, and has larned 'the rights o' women,' and the duties of 'old fogeys' of fathers, and expects to be her own mistress, and theirn too. Obey, indeed! Why should *she* obey,—Haint she come of age,—Haint she been to a female seminary and got her edication finished. It's a runnin' fight arter that; sometimes she's brought to, and some times, bein' a clipper, she gets to windward herself, and larfs at the chase. She don't answer signals no more, and why? all young ladies voted it a bore at 'the boardin'-school.'

"What a pretty wife that critter makes, don't she?—She never heerd that husband and wives was made for each other, but only that husbands was made for wives.—She never heerd that home meant anything but a house to see company in, or that a puss had any eend to it but one, and that was for the hand to go in. Heavens and airth! the feller she catches will find her a man-trap, I know—and one, too, that will hold on like grim death to a dead nigger,—one that he can't lose the grip of, and can't pull out of, but that's got him tight and fast for ever and ever. If the misfortinate wretch has any children, like their dear mamma, they in their turn are packed off to be edicated and ruined,—to be finished and bedeviled, body and soul, to *'a boardin'-school'*."

III

THE REVOLUTIONARY HERO

THE following morning, Mr. Slick, who always made much greater despatch at his meals than any man I ever saw, called for the daily newspaper before I had half-finished my breakfast. "Cotton's ris," said he, "a penny a pound, and that's a'most four dollars a bale or so; I'm five thousand dollars richer than I was yesterday mornin.' I knowd this must be the case in course, for I had an account of last year's crop, and I larnt what stock was on hand here, so I spekilated the other day, and bought a considerable passel. I'll put it off to-day on the enemy. Gauli-opilus! if here aint the Great Western a comin' in;" and he threw down the paper with an air of distress, and sat for some time wholly absorbed with some disagreeable subject. After a while he rose and said, "Squire, will you take a walk down to the docks along with me, if you've done breakfast. I'll introduce you to a person you've often heerd tell of, hut never saw afore. Father's come.—I never was so mad in all my life.—What on airth shall I do with the old man here?—but it sarves me right, it all comes of my crackin' and boastin' so, in my letters to sister Sal, of my great doings to London. Dear, dear, how provokin' this is! I aint a critter that's easy scared off, but I swear to man I feel vastly more like scooterin' off than spunkin' up to face him, that's a fact. You know, Squire, I am a man of fashion now;" and here he paused for a while and adjusted his shirt collar, and then took a lingering look of admiration at a large diamond ring on his fore-finger, before its light was extinguished by the glove—"I'm a man of fashion now; I move in first circles; my *po*sition in socie*ty* is about as tall as any citizen of our country ever had; and I must say I feel kinder proud of it.

"But, heavens and airth what shall I do with father? I warn't broughten up to it myself, and if I hadn't a been as soople as moose wood, I could'nt have gotten the ins and outs of high life as I have. As it was, I most gi'n it up as a bad job; but now I guess I am as well dressed a man as any you see, use a silver fork as if it was nothin' but wood, wine with folks as easy as the best on 'em, and am as free and easy as if I was to home. It's ginirally allowed I go the whole figure, and do the thing genteel. But father, airth and seas! he never see nothin' but Slickville, for Bunkerhill only lasted one night and a piece of next day, and continental troops warn't like Broadway or west-eend folks, I tell you. Then he's considerable hard of heerin', and you have to yell a thing out as loud as a training-gun afore he can understand it. He swears, too, enough for a whole court-house when he's mad. He larnt that in the old war, it was the fashion then, and he's one o' them that won't alter nothin'. But that aint the worst nother, he has some o' them country-fled ways that ryle the Britishers so much. He chaws tobaccy like a turkey, smokes all day long, and puts his legs on the table, and spits like an enjine. Even to Slickville these revolutionary heroes was always reckoned behind the age; but in the great world, like New York, or London, or Paris, where folks go a-head in manners as well as everything else, why it won't go down no longer. I'me a peaceable man when I'me good-natured, but I'me ugly enough when I'me ryled, I tell you. Now folks will stuboy father, and set him on to make him let out jist for a laugh, and if they do, I'me into them as sure: rates. I'll clear the room, I'll be switched if I don't. No man shall insult father, and me stand in' by, without catching it, I know. For old, deaf, and rough as he is, he is father, and that is a large word when its spelt right. Yes, let me see the man that will run a rigg on him, and by the Tarnal"—

Here he suddenly paused, and turning to a man that was passing, said, "What do you mean by that?" "What?" "Why runnin' agin me, you had better look as if you didn't, hadn't you?" "You be hanged," said the man, "I didn't touch you." "D—n you," said Mr. Slick, "I'll knock you into the middle of next week." "Two can play at that game," said the stranger," and in a moment they were both in attitude. Catching the latter's eye, I put my finger to my forehead, and shook my head. "Ah!" said he, "poor fellow! I thought so," and walked away. "You thought so," said Mr. Slick, "did you? Well, it's lucky you found it out afore you had to set down the figures, I can tell you."

"Come, come," I said, "Mr. Slick, I thought you said you were a man of fashion, and here you are trying to pick a quarrel in the street."

"Fashion, sir," said he, "it is always my fashion to fight when I'me mad; but I do suppose, as you say, a street quarrel aint very genteel. Queen might hear it, and it would lower our great nation in the eyes of foreigners. When I'm ready to bust, tho', I like to let off steam, and them that's by must look out for scaldings, that's all. I am ryled, that's a fact, and it's enough to put a man out of sorts to have this old man come a trampousin' here, to set for a pictur to Dickens or some other print maker, and for me to set by and hear folks a snickerin' at it. If he will go a bull-draggin' of me about, I'll resign and go right off home agin, for he'll dress so like old Scratch, we shall have a whole crowd arter our heels whichever way we go. I'me a gone sucker, that's a fact, and shall have a muddy time of it. Pity, too, for I am gettin' rather fond of high life; I find I have a kinder nateral taste for good society. A good tuck out every day, for a man that has a good appetite, aint to be sneezed at, and as much champagne, and hock, and madeiry as you can well carry, and cost you nothin' but the trouble of eatin' and drinkin', to my mind is better than cuttin' your own fodder. At first I didn't care much about wine; it warn't strong enough, and didn't seem to have no flavor, but taste improves, and I am a considerable judge of it now. I always used to think champagne no better nor mean cider, and p'r'aps the imertation stuff we make to New York aint, but if you get the clear grit there is no mistake in it. Lick, it feels handsome, I tell you. Sutherland has the best I've tasted in town, and it's iced down to the exact p'int better nor most has it."

"Sutherland's," I said, "is that the hotel near Mivart's?"

"Hotel, indeed!" said he, "whoever heer'd of good wine at an hotel? and if he did hear of it, what a fool he'd be to go drink it there and pay for it, when he can dine out and have it all free gratis for nothin'. Hotel, indeed!!—no, it's the great Duke of Sutherland's. The 'Socdolager' and I dine there often."

"Oh! the Duke of Sutherland," said I; "now I understand you."

"And I," he replied, "understand you now, too, Squire. Why, in the name of sense, if you wanted to c'rect me, did you go all round about and ax so many questions? Why didn't you come straight up to the mark, and say that word 'Sutherland' has slipt off its handle, and I'd a fixt the helve into the eye, and put a wedge into it to fasten it in my memory. I do like a man to stand up to his lick log, but no matter.

"Well, as I was a-sayin', his champagne is the toploftiest I've seen. His hock aint quite so good as Bobby Peel's (I mean Sir Robert Peel). Lord, he has some from Joe Hannah's,—Bug Metternich's vineyard on the Rhine. It is very sound, has a tall flavour, a good body, and a special handsome taste. It beats the *Bug's*, I tell you. High life is high life, that's a fact, especially for a single man, for it costs him nothin' but for his bed, and cab-hire, and white gloves. He lives like a pet rooster, and actilly saves his board. To give it all up aint no joke; but if this old man will make a show—for I shall feel as striped as a rainbow—of himself, I'me off right away, I tell you,—I won't stand it, for he is my father, and what's more, I can't, for, (drawing himself up, composing his moustache, and adjusting his collar) *I* am 'Sam Slick.'

"What induced him," I said, "at his advanced age, to 'tempt the stormy, deep,' and to leave his comfortable home to visit a country against which I have often heard you say he had very strong prejudices."

"I can't just 'xactly say what it is," said he, "it's a kind of mystery to me,—it would take a great bunch of cipherin' to find that out,—but I'me afeerd. it's my foolish letters to sister Sal, Squire, for I'll tell you candid, I've been braggin' in a way that aint slow to Sal, cause I knowed it would please her, and women do like most special to have a crane to hang their pot-hooks on, so I thought my 'brother Sam' would make one just about the right size. If you'd a-seen my letters to her, you wouldn't a-scolded about leaving out titles, I can tell you, for they are all put in at tandem length. They are full of Queen and Prince, and Lords and Dukes, and Marquisas and Markees, and Sirs, and the Lord knows who. She has been astonishin' the natives to Slickville with Sam and the Airl, and Sam and the Dutchess, and Sam and the Baronet, and Sam and the Devil, and I intended she should; but she, has turned poor old father's head, and that I didn't intend she should. It sarves me right though,—I had no business to brag, for though brag is a good dog, hold-fast is a better one. But Willis bragged, and Rush bragged, and Stephenson bragged, and they all bragged of the Lords they knowed to England; and then Cooper bragged of the Lords he refused to know there; and when they returned every one stared at them, and said, 'Oh he knows nobility,—or he is so great a man he would'nt touch a noble with a pair of tongs.' So I thought I'd brag a little too, so as to let poor Sal say my brother Sam went a-head of them all. There was no great harm in it arter all, Squire, was there? You know, at home, in a family where none but household is by, why we do let out sometimes, and say nobody is good enough for Sal, and nobody rich enough for Sam, and the Slicks are the first people in Slickville, and so on. It's innocent and nateral too, for most folks think more of themselves in a gineral way than any one else does. But, Lord love you, there is no calculatin' on women,—they are the cause of all the evil in the world. On purpose or on accident, in temper or in curiosity, by hook or by crook, some how or another, they do seem as if they couldn't help doin' mischief. Now, here is Sal, as good and kind-hearted a crittur as ever lived, has gone on boastin till she has bust the byler. She has made a proper fool of poor old father, and e'en a-jist ruined me. I'me a gone coon now, that's a fact. Jist see this letter of father's, tellin' me he is a-comin' over in the 'Western.' If it was any one else's case, I should haw-haw right out; but now its come home, I could boo-boo with spite a'most. Here it is,—no that's not it nother, that's an invite from Melb.—Lord Melbourne—no this is it,—no it tainte nother, that's from Lord Brougham,—no, it's in my trunk—I'll shew it to you some other time. I can't 'xactly fathom it: it's a ditch I can't jist pole over;—he's got some crotchet in his head, but the Lord only knows what. I was proud of father to Slickville, and so was every one, for he was the makin' of the town, and he was one of our old veterans too; but here, somehow or another, it sounds kinder odd to have a man a crackin' of himself up as a Bunker Hill, or a revolutionary hero."

IV

THE EYE

AS soon as the "Great Western" was warped into dock I left Mr. Slick, and returned to the hotel. His unwillingness to meet his father I knew arose from the difference of station in which they were adventitiously placed; his pride was evidently wounded, and I was reluctant to increase his mortification by witnessing their first interview. I did not see them until the following day, when we were about to depart for London. It was evident, from the appearance of the Colonel, that his son had caused his whole attire to be changed, for it was perfectly new, and not unlike that of most persons of his age in England. He was an uncultivated man, of rough manners and eccentric habits, and very weak and vain. He had not kept pace with the age in which he lived, and was a perfect specimen of a colonist of the rural districts of Connecticut sixty years ago. I had seen many such persons among the loyalists, or refugees as they were called, who had followed the troops at the peace of 1784 to Nova Scotia. Although quite an original therefore in England, there was but little of novelty either in his manner, appearance, or train of thought, to me. Men who have a quick perception of the ludicrous in others, are always painfully and sensitively alive to ridicule themselves. Mr. Slick, therefore, watched his father with great uneasiness during our passage in the train to town, and to prevent his exposing his ignorance of the world, engrossed the whole conversation.

"There is a change in the fashion here, Squire," said he; "black stocks aint the go no longer for full dress, and white ones aint quite up to the notch nother; to my mind they are a leetle sarvanty. A man of fashion must mind his 'eye' always. I guess I'll send and get some white muslins, but then the difficulty is to tie them neat. Perhaps nothin' in natur' is so difficult as to tie a white cravat so as not to rumfoozle it or sile it. It requires quite a slight of hand, that's a fact. I used to get our beautiful little chamber-help to do it when I first come, for women's fingers aint all thumbs like men's; but the angeliferous dear was too short to reach up easy, so I had to stand her on the foot-stool, and that was so tottlish I had to put one hand on one side of her waist, and one on t'other, to steedy her like, and that used to set her little heart a beatin' like a drum, and kinder agitated her, and it made me feel sort of all overish too, so we had to ginn it up, for it took too long; we never could tie the knot under half an hour. But then, practice makes perfect, and that's a fact. If a feller 'minds his eye' he will soon catch the knack, for the eye must never be let go asleep, except in bed. Lord, its in little things a man of fashion is seen in! Now how many ways there be of eatin' an orange. First, there's my way when I'm alone; take a bite out, suck the juice, tear off a piece of the hide and eat it for digestion, and role up the rest into a ball and give it a shy into the street; or, if other folks is by, jist take a knife and cut it into pieces; or, if gals is present, strip him down to his waist, leavin' his outer garment hanging graceful over his hips, and his upper man standin' in his beautiful shirt; or else quartern him, with hands off, neat, scientific, and workmanlike; or, if its forbidden fruit's to be carved, why tearin' him with silver forks into good sizeable pieces for helpin'. All this is larnt by *mindin' your eye*. And now Squire, let me tell you, for nothin' 'scapes me a'most, tho' I say it that shouldn't say it, but still it taint no vanity in me to say that nothin' never escapes me. *I mind my eye.* And now let me tell you there aint no maxim in natur' hardly equal to that one. Folks may go crackin' and braggin' of their knowledge of Phisionomy, or their skill in Phrenology, but it's all moonshine. A feller can put on any phiz he likes and deceive the devil himself; and as for a knowledge of bumps, why natur' never intended them for signs, or she wouldn't have covered 'em all over with hair, and put them out of sight. Who the plague will let you be puttin' your fingers under their hair, and be a foozlin' of their heads? If it's a man, why he'll knock you down, and if it's a gal, she will look to her brother, as much as to say, if this sassy feller goes a feelin' of my bumps, I wish you would let your foot feel a bump of his'n, that will teach him better manners, that's all. No, it's 'all in my eye.' You must look

there for it. Well, then, some fellers, and especially painters, go a ravin'
and a pratin' about .the mouth, the expression of the mouth, the seat of
all the emotions, the speakin' mouth, the large print of the mouth, and
such stuff; and others are for everlastinly a lecturin' about the nose, the
expression of the nose, the character of the nose, and so on, jist as if the
nose was anything else but a speakin' trumpet that a sneeze blows thro',
and the snuffles give the rattles to, or that cant uses as a flute; I wouldn't
give a piece of tobacky for the nose, except to tell me when my food was
good: nor a cent for the mouth, except as a kennel for the tongue. But
the eye is the boy for me; there's no mistake there; study that well, and
you will read any man's heart, as plain as a book. 'Mind your eye' is the
maxim you may depend, either with man or woman. Now I will explain
this to you, and give you a rule, with examples, as Minister used to say
to night school, that's worth knowing I can tell you. 'Mind your eye' is
the rule; now for the examples. Furst, let's take men, and then women.
Now, Squire, the first railroad that was ever made, was made by natur'.
It runs from the heart to the eye, and it goes so almighty fast, it can't be
compared to nothin' but iled lightening. The moment the heart opens its
doors, out jumps an emotion, whips into a car, and offs like wink to the
eye. That's the station-house and terminus for the passengers, and every
passenger carries a lantern in his hand as bright as an Argand lamp; you
can see him ever so far off. Look, therefore to the eye, if there aint no
lamp there, no soul leaves the heart that hitch; there aint no train runnin',
and the station-house is empty. It taint every one that knows this, but as
I said before, nothin' never 'scapes me, and I have proved it over and over
agin. Smiles can be put on and off like a wig; sweet expressions come and
go like shades and lights in natur'; the hands will squeeze like a fox-trap;
the body bends most graceful; the ear will be most attentive; the manner
will flatter, so you're enchanted; and the tongue will lie like the devil—
but *the eye, never.* And yet there are all sorts of eyes. There's an onmeanin'
eye, and a cold eye; a true eye, and a false eye; a sly eye, a kickin' eye, a
passionate eye, a revengeful eye, a manœuvering eye, a joyous eye, and a
sad eye; a squintin' eye, and the evil eye; and, above all, the dear little lovin'
eye, and so forth. They must be studied to be larnt, but the two important
ones to be known are the true eye and the false eye. Now what do you
think of that statesman that you met to dinner yesterday, that stuck to you
like a burr to a sheep's tail, a-takin' such an interest in your books and in

colony governments and colonists as sweet as sugar-candy? What did you think of him, eh?"

"I thought him," I said, "a well-informed gentlemanlike man, and I believe him to be a sincere friend of mine. I have received too many civilities from him to doubt his sincerity, especially as I have no claims upon him whatever. I am an unknown, obscure, and humble, man; above all, I am a stranger and a colonist; his attentions, therefore, must be disinterested."

"That's all you know, Squire," said he, "he is the greatest humbug in all England. I'll tell you what he wanted:—He wanted to tap you; he wanted information; he wanted your original views for his speech for Parliament; in short, he wanted to know if Nova Scotia was in Canada or New Brunswick, without the trouble of looking it out in the map. You didn't mind his eye; it warn't in tune with his face; the last was up to consart pitch, and t'other one several notes lower. He was readin' you. His eye was cold, abstracted, thoughtful: it had no Argand lamp in it. He'll use you, and throw you away. You can't use him, if you was to try. You are one of the sticks used by politicians; he is the hand that holds you. You support him, he is of no good to you. When you cease to answer his purpose he lays you aside and takes another. He has 'a *manœvring* eye.' The eye of a politician is like that of an old lawyer, a sort of spider-eye. Few things resembles each other more in natur', than an old cunnin' lawyer and a spider. He weaves his web in a corner with no light behind him to show the thread of his nest, but in the shade like, and then he waits in the dark-office to receive visitors. A buzzin', burrin', thoughtless, fly, thinkin' of nothin' but his beautiful wings, and well-made legs, and rather near-sighted withal, comes stumblin' head over heels into the net. 'I beg your pardon,' says fly, 'I reely didn't see this net-work of yours; the weather is so foggy, and the streets so confounded dark—they ought to burn gas here all day. I am afraid I have done mischief.' 'Not at all,' says spider, bowin' most gallus purlite, 'I guess its all my fault; I reckon I had ought to have hung a lamp out; but pray don't move or you *may* do dammage. Allow me to assist you.' And then he ties one leg and then t'other, and furls up both his wings, and has him as fast as Gibraltar. 'Now,' says spider, 'my good friend, (a phrase a feller always uses when he's a-goin' to be tricky,) I am afeard you have hurt yourself a considerable sum; I must bleed you.' 'Bleed me,' says fly, 'excuse me, I am much obliged to you, I don't require it.' 'Oh, yes, you do, my dear friend,' he says, and he gets ready for the operation. 'If you dare to do that,' says fly, 'I'll knock you down you scoundrel, and I'me a man that what I lay down I stand on.' 'You had better get up first, my good friend,' says spider a-laughin'. 'You must be bled; you must pay damages;' and he bleeds him, and bleeds him, and bleeds him, till he gasps for breath, and feels faintin' come on. 'Let me go, my good feller,' says poor fly, 'and I will pay liberally.' 'Pay,' says spider; 'you miserable oncircumcised wretch, you have nothin' left to pay with; take that,' and he gives him the last dig, and fly is a gone coon—bled to death.

"The politician, the lawyer, and the spider, they are all alike, they have the *manœvering eye*. Beware of these I tell *you*. *Mind your eye*. Women is more difficulter still to read than man, because smilin' comes as nateral to them as suction to a snipe. Doin' the agreeable is part of their natur', specially afore folks (for some times they do the Devil to home). The eye tho' is the thing to tell 'em by, its infallible, that's a fact. There is two sorts of women that have the 'manœuvering eye'—one that's false and imprudent, and t'other that's false and cautious. The first is soon found out, by them that live much with them; but I defy old Scratch himself to find the other out without 'mindin' his eye.' I knowed two such women to Slickville, one was all smiles and graces, oh! she was as sweet as candy; oh! dear, how kind she was, She used to kiss me, and oncet gave me the astmy for a week, she hugged me so. She called me dear Sam, always.

"'Oh! Sammy dear,' says she, 'how do you do? How is poor dear old Minister, and the Colonel, your father, is he well? Why don't you come as you used to did to see us? Will you stay dinner to-day?—do, that's a good fellow. I thought you was offended, you staid away so long.' Well, I don't care if I do,' says I, 'seein' that I have nothin' above particular to do; but I must titivate up a leetle first, so I'll jist go into the boy's room and smarten a bit.' Well, when I goes in, I could hear her, thro' the partition, say, 'What possesses that critter to come here so often? he is for ever a botherin' of us; or else that stupid old Minister comes a prosin' and a potterin' all day; and as for his father, he is the biggest fool in the whole State, eh?' Heavens and airth, how I curled inwardly! I felt all up an eend. Father the biggest fool in the State, eh? 'No, you are mistaken there, old crocodile,' says I to myself. 'Father's own son is the tallest fool for allowing of himself to be tooken in this way by you. But keep cool, Sam,' says I to myself, 'bite in

your breath, swaller it all down, and sarve her out her own way. Don't be
in debt, pay all back, principal and interest; get a receipt in full, and be
a free man.' So when I went back, oh! didn't I out-smile her, and out-
compliment her; and when I quit, didn't I return her kiss so hard, she
said, 'oh!' and looked puzzled, as if I was goin' to be a fool and fall in love.
'Now,' says I, 'Sam, study that screech owl in petticoats, and see how it
was you was so took in.' Well, I watched, and, watched, and at last I found
it out. It bust on me; all at once, like. I hadn't 'minded her eye.' I saw the
face and manner, was put on so well, it looked quite nateral, but the eye
had no passengers from the heart. Truth warn't there. There was no lamp,
it was *'a manœuvering eye.'* Such critters are easy found out by those as see
a good deal of them, because they see they talk one way to people's faces,
and another way to their backs. They aint cautious, and, folks soon think;
well, when I'm gone my turn will come next, and I'll get it too, and they
take care not to give 'em a chance. But a cautious false woman can never
be found out but by the eye. I know'd a woman once that was all caution,
and a jinniral favorite, with every one, every one said what a nice woman
she was, how; kind, how agreeable, how sweet, how friendly, and all that,
and so she was. She looked so artless, and smiled so pretty, and listened so
patient, and defended any one you abused, or held her tongue, as if she
would'nt jine you; and jist looked like a dear sweet love of a woman that
was all goodness, good-will to man, charity to woman, and smiles for all.
Well, I thought as everybody did. I aint a suspicious man, at least I usn't
to did to be, and at that time I didn't know all the secrets of the eye as I
do now. One day I was there to a quiltin' frollic, and I was a-tellin' of her
one of my good stories, and she was a-lookin' strait at me, a-takin' aim
with her smiles so as to hit me with every one on 'em, and a-laughin like
anythin'; but she happened to look round for a pair of scissors that was
on t'other side of her, jist as I was at the funnyist part of my story, and lo
and behold! her smiles dropt right slap off like petticoat when the string's
broke, her face looked vacant for a minute, and her eye waited till it
caught some one else's, and then it found its focus, looked right strait for
it, all true agin, but she never look'd back for the rest of my capital story.
She had never heard a word of it. 'Creation!' says I, 'is this all a bamm?—what
a fool I be.' I was stumped, I tell you. Well, a few days arterwards I found
out the eye secret from t'other woman's behaviour, and I applied the test
to this one, and I hope I may never see day-light agin if there wasn't 'the

manœvring eye' to perfection. If I had know'd the world then as I do now, I should have had some misgivings sooner. *No man, nor woman nother, can be a general favorite, and be true.* It don't stand to natur' and common sense. *The world is divided into three classes; the good, the bad, and the indifferent. If a woman is a favorite of all, there is somethin' wrong. She ought to love the good, to hate the wicked, and let the indifferent be. If the indifferent like, she has been pretendin' to them; if the bad like, she must have assented to them; and if the good like, under these circumstances, they are duped. A general favorite don't desarve to be a favorite with no one.* And besides that, I ought to have know'd, and ought to have asked, does she weep with them that weep, because that is friendship, and no mistake. Anybody can smile with you, for it's pleasant to smile, or romp with you, for romping is fine fun; but will they lessen your trouble by takin' some of the load of grief off your shoulders for you and carryin' it? That's the question, for that aint a pleasant task; but it's the duty of a friend though, that's a fact. Oh! cuss your universal favorites, I say! Give me the rael Jeremiah."

"But lord love you! obsarvin' is larning. This aint a deep subject arter all, for this eye study is not rit in cypher like treason, nor in the dead languages, that have been dead so long ago, there is only the hair and the bones of them left. Nor foreign languages, that's only fit for singin', swarin', braggin', and blowin' soup when it's hot, nor any kind of lingo. It's the language of natur', and the language of natur' is the voice of Providence. Dogs and children can larn it, and half the time know it better nor man; and one of the first lessons and plainest laws of natur' is, *'to mind the eye.'*"

V

THE QUEEN

THE Archbishop of Canterbury, according to appointment, called to-day upon Mr. Hopewell, and procured for him the honour of a private audience with the Queen. Her Majesty received him most graciously, and appeared to be much struck with the natural grace and ease of his manner, and the ingenuousness and simplicity of his character. Many anxious enquiries were made as to the state of the Episcopal Church in the States, and the Queen expressed herself much gratified at its extraordinary increase and prosperity of late years. On his withdrawing, her Majesty presented him with a very beautiful snuff-box, having her initials on it set in brilliants, which she begged him to gratify her by accepting, as a token of respect for his many virtues, and of the pleasure she had derived from this interview with the only surviving colonist of the United States she had ever seen.

Of such an event as an introduction at Court, the tale is soon told. They were too short and too uniform, to admit of incident, but they naturally suggest many reflections. On his return he said, "I have had the gratification to-day of being presented to the Queen of England. Her Majesty is the first and only monarch I have ever seen. How exalted is her station, how heavy her responsibilities, and how well are her duties performed! She is an incomparable woman, an obedient daughter, an excellent wife, an exemplary mother, an indulgent mistress, and an intelligent and merciful Sovereign. The women of England have great reason to be thankful to God, for setting before them so bright an example for their imitation; and the men of England that their allegiance is due to a Queen, who reigns in the hearts and affections of the people. My own opinion is, that the descent of the sceptre to her Majesty, at the decease of the late King, was a special interposition of Providence, for the protection and safety of the empire. It was a time of great excitement. The Reformers, availing themselves of the turbulence of the lower orders whose passions they had inflamed, had, about that period, let loose the midnight incendiary to create a distress that did not exist, by destroying the harvests that were to feed the poor; had put the masses into motion, and marched immense bodies of unemployed and seditious men through the large towns of the kingdom, in order to infuse terror and dismay through the land; to break asunder the ties between landlord and tenant, master and servant, parishioner and rector, and subject and sovereign."

"Ignorant and brutal as these people were, and furious and cruel as were their leaders, still they were men and English men, and when they turned their eyes to their youthful sovereign, and their virgin Queen, her spotless purity, her sex, her personal helplessness, and her many virtues, touched the hearts of even these monsters; while the knowledge that for *such a Queen*, millions of swords would leap from their scabbards, in every part of the empire, awakened their fears, and the wave of sedition rolled back again into the bosom of the deep, from which it had been thrown up by Whiggery, Radicalism, and Agitation. Had there at that juncture been a Prince upon the throne, and that Prince unfortunately not been popular, there would in all probability have been a second royal martyr, and a Robespierre, or a Cromwell, would have substituted a reign of terror for the mild and merciful government of a constitutional and legitimate sovereign. The English people owe much to their Queen. The hereditary descent of the crown, the more we consider it, and the more experienced we become, is after all, Squire, the best, the safest, and the wisest mode possible of transmitting it.

"Sam is always extolling the value of a knowledge of human nature. It is no doubt of great use to the philosopher, and the lawgiver; but at last, it is but the knowledge of the cunning man. The artful advocate, who plays upon the prejudices of a jury; the unprincipled politician, who addresses the passions of the vulgar; and the subtle courtier, who works upon the weaknesses and foibles of Princes, may pride themselves on their knowledge of human nature, but, in my opinion, the only knowledge necessary for man, in his intercourse with man, is written in a far different book—the Book of Life.

Now, as respects the subject we are talking of, an hereditary monarchy, I have often and often meditated on that beautiful parable, the first and the oldest, as well as one of the most striking, impressive, and instructive of all that are to be found in the Bible. It occurs in the ninth chapter of Judges. Abimelech, you may recollect, induced his kindred to prepare the way for his ascent to the throne by a most horrible massacre, using those affectionate words, that are ever found in the mouths of all demagogues, for remember he said, 'I am *your* bone and *your* flesh.' His followers are designated in the Holy Record as 'vain and light persons,' who, when they accepted their bribe to commit that atrocious murder, said, *surely he is our brother*. Regicides and rebels use to this day the same alluring language; they call themselves 'the friends of the people,' and those that are vile enough to publish seditious tracts, and cowardly enough not to avow them, always subscribe themselves 'one of the People.' The perpetrators of this awful murder gave rise to the following parrable:

"'The trees went forth on a time to anoint a king over them, and they said unto the olive-tree, Reign thou over us.'

"'But the olive-tree said unto them, Should I leave my fatness, wherewith by me they honour God and man, and go to be promoted over the trees?'

"'And the trees said to the fig-tree, Come thou and reign over us.'

"'But the fig-tree said unto them, Should I forsake my sweetness and my good fruit, and go to be promoted over the trees?'

"'Then said the trees unto the vine, Come thou and reign over us.'

"'And the vine said unto them; should I leave my wine, which cheereth God and man, and go to be promoted over the trees?'

"'Then said all the trees unto the bramble, Come thou and reign over us.'

"'And the bramble said unto the trees, If in truth ye anoint me king over you, then come and put your trust in my shadow; if not, let fire come out of the bramble and devour the cedars of Lebanon.'

"What a beautiful parable, and how applicable is it to all time and all ages. The olive, the fig, and the vine had their several duties to perform, and were unwilling to assume those for which nature had not designed them. They were restrained alike by their modesty and their strong sense of rectitude.

"But the worthless bramble, the poorest and the meanest plant in the forest, with the presumptuous vanity so peculiar to weak and vulgar men, caught at once at the offer, and said, 'Anoint me your king, and repose in my shadow;' and then, with the horrible denunciations which are usually uttered by these low-bred tyrants, said, 'if not, let fire issue from me and destroy all the noble cedars of Lebanon.'

"The shadow of a bramble!—How eloquent is this vain-glorious boast, of a thing so humble, so naked of foliage, so pervious to the sun, as a bramble!!—of one, too, so armed, and so constituted by nature, as to destroy the fleece and lacerate the flesh of all animals incautious enough to approach it. As it was with the trees of the forest, to whom the option was offered to elect a king, so it is with us in the States to this day, in the choice of our chief magistrate. The olive, the fig, and the vine decline the honour. Content to remain in the sphere in which Providence has placed them, performing their several duties in a way creditable to themselves and useful to the public, they prefer pursuing the even tenour of their way to being transplanted into the barren soil of politics, where a poisonous atmosphere engenders a feeble circulation, and a sour and deteriorated fruit. The brambles alone contend for the prize; and how often are the stately cedars destroyed to make room for those worthless pretenders. Republicanism has caused our country to be over-run by brambles. The Reform Bill has greatly increased them in England, and responsible government has multiplied them ten-fold in the colonies. May the offer of a crown never be made to one here, but may it descend, through all time, to the lawful heirs and descendants of this noble Queen.

"What a glorious spectacle is now presented in London—the Queen, the Nobles, and the Commons, assembling at their appointed time, aided by the wisdom, sanctified by the prayers, and honored by the presence, of the prelates of the Church, to deliberate for the benefit of this vast empire! What a union of rank, of wealth, of talent, of piety, of justice, of benevolence, and of all that is good and great, is to be found in this national council. The world is not able to shake an empire whose foundation is laid like that of England. But treason may undermine what force dare not assault. The strength of this nation lies in the union of the Church with the State. To sever this connection, then, is the object of all the evil-disposed in the realm, for they are well aware that the sceptre will fall with the ruin of the altar. The brambles may then, as in days of old, have the offer of power. What will precede, and what will follow, such an event, we all full well know. All Holy Scripture was written, we are informed, 'that we might read, mark, learn, and inwardly digest it;' and we are told therein that such an offer was not made in the instance alluded to till the way as prepared for it by the murder of all those lawfully entitled to the throne, and that it was followed by the most fearful denunciations against all the aristocracy of the land. The *brambles* then as now, were *levellers*: the tall cedars were objects of their hatred.

"It is a holy and blessed union. Wordsworth, whom, as a child of nature I love has beautifully expressed my ideas on this subject:-

> "'Hail to the crown by Freedom shaped to gird
> An English sovereign's brow! and to the throne
> Whereon she sits! whose deep foundations lie
> In veneration and the people's love;
> Whose steps are equity, whose seat is law.
> Hail to the State of England! And conjoin
> With this a salutation as devout,
> Made to the spiritual fabric of her Church,
> Founded in truth; by blood of Martyrdom
> Cemented; by the hands of Wisdom reared
> In beauty of holiness, with ordered pomp,
> Decent and unreproved. The voice that greets
> The majesty of both, shall pray for both;
> That mutually protected and sustained,
> They may endure as long as sea surrounds
> This favoured land, or sunshine warms her soil.'"

After repeating these verses, to which he gave great effect, he slowly rose from his seat—drew himself up to his full height—and lifted up both his hands in a manner so impressive as to bring me at once upon my feet. I shall ever retain a most vivid recollection of the scene. His tall erect figure, his long white hair descending on his collar, his noble forehead and intelligent and benevolent countenance, and the devout and earnest expression of his face, was truly Apostolical. His attitude and manner, as I have before observed, caused me involuntarily to rise, when he gave vent to his feelings in those words, so familiar to the ear and so dear to the heart of every churchman, that I cannot deny myself the satisfaction of transcribing them, for the benefit of those whose dissent precludes them from the honor, and the gratification of constantly uniting with us in their use:—

"Almighty God, whose kingdom is everlasting and power infinite, have mercy upon the whole Church, and so rule the heart of thy chosen servant, Victoria, Queen and Governor, of England, that she, *knowing whose minister she is*, may, above all things, seek thy honor and glory, and that all her subjects, *duly considering whose authority she hath*, may faithfully serve, honor, and humbly obey her, in thee, and for thee, according to thy blessed word and ordinance.—Amen.'"

VI

SMALL TALK

"SQUIRE," said Mr. Slick, "I am a-goin' to dine with Palm—Lord Palmerston, I mean, to-day, and arter that I'me for a grand let off to Belgrave Square," and then, throwing himself into a chair, he said, with an air of languor, "these people will actually kill me with kindness; I feel e'en a'most used up,—I want rest, for I am up to the elbows,—I wish you was a-going too, I must say, for I should like to shew you high life, but, unfortunately, you are a colonist. The British look down upon you as much as we look down upon them, so that you are not so tall as them, and a shocking sight shorter than us.—Lord, I wonder you keep your temper sometimes, when you get them compliments I've heerd paid you by the Whigs 'We'd be better without you by a long chalk,' they say, 'the colonies cost more than they are worth. They only sarve to involve us in disputes, and all such scorny talk; and then to see you coolly sayin', Great Britain without her colonies would be a mere trunk without arms or legs, and then cypherin' away at figures, to show 'em they are wrong, instead of givin' 'em back as good as they send, or up foot and let 'em have it; and this I will say for the Tories, I have never heer'd them talk such everlastin' impudent nonsense, that's a fact, but the Whigs is Whigs, I tell you. But to get back to these parties, if you would let me or your colonial minister introduce you to society, I would give you some hints that would be useful to you, for I have made high life a study, and my knowledge of human natur' and soft sawder has helped me amazingly. I know the ins and outs of life from the palace to the log hut. And I'll tell you now what I call general rules for society. First, it aint one man in a hundred knows any subject thorough, and if he does, it aint one time in a thousand he has an opportunity, or knows how to avail it. Secondly, a smatterin' is better nor deeper knowledge for society, for one is small talk, and the other is lecturin'. Thirdly, pretendin' to know, is half the time as good as knowin', if pretendin' is done by a man of the world cutely. Fourthly, if any crittur axes you if you have been here or there, or know this one or that one, or seen this sight, or t'other sight, always say yes, if you can without lyin', and then turn right short round to him, and say 'What's your opinion on it? I should like to hear your views, for they are always so original' That saves you makin' a fool of yourself by talking nonsense, for one thing, and when a room aint overly well furnished, it's best to keep the blinds down in a general way; and it tickles his vanity, and that's another thing. Most folks like the sound of their own voices better nor other peoples', and every one thinks a good listener and a good laugher, the pleasantest crittur in the world. Fifthly, lead where you know, when you don't, foller, but soft sawder always. Sixthly, never get cross in society, especially where the gals are, but bite in your breath, and swaller all down. When women is by, fend off with fun; when it's only men, give 'em a taste of your breed, delicate like, jist hintin' in a way they can't mistake, for a nod is as good as a wink to a blind horse. Oncet or twice here to London, I've had the rig run on me, and our great nation, among men till I couldn't stand it no longer. Well, what does I do,—why, instead of breakin' out into a uprorious passion, I jist work round, and work round, to turn the talk a little, so as to get a chance to, give 'em a guess what sort of iron I'me made of, and how I'me tempered, by sayin' naterally and accidentally like, 'I was in Scotland the other day goin' from Kelso to Edinboro'. There was a good many men folk on the top of the coach, and as I didn't know one, I jist outs with a cigar, and begins to smoke away all to myself, for company like. Well, one feller began grumblin' and growlin' about smokin', how ongenteel it was, and what a nuisance it was, and so on, and all that, and more too, and then looked right strait at me, and said it hadn't ought to be allowed. Well, I jist took a squint round, and as I seed there was no women folks present—for if there had a-been I'd a-throwed it right away in a minit—but as there warn't, I jist smoked on, folded my arms, and said nothin'. At last the crittur, findin' others agreed with him, and that I didn't give lip, spunks up to me, bullyin' like, and sais, 'What would you think, sir,' sais he, 'if

I was to pull that cigar from your mouth and throw it right down on the ground.' 'I'll tell you,' sais I, quite cool, 'what I'd think, and that is, that it would be most partekilarly d—d odd if you didn't touch ground before the cigar. Try it,' sais I, puttin' my head forward so he might take it, 'and I'll bet you five pounds you are off the coach before the cigar.' I gave the feller but one look, and that was wicked enough to kill the coon, and skin him too. It cut his comb, you may depend; he hauled in his horns, mumbled a leetle, and then sat as silent as a pine stump, and looked as small as if he was screwed into an augur hole. Arter tellin' of this story I jist add, with a smile, 'Since the Judges have given out here they intend to hang for duellin', some folks think they can be rude; but it never troubles me. I'me a good-natered man, and always was. I never could carry malice till next day since I was born, so I punish on the spot.' A leetle anecdote like that, with a delicate elegant leetle hint to the eend on't, stops impudence in a minit. Yes, that's a great rule, never get cross in society; It tante considered good breedin'.

"Now as for small change in society, you know, Squire, I aint a deep larned man, but I know a leetle of everything, a'most, and I try to have a curious fact in each, and that is my stock to trade with. Fust thing in company is dress, no man can pass muster unless he is fust chop in that. Hat, gloves, shoes, from Paris; cloths from Stultz, and so on, and then your outer man is as good as Count Dorsy's. Second thing is talk. Now suppose I call on a lady, and see her at rug-work, or worsteds, or whatever you call it. Well, I take it up, coolly, and say, this is very beautiful, and very difficult, too, for that is the double cross stich with a half slant, and then suggest about tent stich, satin stich, and so on; but above all I swear her stich is the best in the world, whatever it is, and she looks all struck up of a heap, as much as to say where on airth did you larn all that. 'And where did you larn it?' I said in some surprise. 'From mother,' she replied. When she was a gal rug-work was all the edication female women had, besides house-keepin', so in course she talked for ever of the double cross stich, with the half slant, the fine fern stich, the finny stich, the brave bred stich, the smarting whip stich, and the Lord knows how many stiches; and it's a pity they hadn't a stich to it, Squire, for one half on 'em have had all their natur' druv out of them and no art put into them, 'xcept the art of talking, and acting like fools. *I like natur' myself and always did, but if we are so cussed fashionable, we must put a dress of our own on it, for goodness gracious sake, let it be somethin' transparent, that we may get a little peep through it sometimes, at any rate.*

"Well, then, sposin' its picters that's on the carpet, wait till you hear the name of the painter. If it is Rupees, or any one of the old ones,"—"Rubens you mean," I said.—"Oh, yes; cuss that word, I seldom use it," he replied, "for I am sure to make that mistake, and therefore I let others pronounce it fust. If its Rubens, or any o' hem old boys, praise, for its agin the law to doubt them; but if its a new man, and the company aint most special judges, criticise. A leetle out of keepin', sais you, he don't use his greys enough, nor glaze down well; that shadder wants depth; gineral effect is good, tho' parts aint; those eyebrows are heavy enough for stucco, says you, and other unmeanin', terms like them. It will pass, I tell you, your opinion will be thought great. Them that judged the Cartoon, at Westminster Hall, knew plaguy little more nor that. But if there is a portrait of the lady of the house hangin' up, and its at all like enough to make it out, stop,—gaze on it—walk back—close your fingers like a spy-glass, and look thro 'em amazed like,—enchanted—chained to the spot. Then utter, unconscious like, 'that's a'most a beautiful pictur';—by Heavens that's a speakin' portrait. Its well painted, too; but, whoever the artist is, he is an onprincipled man.' 'Good gracious,' she'll say, 'how so?' 'Because, Madam, he has not done you justice, he pretends to have a conscience, and says he wont flatter. The cantin' rascal knew he could not add a charm to that face if he was to try, and has, therefore, basely robbed your countenance to put it on to *his* character. Out on such a villain,' sais you. 'Oh, Mr. Slick,' she'll say, blushin', but lookin' horrid pleased all the time, 'what a shame it is to be so severe, and, besides, you are not just, for I am afeerd to exhibit it, it is so flattered.' 'Flattered!' sais you, turn round, and lookin' at her, with your whole soul in your face, all admiration like:—'flattered!—impossible, Madam.' And then turn short off, and say to yourself aloud, 'Heavens, how unconscious she is of her own power!'

"Well, sposin' its roses; get hold of a moss-rose tree, and say, 'these bushes send up few suckers; I'll tell you how to propagate 'em:—Lay a root bare; insert the blade of a penknife lengthwise, and then put a small peg into the slit, and cover all up again, and it will give you a new shoot there.' 'Indeed,' she'll say, 'that's worth knowin.' Well, if its annuals, say, 'mix saw-dust with the airth and they'll come double, and be of a better color.' 'Dear me!' she'll say, 'I didn't know that.' Or if its a tree-rose, say, 'put a silver-skinned onion to its roots, and it will increase the flavor of the roses, without given out the leastest mossel in the world of its own.' Or if its a tulip, 'run a needleful of yarn thro' the bulb, to variegate it, or some such little information as that.' Oh! its a great thing to have a gineral little assortment, if its only one thing of a kind, so that if its called for, you needn't send your friend to another shop for it. There is nothin' like savin' a customer where you can. In small places they can sound your depth, and tell whether you are a deep nine, or a quarterless six, as easy as nothin'; but here they can't do any such a thing, for circles are too large, and that's the beauty of London. You don't always meet the same people here, and, in course, can use the same stories over and over agin', and not ear-wig folks; nothin' is so bad as tellin' the same story twice. Now that's the way the methodists do. They divide the country into circuits, and keep their preachers a movin from place to place. Well, each one has three or four crack sermons. He puts them into his portmanter, gallops into a town, all ready cocked and primed, fires them off, and then travels on, afore he is guaged and his measure took; and the folks say what a most a grand preacher that is, what a pleasin' man he is, and the next man fust charms, and then breaks their hearts by goin' away agin'. The methodists are actilly the most broken-hearted people I ever see. They are doomed forever to be partin' with the cleverest men, the best preachers, and the dearest friends in the world. I actilly pity them. Well, these little things must be attended to; colored note-paper, filagreed envelopes, with musk inside and gold wafer outside delicate, refined, and uppercrust. Some fashionable people don't use those things, and laugh at them little finikin forms. New men, and, above all, colony men, that's only half way between an African and a white man can't. *I* could but *you* couldn't, that's the difference. Yes, Squire, these are rules worth knowin', they are founded on experience, and experience tells me, that fashionable people, all the world over, are, for the most part, as soft as dough; throw 'em agin' the wall and they actilly stick, they are so soft. But, soft as they be, they won't stick to you if you don't attend to these rules, and, above all things, lay in a good stock of *soft sawder*, and *small talk*."

VII

WHITE BAIT

"I HAVE been looking about all the mornin' for you, Squire," said Mr. Slick, "where on airth have you packed yourself? We are a goin' to make up a party to Blackwall, and eat white bait, and we want you to go along with us. I'll tell you what sot me on the notion. As I was a browsin' about the park this forenoon, who should I meet but Euclid Hogg of Nahant. 'Why, Slick,' says he, 'how do you do? it's a month of Sundays a'most since I've seed you, sposin' we make a day of it, and go to Greenwich or Blackwall; I want to hear you talk, and that's better nor your books at any time.' 'Well,' says I, 'I don't care if I do go, if Minister will, for you know he is here, and so is father, too.' 'Your father!' said he, a-startin' back— 'your father! Land of Goshen! what can you do with *him*?' and his eyes stood still, and looked inward, as if reflecting, and a smile shot right across his cheek, and settled down in the corner of his mouth, sly, funny, and wicked. Oh! how it cut me to the heart, for I knowed what was a passin' in his mind, and if he had a let it pass out, I would have knocked him down—I would, I sware. 'Your father!' said he. 'Yes,' sais I, 'my father, have you any objections, sir?' sais I, a-clinchin' of my fist to let him have it. 'Oh don't talk that way, Sam,' said he, 'that's a good feller, I didn't mean to say nothin' offensive, I was only a thinkin' what under the sun fetched him here, and that he must be considerable in your way, that's all. If repeatin' his name after that fashion hurt you, why I feel as ugly about it as you do, and beg your pardon, that's all.' Well, nothin' mollifies me like soft words; so says I, 'It was me that was wrong, and I am sorry for it; come let's go and start the old folks.' 'That's right,' says he, 'which shall it be, Greenwich or Blackwall?' 'Blackwall,' says I, 'for we have been to t'other one.' 'So it shall be, old feller,' said he, 'we'll go to Lovegrove's and have white bait.' 'White bait,' says I, 'what's that, is it gals? for they are the best bait I know on.' Well, I thought the crittur would have gone into fits, he larfed so. 'Well, you do beat all, Sam,' said he; 'what a droll feller you be! White bait! well that's capital—I don't think it would have raised the idea of gals in any other soul's head but your own, I vow.' I knowed well enough what was a-drivin' at, for in course a man in fashionable life, like me, had eat white bait dinners, and drank iced punch, often and often, tho' I must say I never tasted them any where but on that part of the Thames, and a'most a grand dish it is too, there aint nothin' equal to it hardly. Well, when Euclid had done larfin', says I, 'I'll tell you what put it into my head. When I was last to Nova Scotia, on the Guelph shore, I put up to a farmer's house there, one Gabriel Gab's. All the folks was a haulin' in fish, hand over hand, like any thing. The nets were actilly ready to break with mackerel, for they were chock full, that's a fact. It was a good sight for sore eyes, I tell you, to see the poor people catchin' dollars that way, for a good haul is like fishin' up money, it's so profitable.—Fact I assure you. 'So,' says I, 'uncle Gabe Gab,' says I, 'what a'most a grand haul of fish you have.' 'Oh, Mr. Slick!' sais he, and he turned up the whites of his eyes handsum, 'oh!' said he, (and he looked good enough to eat a'most) 'oh, Mr. Slick! I'me a fisher of men, and not a fisher of fish.' Well it made me mad, for nothin' ryles me so like cant, and the crittur was actilly too infarnal lazy to work, and had took to strollin' preachin' for a livin'. 'I'me a fisher of men and not a fisher of fish,' says he. 'Are you?' sais I. 'Then you ought to be the most fortinate one in these diggins, I know.' 'How so?' said he. 'Why,' sais I, 'no soul ever fished for men that had his hook sot with such beautiful bait as yours,' a-pinetin' to his three splenderiferous gals. Lord, how the young heifers screamed, and larfed, and tee-heed, for they was the rompinest, forredest, tormentenest, wildest, devils ever you see. It's curous, Squire, aint it? But a hypocrite father like Gabe Gab is sure to have rollickin' frolickin' children. They, do well enough when in sight; but out of that, they beat all natur'. Takin' off restraint is like takin' off the harness of a hoss; how they race about the field, squeel, roll over and over on the grass, and kick up their heels, don't they? Gabe Gab's darters were proper sly ones, and up to all sorts of mischief when his back was turned. I never seed them I didn't think of the old song,—

WHITE BAIT   57

'The darter of a fisherman,
That was so tall and slim,
Lived over on the other side,
Just opposite to him.
He saw her wave her handkercher,
As much as for to say,
It's grand time for courtin' now,
For daddy's gone away.'

Yes, hypocracy his enlisted more folks for old Scratch than any recruitin' sergeant he has, that's a fact. But to get back to the white bait, we went and roused out old Minister and father, but father said he had most special business (tho' what onder the sun he is arter, I can't make out for the life of me,) and Minister said he wouldn't go without you, and now it's too late for to-day. So what do say to tomorrow, Squire? Will you go? That's right; then we'll all go to-morrow, and I'll shew you what '*white bait*' is."

VIII

THE CURLING WAVE AND THE OLD OAK TREE

ACCORDING to the arrangements made, as related in the last chapter, we went to Blackwall. Upon these excursions, when we all travelled together, I always ordered private apartments, that the conversation might be unrestrained, and that the freedom of remark, in which we indulged, might neither attract attention nor give offence. Orders having been given for "white bait," Mr. Slick and his father walked into the garden, while the "Minister" and myself were engaged in conversation on various topics suggested by the moving scene presented by the river. Among other things, he pointed to the beautiful pile of buildings on the opposite side of the Thames, and eulogised the munificent provision England had made for the infirmities and old age of those whose lives had been spent in the service of the country. "That palace, sir, he said, "for disabled sailors, and the other, at Chelsea, for decrepid soldiers, splendid as they are, if they were the only charitable institutions of England, might perhaps be said to have had their origin, rather in state policy, than national liberality; but fortunately they are only part of an universal system of benevolence here. Turn which way you will, you find Orphan Asylums, Magdalen Hospitals, Charity Schools, Bedlams, places of refuge for the blind, the deaf, the dumb, the deformed, the destitute, for families reduced by misfortune, and for those whom crime or profligacy have punished with infamy or disease. For all classes of sufferers charity has provided a home, and kindness a nurse, while funds have been liberally bestowed to encourage talent, and educate, promote, and reward merit.

"The amount of capital, permanently invested and annually supplied by voluntary contribution, for those objects, is almost incredible. What are the people who have done all this? and whence does it flow? They are Christians, sir. It is the fruit of their religion; and as no other country in the world can exhibit such a noble spectacle—so pleasing to God, and so instructive and honourable to man, it is fair to infer that that religion is better taught, better understood, and better exemplified here than elsewhere. You shall know a tree by its productions, and this is the glorious fruit of the Church of England.

"Liberals and infidels may ridicule its connexion with the State, and Dissenters may point to the Bench of Bishops, and ask with ignorant effrontery, whether their usefulness is commensurate with their expense. I point to their own establishments and say, let their condition and their effects be your answer. I point to Owen and Irvin, whom they impiously call their apostles, and while declining a comparison, repose myself under the shadow of the venerable hierarchy of the Church. The spires and hospitals and colleges so diffusely spread over this great country, testify in its behalf. The great Episcopal Church of America raises its voice in the defence and praise of its parent; and the colonies of the east and the west, and the north and the south, and the heathen everywhere, implore the blessing of God on a Church, to whose liberality alone they owe the means of grace they now possess. But this is not all. When asked where do you find a justification for this connexion, the answer is short and plain, *I find it written in the character of an Englishman*. With all his faults of manner, Squire, (and it is his manner that is chiefly reprehensible, not his conduct,) shew me a foreigner from any nation in the world, under any other form of Church government, whose character stands so high as *an Englishman's*. How much of greatness and goodness—of liberality, and of sterling worth, is conveyed by that one word. And yet, Squire," he said, "I would not attribute all the elements of his character to his Church, although all the most valuable ones unquestionably must be ascribed to it; for some of them are to be traced to the political institutions of England. There are three things that mould and modify national character—the religion—the constitution—and the climate of a country. There are those who murmur against their God, and would improve their climate if they could, but this is impious; and there are those who would overthrow the altar and the throne, in their reckless thirst for change, and this also is wicked. Avoid the contamination of both.

"May man support the Church of God as here established, for it is the best that is known to the human race; and may God preserve and prosper the constitution as here formed, for it is the perfection of human wisdom."

He then took up his chair, and placing it directly in front of the open window, rested his head on his hands, and seemed to be absorbed in some speculation. He continued in this state of abstraction for some time. I never disturbed him when I saw him in these meditating moods, as I knew that he sought them either as a refuge, or as a resource for the supply of conversation.

He was soon doomed, however, to be interrupted by Mr. Slick, who, returning with his father, at once walked up to him, and, tapping him on the shoulder, said, "Come, Minister, what do you say to the white bait now? I'm getting considerable peckish, and feel as if I could tuck it in in good style. A slice of nice brown bread and butter, the white bait fried dry and crisp, jist laid a-top of it, like the naked truth, the leastest mossel in the world of cayenne, and then a squeeze of a lemon, as delicate as the squeeze of a gal's hand in courting time, and lick! it goes down as slick as a rifle-ball; it fairly makes my mouth water! And then arter laying in a solid foundation of that, there's a glass of lignum-vity for me, a bottle of genuine old cider for you and father, and another of champagne for Squire and me to top off with, and then a cigar all round, and up killock and off for London. Come, Minister, what do you say? Why, what in airth ails him, Squire, that he don't answer? He's off the handle again as sure as a gun. Come, Minister," he said again, tapping him on the shoulder, "won't you rise to my hook, it's got white bait on the eend on't?"

"Oh!" said he, "is that you Sam?"

"Sartain," he replied, "at least what's left of me. What under the sun have you been a thinkin' on so everlastin' deep? I've been a-standin' talking' to you here these ten minits, and I believe, in my soul, you havn't heerd one blessed word."

"I'll tell you Sam," he said, "sit down on this chair. Do you see that 'curling wave?' behold it how it emerges out of the mass of water, increases as it rolls on, rises to a head, and then, curls over, and sinks again into the great flood from which it was forced up, and vanishes from sight for ever. That is an emblem of a public man in America. Society there has no permanency, and therefore wants not only the high polish that the attrition of several generations gives, but one of the greatest stimulants and incentives to action next to religion that we know of—pride of name, and the honor of an old family. Now don't interrupt me, Sam; I don't mean to say that we havn't polished men, and honorable men, in abundance. I am not a man to undervalue my countrymen; but then I am not so weak as you and many others are, as to claim all the advantages of a republic, and deny that we have the unavoidable attendant evils of one. Don't interrupt me. I am now merely stating one of the effects of political institutions on character. We have enough to boast of; don't let us claim all, or we shall have everything disputed. With us a low family amasses wealth, and educates its Sons; one of them has talent, and becomes a great public character. He lives on his patrimony, and spends it; for, politics with us, though they may make a man distinguished, never make him rich. He acquires a great name that becomes known all over America, and is everywhere recognized in Europe. He dies and leaves some poor children who sink under the surface of society from which he accidentally arose, and are never more heard of again. The pride of his name is lost after the first generation, and the authenticity of descent is disputed in the second. Had our institutions permitted his perpetuating his name by an entailment of his estate (which they do not and cannot allow), he would have preserved his property during his life, and there would have arisen among his descendants, in a few years, the pride of name—that pride which is so anxious for the preservation of the purity of its escutcheon, and which generates, in process of time, a high sense of honor. We lose by this equality of ours a great stimulant to virtuous actions. Now look at that oak, it is the growth of past ages. Queen Elizabeth looked upon it as we now do. Race after race have beheld it, and passed away. They are gone, and most of them are forgotten; but there is that noble tree, so deep rooted, that storms and tempests cannot move it. So strong and so sound, that ages seem rather to have increased its solidity than impaired its health. That is an emblem of the hereditary class in England—permanent, useful, and ornamental; it graces the landscape, and affords shelter and protection under its umbrageous branches."

"And pysons all the grain onderneath it," said Mr. Slick, "and stops the plough in the furror, and spiles the ridges; and attracts the lightening, and kills the cattle that run under it from the storm."

"The cattle, Sam," he mildly replied, "sometimes attract the lightning that rends the branches. The tree does not destroy the grass beneath its shelter; but nature, while it refuses to produce both in one spot, increases the quantity of grain that is grown at a distance, in consequence of the protection it enjoys against the wind. Thus, while the cultivation of the soil affords nurture for the tree, and increases its size, the shelter of the tree protects the grain. What a picture of a nobleman and his tenants! What a type of the political world is to be found here in the visible objects of nature! Here a man rises into a great public character—is ennobled, founds a family, and his posterity, in time feel they have the honor of several generations of ancestors in their keeping, and that if they cannot increase, they must at least not tarnish, the lustre of their name. What an incentive to virtuous action! What an antidote to dishonor! But here is the white bait; after dinner we will again discourse of the *Curling Wave* and *The Old Oak Tree*."

IX

NATIONAL CHARACTER

AFTER dinner Mr. Hopewell resumed the conversation referred to in the last chapter. "I observed to you just now, Squire, that there were three things that moulded national character; climate, political institutions, and religion. These are curious speculations my children, and well worthy of study, for we are too apt in this world to mistake effect for cause. Look at the operation of climate on an Englishman. The cloudy sky and humid atmosphere in this country renders him phlegmatic, while the uncertain and variable weather, by constantly driving him to shelter induces him to render that shelter as commodious and agreeable as possible. Hence *home* is predominant with him. Operating on all his household equally with himself, the weather unites all in the *family circle*. Hence his *domestic virtues*. Restricted by these circumstances, over which he has no control, to his own fireside, and constitutionally phlegmatic, as I have just observed, he becomes, from the force of habit, unwilling to enlarge or to leave that circle. Hence a *reserve* and *coldness of manner* towards strangers, too often mistaken for the *pride* of home or purse. His habits are necessarily those of business. The weather is neither too hot for exertion, nor too cold for exposure, but such as to require a comfortable house, abundance of fuel, and warm clothing. His wants are numerous, and his exertions must correspond to them. He is, therefore, both *industrious and frugal*. Cross the channel, and a sunny sky produces the reverse. You have a volatile excitable Frenchman; he has no place that deserves the name of a home. He lives in the gardens, the fields, in the public houses, and the theatres. It is no in convenience to him to know all the world. He has all these places of public resort to meet his acquaintances in, and they meet on equal terms. The climate is such as to admit of light clothing, and slight shelter; food is cheap, and but little more fuel is required than what suffices to dress it; but little exertion is requisite, therefore, to procure the necessaries of life, and he is an idle, thoughtless, merry fellow. So much for climate, now for political institutions that affect character.

"I need only advert to the form of this government, a limited monarchy, which is without doubt the best that human wisdom has yet discovered, or that accidental circumstances have ever conspired to form. Where it is absolute, there can be no freedom; where it is limited, there can be no tyranny. The regal power here (notwithstanding our dread of royalty), varies very little from what is found in the United States conducive to the public good, to delegate to the President. In one case the sceptre is inherited and held for life, in the other it is bestowed by election, and its tenure terminates in four years. Our upper legislative assembly is elective, and resembles a large lake into which numerous and copious streams are constantly pouring, and from which others of equal size are perpetually issuing. The President, the Senators, and the Representatives though differently chosen, all belong to one class; and are in no way distinguishable one from the other. The second branch of the legislature in England is composed of nobility, men distinguished alike for their learning, their accomplishments, their high honour, enormous wealth, munificence, and all those things that constitute, in the opinion of the world, greatness. The Queen, then, and all the various orders of nobility, are not only in reality above all others, but it is freely, fully, and cheerfully conceded that they are so.

"With us all religions are merely tolerated, as a sort of necessary evil; no one church is fostered, protected, or adopted by the State. Here they have incorporated one with the State, and given the name of the kingdom to it, to distinguish it from all others—the Church of England. Excuse my mentioning these truisms to you, but it is necessary to allude to them, not for the purpose of instruction, for no one needs that, but to explain their effect on character. Here then are permanent orders and fixed institutions, and here is a regular well-defined gradation of rank, from the sovereign on the throne to the country squire; known to all, acknowledged by all, and approved of by all. This political stability necessarily imparts stability to the character, and the court and the peerage naturally infuse through society, by the unavoidable influence of the models they present, a high sense of honour, elegance of manners, and great dignity of character and conduct. An English gentleman, therefore, is kind and considerate to his inferiors, affable to his equals, and respectful (not obsequious, for servility belongs to an absolute, and not a limited monarchy, and is begotten of power not of right) to his superiors. What is the case where there are no superiors and no inferiors? Where all strive to be first and none are admitted to be so; where the law, in direct opposition to all nature, has declared those to be equal who are as unequal in their talents as they are in their stature, and as dissimilar in their characters as they are in their pecuniary means? In such a case the tone may be called *an average one*, but what must the average of the masses be in intelligence, in morals, in civilization? to use another mercantile phrase, it must inevitably be '*below par.*' All these things are elements in the formation of character, whether national or individual. There is great manliness, great sincerity, great integrity, and a great sense of propriety in England, arising from the causes I have enumerated. One extraordinary proof of the wholesome state of the public mind here is, the condition of the press.

"By the law of the land, the liberty of the press is here secured to the subject. He has a right to use it, he is punishable only for its abuse. You would naturally suppose, that the same liberty of the press in England and America, or in Great Britain and Russia, would produce the same effect, but this is by no means the case. Here it is safe, but no where else, not even in the Colonies. Here a Court, an Established Church, a peerage, an aristocracy, a gentry, a large army and navy, and last, though not least, an intelligent, moral, and highly respectable middle class, all united by one common interest, though they have severally a distinct sphere, and are more or less connected by ties of various kinds, constitute so large, so powerful, and so influential a body, that the press is restrained. It may talk boldly, but it cannot talk licentiously; it may talk freely, but not seditiously. *The good feeling of the country is too strong.* The law of itself is everywhere unequal to the task. There are some liberal papers of a most demoralising character, but they are the exceptions that serve to show how safe it is to entrust Englishmen with this most valuable but most dangerous engine. In France these checks, though nominally the same, scarcely exist. To the great body of the people a different tone is acceptable. *The bad feeling of the country is too strong.*

"In the United States and in the Colonies these checks are also wanting. Here a newspaper is often a joint-stock property. It is worth thousands of pounds. It is edited by men of collegiate education, and first-rate talents. It sometimes reflects, and sometimes acts, upon the opinions of the higher classes. To accomplish this, its tone must be equal, and its ability, if possible, superior to that of its patrons. In America, a bunch of quills and a quire of paper, with the promise of a grocer to give his advertisements for insertion, is all that is necessary to start a newspaper upon. The checks I have spoken of are wanting. This I know to be the case with us, and I am certain your experience of colonial affairs will confirm my assertion that it is the case in the provinces also. Take up almost any (I won't say all, because that would be a gross libel on both my country and yours); but take up almost any transatlantic newspaper, and how much of personality, of imputation, of insolence, of agitation, of pandering to bad passions, is there to regret in it? The good feeling of the country is not strong enough for it. Here it is safe. With us it is safer than in any other place perhaps, but from a totally different cause,—from the enormous number that are published, which limits the circulation of each, distracts rather than directs opinion, and renders unity of design as well as unity of action impossible. Where a few papers are the organs of the public; the public makes itself heard and understood. Where thousands are claiming attention at the same time, all are confounded, and in a manner disregarded. But to leave illustrations, Squire, which are endless, let us consider the effect of religion in the formation of character.

"The Christian religion is essentially the same everywhere; but the form of Church government, and the persons by whom it is administered, modify national character in a manner altogether incredible to those who have not traced these things up to their source, and down to their consequences. Now, it will startle you no doubt when I say, only tell me the class of persons that the clergy of a country are taken from, and I will tell you at once the stage of refinement it is in.

"In England the clergy are taken from the gentry, some few from the nobility, and some few from the humbler walks of life, but mainly from the gentry. *The clergy of the church of England are gentlemen and scholars.* What an immense advantage that is to a country! What an element it forms in the refinement of a nation! when a high sense of honor is superadded to the obligation of religion. France, before the Revolution, had a most learned and accomplished clergy of gentry, and the high state of civilization of the people testified to their influence. In the Revolution the altar was overturned with the throne—the priesthood was dispersed, and society received its tone from a plebeian army. What a change has since come over the nation. It assumed an entirely new character. Some little improvement has taken place of late; but years must pass away before France can recover the loss it sustained in the long continued absence of its amiable and enlightened hierarchy. A mild, tolerant, charitable, gentle, humble, creed like that of a Christian, should be taught and exemplified by a gentleman; for nearly all his attributes are those of a Christian. This is not theory. An Englishman is himself a practical example of the benefits resulting from the union between the Church and the State, and the clergy and the gentry.

"Take a country, where the small farmers furnish the ministers. The people may be moral, but they are not refined; they may be honest, but they are hard; they may have education, but they are coarse and vulgar. Go lower down in the scale, and take them from the peasantry. Education will not eradicate their prejudices, or remove their vulgar errors. They have too many feelings and passions in common with the ignorant associates of their youth, to teach those, from whom they are in no way distinguished but by a little smattering of languages. While they deprecate the æra of darkness, their conversation, unknown to themselves, fans the flame because their early training has made them regard their imaginary grievances as real ones, and induce them to bestow their sympathy where they should give their counsel—or to give their counsel where they should interpose their authority. A thoroughly low-bred ignorant clergy is a sure indication of the ignorance and degradation of a nation. What a dreadful thing it is when any man can preach, and when any one that preaches, as in Independent or Colonial America, can procure hearers; where no training, no learning is required,—where the voice of vanity, or laziness, is often mistaken for a sacred call,—where an ignorant volubility is dignified with the name of inspiration,—where pandering to prejudices is popular, and where popular preaching is lucrative! How deleterious must be the effect of such a state of things on the public mind.

"It is easy for us to say, this constitution or that constitution is the perfection of reason. We boast of ours that it confers equal rights on all, and exclusive privileges on none, and so on; but there are other things besides rights in the world. In our government we surrender certain rights for the protection yielded by government, and no more than is necessary for this purpose; but there are some important things besides protection. In England they yield more to obtain more. Some concession is made to have an hereditary throne, that the country may not be torn to pieces, as ours is every five years, by contending parties, for the office of chief magistrate; or that the nation, like Rome of old, may not be at the mercy of the legions. Some concession is made to have the advantage of an hereditary peerage, that may repress the power of the crown on one side, and popular aggressions on the other;—and further concession is made to secure the blessings of an Established Church, that the people may not be left to themselves to become the prey of furious fanatics like Cromwell, or murderous infidels like Robespierre; and that superstitious zeal and philosophical indifference may alike be excluded from the temple of the Lord. What is the result of all this concession that Whigs call expensive machinery, Radicals the ignorant blunders of our poor old fore-fathers, and your wholesale Reformers the rapacity of might. What is the result? Such a moral, social, and political state, as nothing but the goodness of God could have conferred upon the people in reward for their many virtues. With such a climate—such a constitution, and such a church, is it any wonder that the national character stands so high that, to insure respect in any part of the world, it is only necessary to say, 'I am an Englishman.'"

X

THE PULPIT AND THE PRESS

IT was late when we returned to London, and Mr. Hopewell and Colonel Slick being both fatigued, retired almost immediately for the night.

"Smart man, Minister," said the Attaché, "aint he? You say smart, don't you? for they use words very odd here, and then fancy it is us talk strange, because we use them as they be. I met Lady Charlotte West to-day, and sais I, 'I am delighted to hear your mother has grown so clever lately.' 'Clever?' sais she, and she colored up like anythin', for the old lady, the duchess, is one of the biggest noodles in all England,—'clever, sir?' 'Yes,' sais I, 'I heerd she was *layin'* all last, week, and is *a-settin'* now.' Oh Soliman! how mad she looked. 'Layin' and settin', sir? I don't understand you.' 'Why,' sais I, 'I heerd she kept her bed last week, but is so much better now, she sot up yesterday and drove out to-day.' 'Oh! better?' sais she, 'now I understand, oh yes! thank you, she is a great deal better:' and she looked as chipper as possible, seein' that I warn't a pokin' fun at her. I guess I used them words wrong, but one good thing is, she won't tell the story, I know, for old marm's sake. I don't know whether smart is the word or no, but clever, I suppose, is.

"Well, he's a clever old man, old Minister, too, aint he? That talk of his'n about the curling wave and national character, to-day, is about the best I've heern of his since you come back agin. The worst of it is, he carries things a leetle too far. A man that dives so deep into things is apt to touch bottom sometimes with his head, stir the mud, and rile the water so, he can hardly see his way out himself much less show others the road. I guess he went a leetle too low that time, and touched the sediment, for I don't 'xactly see that all that follows from his pre*my*ses at all. Still he is a book, and what he says about the pulpit and the press is true enough, that's a fact. Their influence beats all natur'. The first time I came to England was in one of our splendid liners. There was a considerable number of passengers on board, and among them two outlandish, awkward, ongainly looking fellers, from Tammer Squatter, in the State o' Main. One on 'em was a preacher, and the other a literary gentleman, that published a newspaper. They was always together a'most like two oxen in a parstur, that are used to be yoked together. Where one was t'other warn't never at no great distance. They had the longest necks and the longest legs of any fellers I ever see,—reg'lar cranes. Swaller a frog whole at a gulp, and bein' temperance chaps, would drink cold water enough arter for him to swim in. The preacher had a rusty suit of black on, that had grown brown by way of a change. His coat had been made by a Tammer Squatter tailor, that carried the fashions there forty years ago, and stuck to 'em ever since. The waist was up atween the shoulders, and the tails short like a boy's jacket; his trousers was most too tight to sit down comfortable, and as they had no straps, they wriggled, and wrinkled, and worked a'most up to his knees. Onderneath were a pair of water-proof boots, big enough to wade across a lake in a'most. His white cravat looked as yaller as if he'd kept it in the smoke-house where he cured his hams. His hat was a yaller white, too, enormous high in the crown, and enormous short in the rim, and the nap as close fed down as a sheep pastur'—you couldn't pull enough off to clot your chin, if you had scratched it in shavin'. Walkin' so much in the woods in narror paths, he had what we call the surveyor's gait; half on him went first to clear the way thro' the bushes for t'other half to follow—his knees and his shoulders bein' the best part of a yard before him. If he warn't a droll boy it's a pity. When he warn't a talkin' to the editor, he was walkin' the deck and studyin' a book for dear life, sometimes a lookin' at it, and then holdin' it down and repeatin', and then lookin' agin for a word that had slipt thro' his fingers. Confound him, he was always runnin' agin me, most knockin' me down; so at last, 'stranger,' sais I, you always talk when you sit, and always read when you walk; now jist reverse the thing, and make use of your eyes, or some of them days you'll break your nose.' 'I thank you for the hint, Mr. Slick,' sais he, 'I'll take your advice.' 'Mr. Slick,' sais I, 'why, how do you know me?' 'Oh,' sais he, 'every body knows you. I was told when I came on board you was the man that wrote the Clockmaker, and a very cute book it is too; a great deal of human natur' in it. Come, s'pose we sit down and talk a leetle.' Sais I, 'that must be an entertainin' book you are a-readin' of,—what is it?' 'Why,' sais he, 'it's a Hebrew Grammar.' 'A Hebrew Grammar,' sais I, 'why what on airth do you l arn Hebrew for?' Says he, 'I'm a-goin' to the Holy Land for the sake of my health, and I want to larn a leetle of their gibberish afore I go.' 'Pray,' sais I, ''xcuse me, stranger, but what line are you in?' 'I'm,' sais he, 'a leader of the Christian band at Tammer Squatter.' 'Can you play the key bugle?' sais I, 'I have one here, and it sounds grand in the open air; its loud enough to give a pole-cat the ague. What instruments do you play on? Oh lord!' sais I, 'let's have the gals on deck, and get up a dance. Have you a fiddle?' 'Oh,' sais he, 'Mr. Slick, don't bamm, I'm a minister.' 'Well, why the plague didn't you say so,' sais I, 'for I actually misunderstood you, I did indeed. I know they have a black band at Boston, and a capital one it is too, for they have most excellent ears for music has those niggers, but then they pyson a room so, you can't set in it for five minutes; and they have a white band, and they *are* Christians, which them oncircumcised imps of darkness aint; and I swear to man, I thought you meant you was a leader of one of those white Christian bands.' 'Well,' sais he, 'I used that word leader because it's a humble word, and I am a humble man; but minister is better, 'cause it aint open to such a droll mistake as that.' He then up and told me he was in delicate health, and the Tammer Squatter ladies of his congregation had subscribed two thousand dollars for him to take a tower to Holy Land, and then lecturin' on it next winter for them. 'Oh!' sais I, 'I see you prefer bein' paid for omission better than a mission.' 'Well,' says he, 'we airn it, and work awful hard. The other day as I passed thro' Bosting, the reverend Mr. Funnyeye sais to me,—Hosiah, sais he, I envy you your visit. I wish I could get up a case for the women too, for they would do it for me in a minit; but the devil of it is, sais he, I have a most ungodly appetite, and am so distressin' well, and look so horrid healthy, I am afeerd it won't go down. Do give me a receipt for lookin' pale.—Go to Tammer Squatter, sais I, and do my work in my absence, and see if the women won't work you off your legs in no time; women havn't no marcy on hosses and preachers. They keep 'em a goin' day and night, and think they can't drive 'em fast enough. In long winter nights, away back in the country there, they aint content if they havn't strong hyson tea, and preachin' every night; and no mortal man can stand it, unless his lungs was as strong as a blacksmith's bellows is. They aint stingy though, I tell *you*, they pay down handsome, go the whole figur', and do the thing genteel. Two thousand dollars is a pretty little sum, aint it? and I needn't come back till it's gone. Back-wood preachin' is hard work, but it pays well if there aint too many feedin' in the same pastur'. There aint no profession a'most in all our country that gives so much power, and so much influence as preachin'. A pop'lar preacher can do anything, especially if he is wise enough to be a comfort, and not a caution to sinners.

"Well, the Editor looked like a twin-brother. He wore a long loose brown great-coat, that hung down to his heels. Once on a time it had to mount guard over an under-coat; now it was promoted. His trowsers was black, and shined in the sun as if they had been polished by mistake for his boots. They was a leetle of the shortest, too, and show'd the rim of a pair of red flannel drawers, tied with white tape, and a pair of thunder and lightning socks. He wore no shoes, but only a pair of Indian Rubbers, that was too big for him, and every time he took a step it made two beats, one for the rubber, and the other for the foot, so that it sounded like a four-footed beast.

"They were whappers, you may depend. They actilly looked like young canoes. Every now and then he'd slip on the wet deck, pull his foot out of the rubber, and then hop on one leg to t'other side, 'till it was picked up and handed to him. His shirt collar nearly reached his ear, and a black stock buckled tight round his throat, made his long neck look as if it had outgrown its strength, and would go into a decline, if it didn't fill out as it grew older. When he was in the cabin he had the table covered with long strips of printed paper that looked like columns cut out of newspapers. He, too had got on a mission. He was a delegate from the Tammer Squatter Anti Slavery Society that had subscribed to send him to attend the general meetin' to London. He was full of importance, and generally sat armed with two steel pens; one in his hand, for use, and another atween his ear and his head, to relieve guard when the other was off duty. He was a composin' of his speech. He would fold his arms, throw himself back in his chair, look intently at the ceiling, and then suddenly, as if he had caught an idea by the tail, bend down and write as fast as possible, until he had recorded it for ever. Then, relapsin' again into a brown study, he would hum a tune until another bright thought again appeared, when he'd pounce upon it like a cat, and secure it. If he didn't make faces, it's a pity, workin' his lips, twitchin' his face, winkin' his eye, lightin' up his brows, and wrinklin' his forehead, awful. It must be shocking hard work to write, I tell you, if all folks have such a time on it as he had. At last he got his speech done, for he ginn over writin', and said he had made up his mind. He supposed it would cost the Union the loss of the Southern States, but duty must be done. Tammer Squatter was not to be put down and terrified by any power on airth. One day, as I was a laying on the seats, taking a stretch for it, I heerd him say to the Preacher, 'you have not done your duty, sir. The Pulpit has left abolition to the Press. The Press is equal to it, sir, but of course it will require longer time to do it in. They should have gone together, sir, in the great cause. I shall tell the Christian ministry in my speech, they have not sounded the alarm as faithful sentinels. I suppose it will bring all the churches of the Union on me, but the Press is able to bear it alone. It's unfair tho', sir, and you don't know your power. The Pulpit and the Press can move the world. That, sir, is the Archimedean lever.' The crittur was right, Squire, if two such gonies as them could talk it into 'em, and write it into 'em, at such an outlandish place as Tammer Squatter, that never would have been heerd of to the sea-board, if it hadn't a-been the boundary question made it talked of; and one on 'em got sent to Holy Land, 'cause he guessed he looked pale, and know'd he felt lazy, and t'other sent to have a lark to London, on a business all the world knows London hante got nothin' to do with; I say then, there can't be better proof of the power of the Pulpit and the Press than that. Influence is one thing, and power another. Influence is nothin,' any man can get votes; with us, we give them away, for they aint worth sellin'. But power is shown in makin' folks shell out their money; and more nor half the subscriptions in the world are preached out of folks, or 'pressed' out of 'em—that's a fact. I wish they would go in harness together always, for we couldn't do without either on them; but the misfortune is, that the Pulpit, in a gineral way, pulls agin' the Press, and if ever it succeeds, the world, like old Rome, will be all in darkness, and bigotry and superstition will cover the land. Without the Pulpit we should be heathens; without the Press we should be slaves. It becomes us Protestants to support one, and to protect the other. Yes! they are great engines, are *the Pulpit and the Press*."

XI

WATERLOO AND BUNKER-HILL

AS soon as breakfast was over this morning, Colonel Slick left the house as usual, alone. Ever since his arrival in London his conduct has been most eccentric. He never informs his son where he is going, and very seldom alludes to the business that induced him to come to England, and when he does, he studiously avoids any explanation. I noticed the distress of the *attaché*, who evidently fears that he is deranged; and to divert his mind from such a painful subject of conversation, asked him if he had not been in Ireland during my absence. "Ah," said, he, "you must go to Ireland, Squire. It is one of the most beautiful countries in the world,—few people see it, because they fear it. I don't speak of the people, for agitation has ruined them: but I speak of the face of natur', for that is the work of God. It is splendid—that's a fact. There is more water there than in England, and of course more light in the landscape. Its features are bolder, and of course more picturesque, you must see Killarney,—we haven't nothin' to compare to it. The Scotch lakes aint fit to be named on the same day with it,—our'n are longer and broader, and deeper and bigger, and everything but prettier.' I don't think there is nothin' equal to it. Loch Katrein and Loch Lomond have been bedeviled by poets, who have dragged all the world there to disappoint 'em, and folks come away as mad as hatters at bein' made fools of, when, if they had been let alone, they'd a–lied as bad perhaps as the poets have, and overpraised them themselves most likely. If you want a son not to fall in love with any splenderiferous gal, praise her up to the skies, call her an angel, say she is a whole team and a horse to spare, and all that: the moment the crittur sees her, he is a little grain disappointed, and says, 'well, she *is* handsome, that's a fact, but she *is* not so *very very* everlastin' pretty arter all.' Then he criticises her:—'Her foot is too thick in the instep—her elbow bone is sharp—she rouges—is affected, and so on' and the more you oppose him, the more he abuses her, till he swears she is misreported, and aint handsome at all;—say nothin' to him, and he is spooney over head and ears in a minute; he sees all beauties and no defects, and is for walkin' into her affections at oncet. Nothin' damages a gal, a preacher, or a lake, like over-praise; a hoss is one of the onliest things in natur' that is helpet by it. Now Killarney aint overpraised—it tante praised half enough;—the Irish praise it about the toploftiest, the Lord knows—but then nobody minds what they say—they blarney so like mad. But it's safe from the poets. My praise won't hurt it, 'cause if I was to talk till I was hoarse, I couldn't persuade people to go to a country where the sting was taken out of the snakes, and the pyson out of the toads, and the venom out of reptiles of all kinds, and given to whigs, demagogues, agitators, radicals, and devils of all sorts and kinds, who have biled it down to an essence, and poured it out into the national cup, until all them that drink of it foam at the mouth and rave like madmen. But you are a stranger, and no one there will hurt the hair of a stranger's head. It's only each other they're at. Go there and see it. It was Minister sent me there.—Oh, how he raved about it! 'Go,' said he, 'go there of a fine day, when the Lake is sleeping in the sunbeams, and the jealous mountain extends its shadowy veil, to conceal its beautiful bosom from the intrusive gaze of the stranger. Go when the light silvery vapour rises up like a transparent scarf, and folds itself round the lofty summit of Mangerton, till it is lost in the fleecy clouds of the upper regions. Rest on your oars, and drift slowly down to the base of the cliff, and give utterance to the emotions of your heart, and say, 'Oh, God, how beautiful!' and your voice will awaken the sleeping echoes from their drowsy caverns, and every rock and every cave, and every crag, and every peak of the mountain will respond to your feelings, and echo back in a thousand voices, 'Oh, God, how beautiful!' Then trim your bark to the coming breeze, and steer for Muckross Abbey. Pause here again, to take a last, long, lingering look at this scene of loveliness—and with a mind thus elevated and purified, turn from nature to nature's God, and entering upon the awful solitude that reigns over this his holy temple, kneel on its broken altar, and pray to Him that made this island so beautiful, to vouchsafe in his goodness and mercy to make it also tranquil and happy. 'Go,' he said, 'and see it as I did, at such a time as this, and then tell me if you were not reminded of the Garden of Eden, and the passage of light whereby Angels descended and ascended,—when man was pure and woman innocent.'"

"Well done, Mr. Slick," I said, "that's the highest flight I ever heard you undertake to commit to memory yet. You are really quite inspired, and in your poetry have lost your provincialism."

"My pipe is out, Squire," he said, "I forgot I was talkin' to you; I actilly thought I was a-talkin to the gals; and they are so romantic, one must give 'em a touch above common, 'specially in the high circles I'me in. Minister always talks like a book, and since you've been gone I have been larnin' all our own na*tive* poets over and over, so as to get pieces by heart, and quote 'em, and my head runs that way like. I'll be hanged if I don't think I could write it myself, if it would pay, and was worth while, which it aint, and I had nothin' above partickelar to do, which I have. I am glad you checked me, tho'. It lowers one in the eyes of foreigners to talk galish that way to men. But raelly it is a fust chop place; the clear thing, rael jam, and no mistake; you can't ditto Killarney nowhere, I know."

Here the Colonel entered abruptly, and said, "I have seed him, Sam, I have seed him, my boy."

"Seen whom?" said the Attaché.

"Why Gineral Wellington, to be sure, the first man of the age, and well worth seein' he is too, especially to a military man like me. What's a prize ox to him, or a calf with two heads, or a caravan, or any other living show?"

"Why surely, father, you haven't been there to his house, have you?"

"To be sure I have. What do you think I came here for, but to attend to a matter of vast importance to me and you, and all of us; and, at spare time, to see the Tunnel, and the Gineral, and the Queen, and the Tower, and such critturs, eh? Seen him, why, in course I have; I went to the door of his house, and a good sizable one it is too, most as big as a state house, (only he has made the front yard look like a pound, with them horrid nasty great ugly barn-yard gates,) and rung the bell, and sais a gentleman that was there, 'Your name, sir, if you please;' 'Lieutenant Colonel Slick,' sais I, 'one of the Bunker Hill heroes.' 'Walk in here, sir,' sais he, 'and I will see if his grace is at home,' and then in a minute back he comes, and treats me most respectful, I must say, bowin' several times, and sais 'this

way, sir,' and he throws open a door and bawls out, 'Lieutenant Colonel
Slick.' When I come in, the Gineral was a sittin' down readin', but as soon
as he heerd *my* name, he laid down the paper and rose up, and I stood still,
threw up old Liberty, (you know I call this here old staff old Liberty, for
it is made out of the fust liberty pole ever sot up in Slickville,)—threw
up old Liberty, and stood on the salute, as we officers do in reviews on
Independence day, or at gineral trainin's. When he seed that, he started
like. 'Don't be skeered,' sais I, 'Gineral, don't be skeered; I aint a-goin'
for to hurt you, but jist to salute you as my senior officer, for it tante
often two such old heroes like you and me meet, I can tell you. You fit at
Waterloo, and I fit at Bunker's Hill; you whipt the French, and we whipt
the English; p'raps history can't show jist two such battles as them; they
take the rag off, quite. I was a Sargint, then,' sais I. 'So I should think,'
sais he. Strange, Squire, aint it, a military man can tell another military
with half an eye?—'So I should think,' sais he.—There aint no deceivin'
of them. They can tell by the way you stand, or walk, or hold your head;
by your look, your eye, your voice; by everythin'; there is no mistake
in an old veteran. 'So I should think,' sais he. 'But pray be seated. I have
seen your son, sir,' sais he, 'the Attaché; he has afforded us a great deal of
amusement.' 'Sam is a cute man, Gineral,' sais I, 'and always was from a
boy. It's ginerally allowed a man must rise airly in the mornin' to catch
him asleep, I can tell you. Tho' I say it that shouldn't say it, seein' that I am
his father; he is a well-informed man in most things. He is a'most a grand
judge of a hoss, Gineral; he knows their whole shape, make, and breed;
there's not a p'int about one he don't know; and when he is mounted on
'Old Clay,' the way he cuts dirt is cautionary; he can make him pick up
miles with his feet, and throw 'em behind him faster than any hoss that
ever trod on iron. He made them stare a few in the colonies, I guess. It
aint every corn-field you can find a man in 'xactly like him, I can tell
you. He can hoe his way with most any one I ever see. Indeed few men
can equal him in horned cattle, either; he can lay an ox with most men;
he can actilly tell the weight of one to five pounds. There is no horned
cattle here, tho', for it's all housen.' 'There are more in the high circles
he moves in,' sais the Gineral, smilin', 'than you would suppose.' Oh, he
smiled pretty! he don't look fierce as you'd guess that an old hero would.
It's only ensigns do that, to look big. 'There are more in the high circles
he moves in,' sais the Gineral smilin', 'than you would suppose.' 'There

mought be,' sais I, 'but I don't see none on 'em, for the high circles are all big squares here, and the pastur's are all built over, every inch on 'em, with stone and brick. I wonder if I could get some of the calves, they would improve the breed to Slickville amazingly. Sam sent me a Bedford pig, last year, and raelly it was a sight to behold; small bone, thick j'int, short neck, broad on the back, heavy on the ham, and took next to nothin' to feed him, nother; I sold the young ones for twenty dollars a-piece, I did upon my soul, fact, I assure you, not a word of a lie in it.'

"'Well, well,' sais I, "only think, that I, a hero of Bunker Hill, should have lived to see the hero of Waterloo. I wish you would shake hands along with me, Gineral, it will be somethin' to brag of, I can tell you; it will show our folks you have forgiven us.' 'Forgiven you?' said he, lookin' puzzled. 'Yes,' says I, 'forgiven us for the almighty everlastin' whippin' we give you, in the Revolutionary war.' 'Oh!' said he, smilin' again, 'now I understand—oh! quite forgiven, I assure you,' sais he, 'quite.' 'That's noble,' sais I, 'none but a brave man forgives—a coward, Gineral, never does; a brave man knows no fear, and is above all revenge. That's very noble of you, it shows the great man and the hero. It was a tremendous fight that, at Bunker Hill. We allowed the British to come on till we seed the whites of their eyes, and then we let 'em have it. Heaven and airth! what capers the first rank cut, jumpin', rearin', plungin', staggerin', fallin'; then, afore they formed afresh, we laid it into 'em agin and agin, till they lay in winrows like. P'raps nothin' was ever seen done so beautiful in this blessed world of our'n. There was a doctor from Boston commanded us, and he was unfortunately killed there. Tho' it's an ill wind that don't blow somebody good; if the doctor hadn't got his flint fixed there, p'raps you'd never a-heerd of Washington. But I needn't tell you, in course you know all about Bunker Hill; every one has heerd tell of that sacred spot.' 'Bunker Hill! Bunker Hill!' sais the Gineral, pertendin' to roll up his eyes, "Bunker Hill? think I have—where is it?' 'Where is it, eh?' sais I. 'So you never heerd tell of Bunker Hill, eh? and p'raps' you never heerd tell of Lexington, nother?' 'Why,' sais he, 'to tell you the truth, Colonel Slick, the life I have led has been one of such activity, I have had no time to look into a lexicon since I give up schoolin', and my Greek is rather rusty I confess.' 'Why, damnation! man,' sais I, 'Lexington aint in any of them Greek republics at all, but in our own everlastin' almighty one.' 'P'raps you mean Vinegar Hill,' sais he, 'where the rebels fought, in

Ireland? It is near Inniscorthy. 'Vinegar devil,' sais I, for I began to get wrathy for to come for to go for to pertend that way. 'I don't wonder it is sour to you, and the Vinegar has made your memory a little mothery. No it aint in Ireland at all, but in Massachusetts, near Boston.' 'Oh, I beg your pardon,' he sais, 'Oh, yes! I do recollect now. Oh, yes! the Americans fought well there, very well indeed.' 'Well sir,' sais I, 'I was at that great and glorious battle; I am near about the sole survivor,—the only one to tell the tale. I am the only man, I guess, that can say,—I have seed Waterloo and Bunker's Hill—Wellington and Washington. (I put them two forrard first, tho' our'n was first in time and first in renown, for true politeness always says to the stranger, after you, sir, is manners.) And I count it a great privilege too, I do indeed, Gineral. I heerd of you afore I come here, I can tell you; your name is well known to Slickville, I assure you.' 'Oh, I feel quite flattered!' said Duke. 'Sam has made you known, I can assure you.' 'Indeed,' sais he, smilin', (there aint nothin' ferocious about that man, I can tell you,) 'I am very much indebted to your son.' He did upon my soul, them were his very words, 'I am much indebted to your son.' I hope I may be darned to darnation if he didn't, 'very much indebted' he said. 'Not at all,' sais I, 'Sam would do that, and twice as much for you any day. He writes to my darter all his sayin's and doin's, and I am proud to see you and he are so thick, you will find him a very cute man, and if you want a hoss, Sam is your man. You've heern tell of Doctor Ivory Hovey, Gineral, hante you, the tooth doctor of Slickville?' 'No,' sais he, 'no!' 'Not hear of Doctor Ivory Hovey, of Slickville?' sais I. 'No; I never heern of him,' he sais. 'Well, that's strange too,' sais I, 'I thought every body had heerd tell of him. Well, you've sartinly heern of Deacon Westfall, him that made that grand spec at Alligator's lick?' 'I might,' sais' he, 'but I do not recollect.' 'Well, that's 'cussed odd,' sais I, 'for both on 'em have heern of you and Waterloo too, but then we are an enlightened people. Well, they are counted the best judges of hoss flesh in our country, but they both knock under to Sam. Yes! if you want a hoss, ax Sam, and he'll pick you out one for my sake, that won't stumble as your'n did t'other day, and nearly broke your neck. Washington was fond of a hoss; I suppose you never seed him? you mought, for you are no chicken now in age—but I guess not.' 'I never had that honor,' he said. 'He said 'honor,' he did upon my soul. Heroes are never jealous; it's only mean low-spirited scoundrels that are jealous. 'I never had that honor,' he said.

"Now I must say I feel kinder proud to hear the fust man in the age call it an 'honor' jist to have seed him—for it is an honor, and no mistake; but it aint every one, especially a Britisher, that is high-minded enough to say so. But Wellington is a military man, and that makes the hero, the statesman, and the gentleman—it does, upon my soul. Yes, I feel kinder proud, I tell you. 'Well,' sais I, 'Washington was fond of a hoss, and I'll tell you what Gineral Lincoln told me that he heard Washington say himself with his own lips,—Shew me a man that is fond of a hoss, and I'll show you the makins of a good dragoon.

"'Now, Sam always was fond of one from a boy. He *is* a judge, and no mistake, he caps all, that's a fact. 'Have you ever slept with him, Gineral?' says I. 'What, sir?' said he. 'Have you ever slept with him?' says I. 'I have nev—,'

"Oh, heavens and airth!" said his son; "Surely, father, you didn't say that to him, did you?" And then turning to me, he said in a most melancholy tone, "Oh, Squire, Squire, aint this too bad? I'm a ruined man, I'm a gone sucker, I am up a tree, you may depend. Creation! only think of his saying that, I shall never hear the last of it. Dickens will hear of it; H.B. will hear of it, and there will be a caricature, 'Have you slept with him, Gineral?' 'Speak a little louder,' said the Colonel, 'I don't hear you.' "I was a sayin', sir," said the Attache, raising his voice; "I hoped to heavens you hadn't said that."

"Said it? to be sure I did, and what do you think he answered? 'I never had that honor, sir,' he said, a-drawin' himself up, and lookin' proud-like, as if he felt hurt you hadn't axed him,—he did, upon my soul! 'I never had that honor,' he said. So you see where you stand, Sam, letter A, No. 1, you do indeed. 'I never had *the honor*, sir, to see Washington. I never had *the honor* to sleep with Sam.' Don't be skeered, boy, your fortin is made, I thought you might have bragged and a boasted a leetle in your letters, but I now see I was mistakened. I had no notion you stood so high, I feel quite proud of your *position* in *society*.

"'As for the honour,' sais I, 'Gineral, it will be all the other way, though the advantage will be mutual, for he can explain Oregon territory, right of sarch, free trade, and them things, better nor you'd s'pose; and now,' sais I, 'I must be a-movin', Duke, for I guess dinner is waitin', but I am happy to see you. If you ever come to Slickville I will receive you with all due military honors, at the head of our Volunteer Corps, and shew you the boys the Bunker Hill heroes have left behind 'em, to defend the glorious country they won for 'em with the sword. Good-bye, good-bye. I count it a great privilege to have seed you,' and I bowed myself out. He is a great man, Sam, a very great man. He has the same composed, quiet look Washington had, and all real heroes have. I guess he is a great man all through the piece, but I was very sorry to hear you hadn't slept with him—very sorry indeed. You might sarve our great nation, and raise yourself by it too. Daniel Webster slept with the President all the time he was to Slickville, and he made him Secretary of State; and Deacon Westfall slept with Van Buren at Alligator's Lick, and talked him over to make him Postmaster General. Oh! the next time you go to Duke's party, sais you, 'Gineral,' sais you, 'as there is no Miss Wellington, your wife, now livin', I'll jist turn in with you to-night, and discuss national matters, if you aint sleepy.'"

"Airth and seas!" said the Attaché to me, "did ever any one hear the beat of that? Oh dear, dear! what will folks say to this poor dear old man? I feel very ugly, I do indeed." "I don't hear you," said the Colonel. "Nothin', sir," said the Attaché, "go on." "Sleep with him, Sam, and if he is too cautious on politics, why ax him to tell you of *Waterloo*, and do you tell him all about *Bunker Hill*."

XII

HOOKS AND EYES—PART I

AFTER our return from dinner to-day, Mr. Slick said, "Squire, what did you think of our host?" I said, "I thought he was a remarkably well informed man, and a good talker, although he talked rather louder than was agreeable."

"That feller," said he "is nothin' but a cussed Hook, and they are critturs that it ought to be lawful to kick to the north eend of creation, wherever you meet 'em as it is to kick a dog, an ingian or a nigger." "A Hook," I said, "pray what is that?" "Did you never hear of a Hook," he replied; and, upon my answering in the negative, he said, "well, p'raps you hante, for I believe 'hooks and eyes' is a tarm of my own; they are to be found all over the world; but there are more on 'em to England, than any other part of the globe a'most. I got that wrinkle, about hooks and eyes, when I was just one and twenty, from a gal, and since then I find it goes thro' all natur'. There are Tory hooks, and Whig hooks, and Radical hooks, and rebel hooks, and so on, and they are all so mean it tante easy to tell which is the dirtiest or meanest of 'em. But I'll tell you the first thing sot me to considerin' about hooks and eyes, and then you will see what a grand lesson it is.

"I was always shockin' fond of gunnin' and p'raps to this day there aint no one in all Slickville as good at shot, or bullet as I be. Any created thing my gun got a sight of was struck dead afore it knew what was the matter of it. Well, about five miles or so from our house, there was two most grand duck-ponds, where the blue-winged duck and the teal used to come, and these ponds was on the farm of Squire Foley. Sometimes, in the wild fowl season, I used to go over there and stay at the Squire's three or four days at a time, and grand sport I had too, I can tell you. Well, the Squire had but one child, and she was a darter, and the most beautiful crittur that ever trod in shoe-leather. Onion county couldn't ditto her nowhere, nor Connecticut nother. It would take away your breath a'most to look at her she was so handsum. Well, in course, I was away all day and didn't see much of Lucy, except at feedin' times, and at night, round the fire. Well, what does Lucy do, but say she should like to see how ducks was shot, and that she would go with me some day and look on. Well, we went the matter of three different mornin's, tho' not hard runnin', and sot down in the spruce thickets, that run out in little points into the ponds, which made grand screens for shootin' from, at the birds. But old Marm Foley—Oh! nothin' never escapes a woman;—old Marm observed whenever Lucy was with me, I never shot no birds, for we did nothin' but talk, and that frightened 'em away; and she didn't half like this watchin' for wild ducks so far away from home. 'So,' sais she, (and women know how to find excuses, beautiful, it comes nateral to 'em,) 'so,' sais she 'Lucy, dear, you mustn't go a gunnin' no more. The dew is on the grass so airly in the mornin', and the bushes is wet, and you are delicate yourself; your great grandmother, on your father's side, died of consumption, and you'll catch your death a-cold, and besides,' sais she, 'if you must go, go with some one that knows how to shoot, for you have never brought home no birds yet.' Lucy, who was as proud as Lucifer, understood the hint at oncet, and was shockin' vext, but she wouldn't let on she cared to go with me, and that it was young Squire Slick she wanted to see, and not the ducks. 'So,' she sais, 'I was a thinkin' so too, Ma, for my part, I can't see what pleasure there can be settin' for hours shiverin' under a wet bush jist to shoot a duck. I shan't go no more.' Well, next mornin' arter this talk, jist as I was ready to start away, down comes Lucy to the keepin'-room, with both arms behind her head a-fixin' of the hooks and eyes. 'Man alive,' sais she, 'are you here yet, I thought you was off gunnin' an hour ago; who'd a thought you was here?' 'Gunnin'?' says I 'Lucy, my gunnin' is over, I shan't go no more now, I shall go home; I agree with you; shiverin' alone under a wet bush for hours is no fun; but if Lucy was there'——'Get out,' sais she, 'don't talk nonsense, Sam, and just fasten the upper hook and eye of my frock, will you?' She turned round her back to me. Well, I took the hook in one hand and the eye in the other; but airth and seas! my eyes fairly snapped agin; I never see such a neck since I was raised. It sprung right out o' the breast and shoulder, full and round, and then tapered up to the head like a swan's, and the complexion would beat the most delicate white and red rose that ever was seen. Lick, it made me all eyes! I jist stood stock still, I couldn't move a finger if I was to die for it. 'What ails you, Sam,' sais she, 'that you don't hook it?' 'Why,' sais I, 'Lucy dear, my fingers is all thumbs, that's a fact, I can't handle such little things as fast as you can.' 'Well, come' sais she, 'make haste, that's a dear, mother will be a-comin' directly;' and at last I shot too both my eyes, and fastened it, and when I had done, sais I, 'there is one thing I must say, Lucy.' 'What's that?' sais she. 'That you may stump all Connecticut to show such an angeliferous neck as you have—I never saw the beat of it in all my born days—its the most'—'And you may stump the State, too,' sais she 'to produce such another bold, forward, impedent, onmannerly, tongue as you have,—so there now—so get along with you.'—'Well sais I, if—'

    "Hold your tongue,' sais she, 'this moment, or I'll go right out of the room now.' 'Well,' sais I, 'now I am mad, for I didn't mean no harm, and I'll jist go and kill ducks out of spite.' 'Do,' sais she, 'and p'raps you'll be in good humour at breakfast.' 'Well, that night I bid 'em all good bye, and said I should be off airly and return to my own home to breakfast, as there was some considerable little chores to be attended to there; and in the mornin', as I was rakin' out the coals to light a cigar, in comes Lucy agin, and sais she, 'good bye, Sam, take this parcel to Sally; I had to git up a-purpose to give it to you, for I forgot it last night. I hope you will bring Sally over soon, I am very lonesome here.' Then she went to the glass and stood with her back to it, and turned her head over her shoulders and put both hands behind her, a-tryin' to fix the hooks and eyes agin, and arter fussin' and fumblin' for awhile, sais she, 'I believe I must trouble you agin, Sam, for little Byney is asleep and mother won't be down this half hour, and there is no one to do it; but don't talk nonsense now as you did yesterday.' 'Sartinly,' sais I, 'but a cat may look at a king, I hope, as grandfather Slick used to say, mayn't he?' 'Yes, or a queen either,' sais she, 'if he only keeps his paws off.' 'Oh, oh!' sais I to myself, sais I, 'mother won't be down for half an hour, little Byney is asleep, and it's paws off, is it?' Well, I fastened the hooks and eyes, though I was none of the quiet about it nother, I tell you, for it warn't easy to shut out a view of such a

neck as that, and when I was jist finishin', 'Lucy,' sais I, 'don't ask me to
fasten that are agin.' 'Why not?' sais she. 'Why, because if you do, I'll, I'll,
I'll,'—'What will you do?' sais she.—'I'll, I'll, I'll do that,' sais I, puttin'
my arms round her neck, turnin' up her face, and givin' her a smack that
went off like a pistol. 'Well, I never!' sais she, 'mother heard that as sure
as you are born! you impedent wretch you! I'll never speak to you agin
the longest day I ever live. You ought to be ashamed of yourself to act
that way, so you ought. So there now. Oh I never in all my life! Get out
of my sight, you horrid impedent crittur, go out this minute, or I'll call
mother.' Well, faith, I began to think I had carried it too far, so sais I, 'I
beg pardon, Lucy, I do indeed; if you only knew all, you wouldn't keep
angry, I do assure you.' 'Hold your tongue,' sais she, 'this very minit; don't
you ever dare to speak to me agin.' 'Well,' sais I, 'Lucy, I don't return no
more,—shall go home,—we never meet again, and in course if we don't
meet, we can't speak.' I saw her colour up at that like anything, so, sais
I to myself, its all right, try a leetle longer, and she'll make it up. 'I had
something,' sais I, 'to say, but it's no use now. My heart'—'Well I don't
want to hear it,' sais she, faintly. 'Well then, I'll lock it up in my own breast
for ever,' sais I, 'since you are so cruel,—it's hard to part that way. My
heart, Lucy,'—'Well, don't tell me now, Sam,' sais she, 'you have frightened
me most to death.' 'Oh, I shall never tell you, you are so cruel,' says I. 'I
have a proposal to make. But my heart,—but never mind, good bye;' and
I put my hat on, and moved to the door. 'Had you heerd my proposal, I
might have been happy; but it's past now. I shall sail for Nova Scotia to-
morrow; good bye.' 'Well, what is it then?' sais she, 'I'm in a tittervation
all over.' 'Why, Lucy, dear,' sais I, 'I confess I was very very wrong indeed,
I humbly axe your pardon, and I have a proposal to make, as the only way
to make amends.' 'Well,' sais she, a-lookin' down and colourin' all over,
and a-twistin' o' the corner of her apron frill, 'well,' sais she, 'what is it,
what is it, for mother will be here directly?' 'No,' sais I, 'my lips is sealed
for ever; I know you will refuse me, and that will kill me quite.' 'Refuse
you, dear Sam,' sais she, 'how can you talk so unkind? Speak, dear, what
is it?' 'Why,' sais I, 'my proposal is to beg pardon, and restore what I have
stolen. S'posin' I give you that kiss back again; will you make up and be
friends?' Oh, Lord, I never saw anythin' like her face in all my life; there
was no pretence there; she raelly was all taken a-back, for she thought I
was a-goin' to offer to her in airnest, and it was nothin' but to kiss her

agin. She was actually bung fungered. 'Well, I never!' sais she; and she
seemed in doubt for a space, whether to be angry or good-natured, or
how to take it; at last she sais, 'Well, I must say you desarve it, for your
almighty everlastin' imperence, will you promise never to tell if I let
you?' 'Tell!' sais I, 'I scorn it as I do a nigger.' 'Well, there then,' said she,
standin,' with her face lookin' down, and I jist put my arm round her,
and if I didn't return that kiss with every farthin' of interest that was due,
and ten per cent of premium too, it's a pity, I tell you, that's all! It was
like a seal on wax; it left the impression on her lips all day. 'Ah!' sais she,
'Sam, it's time we did part, for you are actin' foolish now; come, here's
your powder-horn and shot-bag, take your gun and be off. I hear mother.
But, Sam, I rely on your honor; be off.' And she pushed me gently on the
shoulder, and said 'what a sarcy dear you be,' and shot to the door arter
me, and then opened it agin and called arter me, and said, 'Mind you
bring Sally over to see me soon, I'm very lonely here. Bring her soon,
Sam.' As I went home, I began to talk to myself.—Sam, sais I, "hooks and
eyes" is dangerous things, do you jist mind what you are about, or a sartin
young lady with a handsome neck will clap a hook on you, as sure as
you're born. So mind your eye—this was a grand lesson; it has taught me
to watch *hooks* and *eyes* of all kinds, I tell *you*."

"Sam," said Colonel Slick, rising from his chair with some difficulty,
by supporting himself with both hands on its arms; "Sam you are a d—d
rascal."

"Thank you, sir," said his son, with a quick and inquisitive glance at
me, expressive of his impatience and mortification. "Thank you sir, I am
obleeged to you for your good opinion."

"You are welcome sir," said his father, raising himself to his full height.
"To take advantage of that young lady and kiss her, sir, as you did, was
a breach of good manners, and to kiss her under her father's roof was a
breach of hospitality; but to talk of your havin' a proposal to make, and
so on, to induce her to let you repeat it, was a breach of honor. You must
either marry that girl or fight her father, sir."

"Well sir," said Mr. Slick, "considerin' I am the son of a Bunker Hill
hero and one, too, that fought at Mud Creek and Peach Orchard, for the
honor of the name I will fight her father."

"Right," said the Colonel, "seein' she dispises you, as I'm sure she must,
p'raps fightin' is the best course."

"Oh, I'll fight him," said his son, "as soon as we return. He's a gone 'coon, is the old Squire, you may depend."

"Give me your hand, Sam," said his father, "a man desarves to kiss a gal that will fight for her, that's a fact. That's a military rule, lovin' and fightin', sir, is the life of a soldier. When I was a-goin' to Bunker Hill there was a gal"—

"Hem!" said Mr. Hopewell, turning restlessly in his chair. "Sam, give me a pipe, I hardly know which to disapprove of most, your story or your father's comments. Bring me a pipe, and let us change the subject of conversation. I think we have had enough to-day of *'hooks and eyes.'"*

XIII

HOOKS AND EYES—PART II

"IF you recollect," said Mr. Slick, "I was a-tellin' of you yesterday about hooks and eyes, and how I larnt the fust lesson in that worldly wisdom from Lucy Foley. Now, our friend that entertained us yesterday, is a hook, a Tory hook, and nothin' else, and I must say if there is a thing I despise and hate in this world, it is one o' them critturs. The Tory party here, you know, includes all the best part of the upper crust folks in the kingdom,—most o' the prime o' the nobility, clargy, gentry, army, navy, professions and rael marchants. It has, in course, a vast majority of all the power, talent, vartue, and wealth of the kingdom a'most natur' of things, therefore, it has been in power most o' the time, and always will be in longer than the Whigs, who are, in fact, in a gineral way not Liberals on principle, but on interest,—not in heart, but in profession.

"Well, such a party is the eye, or the power, and the 'hook' is a crooked thing made to hitch on to it. Every Tory jungle has one or more of these beasts of prey in it. Talk of a tiger hunt, heavens and airth! it would be nothin' to the fun of huntin one of these devils. Our friend is one; he is an adventurer in politics and nothin' else,—he talks high Tory, and writes high Tory, and acts high Tory, about the toploftiest; not because he is one, for he is nothin', but because it curries favour, because it enables him to stand where he can put his hook in when a chance offers. He'll stoop to anythin', will this wretch. If one of his Tory patrons writes a book, he writes a review of it, and praises it up to the skies. If he makes a speech, he gets a leadin' article in its favour inserted in a paper. If his lady has a lap-dog, he takes it up and fondles it, and swears it is the sweetest one he ever seed in his life; and when the cute leetle divil, smellin' deceit on his fingers, snaps at 'em and half bites 'em off, he gulps down the pain without winkin', and says, oh! you are jealous, you little rogue, you know'd I was a-goin to import a beautiful one from Cuba for your mistress. He is one o' them rascals that will crouch but not yelp when he is kicked,—he knows the old proverb, that if a feller gets a rap from a jackass, he hadn't ought to tell of it. If 'the eye' has an old ugly darter, he dances with her, and takes her in to dinner; whatever tastes her'n is, his'n is the same. If she plays he goes into fits, turns up the whites of his eyes, twirls his thumbs, and makes his foot move in time. If she sings, then it's a beautiful song, but made twice as sweet by the great effect she gives to it. After dinner he turns up his nose at cotton lords, and has some capital stories to tell of their vulgarity; talks of the Corn-law League people havin' leave to hold their meetin's in Newgate; speaks of the days of Eldon and Wetherall as the glorious days of old England, and the Reform Bill as its sunset. Peel wants firmness, Stanley wants temper, Graham consistency, and all want somethin' or another, if 'the eye' only thinks so. If there is anythin' to be done, but not talked of, or that can be neither done nor talked of, he is jist the boy for the dirty job, and will do it right off. That's the way you know the hook when the eye is present. When the eye aint, there you will know him by his arrogance and impedence, by his talkin' folks down, by his overbearin' way, by his layin' down the law, by his pertendin' to know all State secrets, and to be oppressed by the weight of 'em; and by his pertendin' things aint good enough for him by a long chalk. He talks big, walks big, and acts big. He never can go anywhere with you, for he is engaged to the Duke of this, and the Marquis of that, and the Airl of t'other. He is jist a nuisance, that's a fact, and ought to be indicted. Confound him, to-day he eyed me all over, from head to foot, and surveyed me like, as much as to say, what a Yankee scarecrow you be, what standin' corn, I wonder, was you taken out of? When I seed him do that, I jist eyed him the same way, only I turned up my nose and the corner of my mouth a few, as much as for to say, I'me a sneeser, a reg'lar ring-tailed roarer, and can whip my weight in wild cats, so look out for scaldin's, will you. When he seed he was as civil as you please. Cuss how I longed to feel his short ribs, an tickle his long ones for him. If folks could only read men as I can, there wouldn't be many such cattle a-browsin' about in other men's pastur's, I know. But then, as Minister says, all created crittus have their use, and must live, I do suppose. The toad eats slugs, the swaller eats muskeeters, and the hog eats rattle-snakes; why shouldn't these leeches fasten on to fat old fools, and bleed them when their habit is too full.

"Well, bad as this crittur is, there is a wus one, and that is a Whig hook. The Whigs have no power of themselves, they get it all from the Radicals, Romanists, Republicans, Dissenters, and lower orders, and so on. Their hook, therefore, is at t'other eend, and hooks up. Instead of an adventurer, therefore, or spekelator in politics, a Whig hook is a statesman, and fastens on to the leaders of these bodies, so as to get their support. Oh dear! it would make you larf ready to split if you was to watch the menouvres of these crittus to do the thing, and yet not jist stoop too low nother, to keep their own position as big bugs and gentlemen, and yet flatter the vanity of these folks. The decentest leaders of these bodies they now and then axe to their tables, takin' care the company is all of their own party, that they mayn't be larfed at for their popularity-huntin'. If they aint quite so decent, but jist as powerful, why they take two or three on 'em at a time, bag 'em, and shake 'em out into a room chock full of people, where they rub the dust off their clothes agin other folks afore long, and pop in the crowd. Some on 'em axe a high price. Owen and his Socialists made an introduction to the Queen as their condition. They say Melbourne made awful wry faces at it, like a child takin' physic; but it was to save life, so he shot to his eyes, opened his mouth and swallered it. Nothin' never shocked the nation like that. They love their Queen, do the English, and they felt this insult about the deepest. It was one o' them things that fixed the flint of the Whigs. It fairly frighten'd folks, they didn't know what onder the sun would come next. But the great body of these animals aint fit for no decent company whatsomever, but have them they must, cost what it will; and what do you think they do now to countenance, and yet not to associate,—to patronize and not come too familiar? Why they have a half-way house that saves the family the vexation and degradation of havin' such vulgar fellers near 'em, and answers the purpose of gratifyin' these crittus' pride. Why they go to the Reform Club and have a house dinner, to let these men feast their eyes on a lord, and do their hearts good by the sight of a star or a ribbon. Then they do the civil—onbend—take wine with them—talk about enlightened views—removing restrictions—ameliorating the condition of the people—building an altar in Ireland and sacrificing seven church bishops on it, to pacify the country—free trade—cheap bread, and all other stuff that's cheap talkin'—preach up unity—hint to each man if the party comes in he must have office—drink success to reform, shake hands and part. Follow them out arter dinner, and hear the talk of both 'hooks and eyes.' Says the hook, 'What a vulgar wretch that was; how he smelt of tobacco and gin. I'm glad it's over. I think we have these men, though, eh? Staunch reformers, those. 'Gad, if they knew what a sacrifice it was to dine with such brutes, they'd know how to appreciate their good luck.' This, I estimate, is about the wust sight London has to shew; rank, fortin, and station, degradin' itself for party purposes. Follow out the 'eyes,' who, in their turn, become 'hooks' to those below 'em. 'Lucky in gainin' these lords,' they say. 'We must make use of them; we must get them to us to pull down the pillars of their house that's to crush them. They are as blind as Sampson, it's a pity they aint quite as strong. Go to public meetin's and hear their blackguard speeches; hear 'em abuse Queen, Albert, nobles, clargy, and all in a body for it. It wont do for them to except their friends that honoured 'em at the "House dinner." They are throwed into a heap together, and called every name they can lay their tongues to. Talk of our stump orators, they are fools to these fellers, they arn't fit to hold a candle to 'em. We have nothin'·to pull down, nothin' but party agin party, and therefore envy, especially envy of superiors which is an awful feelin', don't enter into their heads and pyson their hearts. It's 'great cry and little wool' with us, and a good deal of fun, too; many of these leaders here are bloodhounds; they snuff gore, and are on the trail; many of our'n snuff whiskey and fun, and their talk is Bunkum. I recollect oncet heerin' one of our western orators, one Colonel Hanibel Hornbeak, of Sea-conch, argue this way: 'Whar was General Jackson, then? a givin' of the British a'most an almighty lickin' at New Orleans, and whar was Harrison? a-fattin' of hogs, makin' bad bacon, and gettin' more credit than he desarved for it; and whar was our friend here? a-drawin' of bills on Baltimore as fast as he could, and a-gettin' of them discounted; and for these reasons I vote for nullification.' But here it is different talk. I heerd one reformer say, 'when the king was brought to the block the work was well begun, but they stopt there; his nobles and his bishops should have shared the same fate. Then, indeed, should we have been free at this day. Let us read history, learn the lesson by heart, and be wise.' Now don't let these folks talk to us of Bowie knives and Arkansau toothpicks. In our country they are used in drunken private quarrels; here they are ready to use 'em in public ones. 'Hooks and eyes!!' I'll count the chain for you. Here it is: 1st. link,—Masses; 2nd.—Republicans; 3rd.—Agitators; 4th.—Repealers; 5th.—Liberals; 6th.—Whigs. This is the great reform chain, and a pretty considerable tarnation precious chain it is, too, of 'hooks and eyes.'"

XIV

RESPONSIBLE GOVERNMENT—PART I

DESPATCHES having been received from Canada, announcing the resignation of the Local Cabinet, responsible government became, as a matter of course, a general topic of conversation. I had never heard Mr. Hopewell's opinion on this subject, and as I knew no man was able to form so correct a one as himself, I asked him what he thought of it.

"If you will tell me what responsible government is," he said, "then I will tell you what I think of it. As it is understood by the leaders of the liberal party in Canada, it is independence and republicanism; as it is understood here, it is a cant term of Whig invention, susceptible of several interpretations, either of which can be put upon it to suit a particular purpose. 'It is a Greek incantation to call fools into a circle.' It is said to have originated from Lord Durham; that alone is sufficient to stamp its character. Haughty, vain, impetuous, credulous, prejudiced, and weak, he imagined that theories of government could be put into practice with as much ease as they could be put upon paper. I do not think myself he attached any definite meaning to the term, but used it as a grandiloquent phrase, which, from its size, must be supposed to contain something within it; and from its popular compound, could not fail to be acceptable to the party he acted with. It appears to have been left to common parlance to settle its meaning, but it is not the only word used in a different and sometimes opposite sense, on the two sides of the Atlantic. All the evil that has occurred in Canada since the introduction of this ambiguous phrase is attributed to his Lordship. But in this respect the public has not done him justice; much good was done during his dictatorship in Canada, which, though not emanating directly from him, had the sanction of his name. He found on his arrival there a very excellent council collected, together by Sir John Colborne, and they enabled him to pass many valuable ordinances, which it has been the object of the Responsibles ever since to repeal. The greatest mischief was done by Poulett Thompson; shrewd, sensible, laborious, and practical, he had great personal weight, and as he was known to have unlimited power delegated to him, and took the liberty of altering the tenure of every office of emolument in the country, he had the greatest patronage ever known in a British province, at his command, and of course extraordinary official influence.

"His object evidently was not to lay the foundation of a permanent system of government there. That would have taken a longer period of time than he intended to devote to it. It was to reorganise the legislative body under the imperial act, put it into immediate operation, carry through his *measures at any cost* and *by any means*, produce a temporary pacification, make a dashing and striking effect, and return triumphant to Parliament, and say, 'I have effaced all the evils that have grown out of years of Tory misrule, and given to the Canadians that which has so long and so unjustly been withheld from them by the bigotry, intolerance, and exclusiveness of that party "Responsible Government." That short and disastrous Administration has been productive of incalculable mischief. It has disheartened and weakened the loyal British party. It has emboldened and strengthened the opposite one, and from the extraordinary means used to compel acquiescence, and obtain majorities, lowered the tone of moral feeling throughout the country.

"He is now dead, and I will not speak of him in the terms I should have used had he been living. The object of a truly good and patriotic man should have been not to create a triumphant party to carry his measures, (because he must have known that to purchase their aid, he must have adopted too many of their views, or modified or relinquished many of his own,) but to extinguish all party, to summon to his council men possessing the confidence of every large interest in the country, and by their assistance to administer the government with fairness, firmness, and impartiality. No government based upon any other principle will ever give general satisfaction, or insure tranquillity in the Colonies, for in politics as in other things, nothing can be permanent that is not built upon the immutable foundations of truth and justice. The fallacy of this 'Responsibility System' is that it consists, as the liberals interpret it, of two antagonist principles, Republican and Monarchical, the former being the active, and the latter the passive principle. When this is the case, and there is no third or aristocratic body, with which both can unite, or which can prevent their mutual contact, it is evident the active principle will be the ruling one.

"This is not a remote but an immediate consequence, and as soon as this event occurs, there is but one word that expresses the result—independence. One great error of Poulett Thompson was, in strengthening, on all occasions, the democratic, and weakening the aristocratic, feeling of the country, than which nothing could be more subversive of the regal authority and influence. Pitt wisely designed to have created an order in Canada, corresponding as far as the different situations of the two countries would admit, to the hereditary order in England, but unfortunately listened to Whig reasoning and democratic raillery, and relinquished the plan. The soundness of his views is now apparent in the great want that is felt of such a counterpoise, but will talk to you of this subject some other time.

"I know of no colony to which Responsible Government, as now demanded, is applicable; but I know of few to which it is so wholly unsuitable as to Canada. If it means anything, it means a government responsible to the people for its acts, and of course pre-supposes a people capable of judging.

"As no community can act for itself, in a body, individual opinion must be severally collected, and the majority of votes thus taken must be accepted as the voice of the people. How, then, can this be said to be the case in a community where a very large portion of the population surrenders the right of private judgement to its priests, and where the politics of the priesthood are wholly subservient to the advancement of their church, or the preservation of their nationality? A large body like this in Canada will always be made larger by the addition of ambitious and unscrupulous men of other creeds, who are ever willing to give their talents and influence in exchange for its support, and to adopt its views, provided the party will adopt them. *To make the Government responsible to such a party as this, and to surrender the patronage of the Crown to it, is to sacrifice every British and every Protestant interest in the country.*

"The hope and the belief, and indeed the entire conviction that such would be the result, was the reason why the French leaders accepted responsible government with so much eagerness and joy, the moment it was proffered. They felt that they had again, by the folly of their rulers, become sole masters of a country they were unable to reconquer, and were in the singular and anomalous company of having a monopoly of all the power, revenue, authority, and patronage of the Government, without any possibility of the real owners having any practical participation in it. *The French, aided by others holding the same religious views, and a few Protestant Radicals, easily form a majority; once establish the doctrine of ruling by a majority, and then, they are lawfully the government, and the exclusion and oppression of the English, in their own colony, is sanctioned by law, and that law imposed by England on itself. What a monstrous piece of absurdity, cruelty, and injustice!* In making such a concession as this, Poulett Thompson proved himself to have been either a very weak or a very unprincipled man. Let us strive to be charitable, however difficult it be in this case, and endeavour to hope it was an error of the head rather than the heart.

"The doctrine maintained here is, that a governor, who has but a delegated authority, must be responsible to the power that delegates it, namely, the Queen's Government; and this is undoubtedly the true doctrine, and the only one that is compatible with colonial dependence. The Liberals (as the movement party in Canada style themselves) say he is but the head of his executive council, and that that council must be responsible to the people. Where, then, is the monarchical principle? or where is the line of demarcation between such a state and independence? The language of these trouble some and factious men is, 'Every Government ought to be able to possess a majority in the legislature powerful enough to carry its measures;' and the plausibility of this dogmatical assertion deludes many persons who are unable to understand the question properly. *A majority is required, not to carry Government measures, but to carry certain personal office and power.* A colonial administration neither has, nor ought to have, any government; and this is undoubtedly the government measures. Its foreign policy and internal trade, its post-office and customs departments, its army and navy, its commissariat and mint, are imperial services provided for here. Its civil list is, in most cases, established by a permanent law. All local matters should be left to the independent action of members, and are generally better for not being interfered with. If they are required, they will be voted, as in times past; if not, they will remain unattempted. No difficulty was ever felt on this score, nor any complaint ever made, until Lord Durham talked of Boards of Works, Commissionerships, Supervisors, Lord Mayors, District Intendants, and other things that at once awakened the cupidity of hungry demagogues and rapacious patriots, who forthwith demanded a party Government, that they might have party-jobs, and the execution of these lucrative affairs. A Government by a majority has proved itself, with us, to be the worst of tyrannies; but it will be infinitely more oppressive in the Colonies than in the States, for *we have republican institutions to modify its evils.* Neither that presumptuous man, Lord Durham, nor that reckless man Thompson, appear to have had the slightest idea of this difference. With us the commission of a magistrate expires of itself in a few years. The upper branch of the legislature is elective, and the members are constantly changed; while everything else is equally mutable and republican. In the Colonies the magistrates are virtually appointed for life, and so is a legislative councillor, and the principle has been, in times past, practically applied to every office in the country. Responsible Government then, in the Colonies, where the elective franchise is so low as to make it almost universal suffrage, is a great and unmitigated republican principle, introduced into a country not only dependant on another, but having monarchical institutions wholly incompatible with its exercise. The magistrate in some of the provinces has a most extensive judicial as well as ministerial jurisdiction, and I need not say how important the functions of a legislative councillor are. A temporary majority, having all the patronage, (for such is their claim, in what ever way they may attempt to explain it,) is by this new doctrine to be empowered to appoint its partisans to all these permanent offices,—an evil that a change of party cannot remedy, and therefore one that admits of no cure. This has been already severely felt wherever the system has been introduced, for reform has been so long the cover under which disaffection has sheltered itself, that it seldom includes among its supporters any of the upper class of society. The party usually consists of the mass of the lower orders, and those just immediately above them. Demagogues easily and constantly persuade them that they are wronged by the rich, and oppressed by the great, that all who are in a superior station are enemies of the people, and that those who hold office are living in idle luxury at the expense of the poor. Terms of reproach or derision are invented to lower, and degrade them in the public estimation; cliques, family compacts, obstructionists, and other nicknames, are liberally applied; and when facts are wanting, imagination is fruitful, and easily supplies them. To appoint persons from such a party to permanent offices, is an alarming evil. To apply the remedy we have, of the elective principle and short tenure of office, is to introduce republicanism into every department. *What a delusion, then, it is to suppose that Responsible Government is applicable to the North American provinces, or that it is anything else than practical independence as regards England, with a practical exclusion from influence and office of all that is good or respectable, or loyal, or British, as regards the colony!*

   "The evil has not been one of your own seeking, but one that has been thrust upon you by the quackery of English states men. The remedy is beyond your reach; it must be applied by a higher power. The time is now come when it is necessary to speak out, and speak plainly. If the Secretary for the Colonies is not firm, *Canada is lost for ever!*"

XV

RESPONSIBLE GOVERNMENT—PART II

THE subject of Responsible Government, which had now become a general topic of conversation, was resumed again to-day by Mr. Slick.

"Minister," said he, "I quite concur with you in your idee of that form of colony government. When I was to Windsor, Nova Scotia, a few years ago, Poulett Thompson was there, a-waitin' for a steamer to go to St. John, New Brunswick; and as I was a-passin' Mr. Wilcox's inn, who should I see but him. I knowed him the moment I seed him, for I had met him to London the year before, when he was only a member of parliament; and since the Reform Bill, you know, folks don't make no more account of a member than an alderman; indeed since I have moved in the first circles I've rather kept out of their way, for they arn't thought very good company in a gineral way, I can tell you. Well, as soon as I met him I knowed him at once, but I warn't a-goin' for to speak to him fust, seem' that he had become a big bug since, and p'raps wouldn't talk to the likes of me. But up he comes in a minit, and makes a low bow. He had a very curious bow. It was jist a stiff low bend forrard, as a feller does afore he goes to take an everlastin' jump; and sais he, 'How do you do, Mr. Slick? will you do me the favour to walk in and sit down awhile, I want to talk to you. We are endeavourin', you see,' sais he, 'to assimilate matters here as much as possible to what exists in your country.' So I see,' sais I; 'but I am ashamed to say, I don't exactly comprehend what responsible government is in a colony.' 'Well,' sais he, 'it aint easy of definition, but it will work itself out, and adjust itself in practice. I have given them a fresh hare to run, and that is a great matter. Their attention is taken off from old sources of strife, and fixed on this. I have broken up all old parties, shuffled the cards, and given them a new deal and new partners.' 'Take care,' sais I, 'that a knave doesn't turn up for trump card.' He looked thoughtful for a moment, and then sais, 'Very good hit, Mr. Slick; very good hit indeed; and between ourselves, in politics I am afraid there are, everywhere, more knaves than honors in the pack.' I have often thought of that expression since—'a fresh hare to run;' what a principle of action for a statesman, warn't it? But it was jist like him; he thought everybody he met was fools. One half the people to Canada didn't know what onder the sun he meant; but they knowed he was a radical, and agin the Church, and agin all the old English families there, and therefore *they* followed him. Well, he seed that, and thought them fools. If he'd a-lived a little grain longer, he'd a-found they were more rogues than fools, them fellers, for they had an axe to grind as well as him. Well, t'other half seed he was a schemer, and a schemer, too, that wouldn't stick at nothin' to carry out his eends; and *they* wouldn't have nothin' to say to him at all. Well, in course he called them fools too; if he'd a-lived a little grain longer I guess he'd a found out whose head the fool's cap fitted best. 'Well,' sais I, 'it warn't a bad idee that, of givin' 'em a fresh hare to run; it was grand. You had nothin' to do but to start the hare, say 'stuboy,' clap your hands ever so loud, and off goes the whole pack of yelpin' curs at his heels like wink. It's kept them from jumpin' and fawnin', and cryin', and cravin', and pawin' on you for everlastin', for somethin' to eat, and a botherin' of you, and a spilin' of your clothes, don't it? You give 'em the dodge properly that time; you got that lesson from the Indgin dogs on the Mississippi, I guess, didn't you?' 'No,' sais he, lookin' one half out of sorts and t'other half; 'no, I was never there,' sais he. 'Not there?' sais I, 'why, you don't say so! Not there? well, it passes all; for it's the identical same dodge. When a dog wants to cross the river there, he goes to a p'int of land that stretches away out into the water, and sits do on his hind legs, and cries at the tip eend of his voice, most piteous, and howls so it would make your heart break to hear him. It's the most horrid dismal, solemcoly sound you ever knowed. Well, he keeps up this tune for the matter of half-an-hour, till the river and the woods ring again. All the crocodiles for three miles up and three miles down, as soon as they hear it, run as hard as they can lick to the spot, for they are very humane boys them, cry like women at nothin' a'most, and always go where any crittur is in distress, and drag him right out of it. Well, as soon as the dog has em all collected, at a charity-ball like, a-waitin' for their supper, and a-lickin' of their chops, off he starts, hot foot, down the bank of the river, for a mile or so, and then souses right in and swims across as quick as he can pull for it, and gives them the slip beautiful. Now your dodge and the Mississippi dog is so much alike, I'd a bet anything, a'most, you took the hint from him.'

"'What a capital story!' sais he; 'how oncommon good! upon my word it's very apt;' jist then steam-boat bell rung, and he off to the river too, and give me the dodge.'

"I'll tell you what he put me in mind of. I was to Squire Shears, the tailor, to Boston, oncet, to get measured for a coat. 'Squire,' sais I, 'measure me quick, will, you, that's a good soul, for I'm in a horrid hurry.' 'Can't,' sais he, 'Sam; the designer is out—sit down, he will be in directly.' 'The designer,' sais I, 'who the devil is that, what onder the sun do you mean?' Well, it raised my curiosity—so I squats down on the counter and lights a cigar. 'That word has made my fortin' Sam,' sais he. 'It is somethin' new. He designs the coat, that is what is vulgarly called—cuts it out;—and a nice thing it is too. It requires a light hand, great freedom of touch, a quick eye, and great taste. Its all he can do, for he couldn't so much as sow a button on. He is an Englishman of the name of Street. Artist is a common word—a foreman is a common word—a measurer is low, very low; but 'a designer,' oh, its fust chop—its quite the go. 'My designer'— Heavens what a lucky hit that was!' Well, Mr. Thompson put me in mind of Street, the designer, he didn't look onlike him in person nother, and he was a grand hand to cut out work for others to do. A capital hand for makin' measures and designin'. But to get back to my story. He said 'he had given 'em to Canada a fresh hare to run.' Well, they've got tired of the chace at last arter the hare, for they hante been able to catch it. They've returned on the tracks from where they started, and stand starin' at each other like fools. For the fust time they begin' to ax themselves the question, what is responsible government? Well, they don't know, and they axe the Governor, and he don't know, and he axes Lord John, the Colonial Secretary, and he don't know. At last Lord John looks wise and sais, 'its not onlike prerogative—its existence is admitted—its only its exercise is questioned.' Well, the Governor looks wise and sais the same, and the people repeat over the words arter him—look puzzled, and say they don't exactly onderstand the answer nother. It reminds me of what happened to me oncet to Brussels. I was on the top of a coach there, a-goin' down that dreadful steep hill there, not that it is so awful steep nother; but hills are curiosities there, they are so scarce, and every little sharp pinch is called a high hill—jist as every sizeable hill to Nova Scotia is called a mountain. Well, sais the coachman to me, 'Tournez le Mechanique.' I didn't know what the devil he meant—I didn't onderstand French when its talked that way, and don't now. A man must speak very slow in French for me to guess what he wants. 'What in natur' is that?' sais I; but as he didn't onderstand English he just wrapt it up in three yards more of French, and give it back to me agin. So there was a pair of us. Well, the coach began to go down hill like winky, and the passengers put their heads out of the windows and bawled out 'Tournez le Mechanique,' and the coachman roared it out, and so did people on the streets, so what does I do but screams out too, 'Tournez le Mechanique.' Well, coachman seein' it war no use talkin', turned right about, put the pole thro' a pastry cook's window—throwed down his hosses, and upsot the coach, and away we all went, body and bones into the street. When I picked myself up, the coachman comes up and puts his fist into my face, and sais, 'You great lummakin fool, why didn't you Tournez le Mechanique,' and the passengers got all round me shakin' their fists too, sayin', 'Why didn't you Tournez le Mechanique?' I didn't know what the plague they meant, so I ups fist and shakes it at them, too, and roars out, 'Why in the name of sense,' sais I, 'didn't you Tournez le Mechanique?' Well, they began to larf at last, and one on 'em that spoke a little English, sais 'It meant to turn the handle of a little machine that put a drag on the wheels.' 'Oh!' sais I, 'is that it? What the plague's got into the feller not to speak plain English, if he had a-done that I should have onderstood him then.'

"Now that's the case with this Responsible Government, *it tante plain English, and they don't onderstand it.* As soon as the state coach begins to run down hill the people call out to the Governor 'Tournez le Mechanique,' and he gets puzzled and roars out to Secretary, 'Tournez le Mechanique,' and he gets mad, and sais, 'D—n you, Tournez le Mechanique yourself.' None on 'em knows the word—the coach runs down the hill like lightnin', upsets and smashes everything. *That comes a not speakin' plain English.* There is only one party pleased, and that's a party that likes to see all governments upsot. They say 'Its goin' on beautiful. It don't want a turn of the Mechanique at all,' and sing out, as the boatman did to his son when the barge was a-goin' over the falls to Ohio—'Let her went Peter, don't stop her, she's wrathy.'—What Minister sais is true enough. Government is intended for the benefit of all. All parties, therefore, should, as far as possible, have a voice in the Council—and equal justice be done to all—so that as all pay their shot to its support, all should have a share in its advantages. Them fellers to Canada have been a howlin' in the wilderness for years—'We are governed by a party—a clique—a family compact.' Well, England believed 'em, and the party—the clique—and the family compact was broken up. No sooner said than done—they turn right round, as quick as wink, and say—'We want a party government now—not that party, but our party—not that clique, but this clique—not that family compact, but this family compact. For that old party, clique, and compact were British in their language—British in their feelings, and British in their blood. Our party clique and compact is not so narrow and restricted, for it is French in its language, Yankee in its feelin', and Republican in its blood.'"

"Sam," said Mr. Hopewell, with that mildness of manner which was his great characteristic and charm, "that is strong language, very."

"Strong language, sir!" said the Colonel, rising in great wrath, "it's infamous,—none but a scoundrel or a fool would talk that way. D—n me, sir! what are them poor benighted people strugglin' for, but for freedom and independence? They want a leader, that's what they want. They should fust dress themselves as Indgins,—go to the wharves, and throw all the tea in the river, as we did; and then, in the dead of the night, seize on the high hill back of Montreal and fortify it, and when the British come, wait till they see the whites of their eyes, as we did at Bunker Hill, and give them death and destruction for breakfast, as we did. D—n me, sir!" and he seized the poker and waved it over his head, "let them do that, and send for me, and, old as I am, I'll lead them on to victory or death. Let 'em send for me, sir, and, by the 'tarnal, I'll take a few of my 'north-eend boys' with me, and shew 'em what clear grit is. Let the British send Wellington out to command the troops if they dare, and I'll let him know Bunker Hill! aint Waterloo, I know. Rear rank, take open order—right shoulders forward—march;" and he marched round the room and sat down.

"It's very strong language that, Sam," continued Mr. Hopewell, who never noticed the interruptions of the Colonel, "very strong language indeed, too strong I fear. It may wound the feelings of others, and that we have no right to do unnecessarily. Squire, if you report this conversation, as I suppose you will, leave out all the last sentence or two, and insert this: 'Responsible Government is a term not well defined or understood, and appears to be only applicable to an independent country. But whatever interpretation is put upon it, one thing is certain, the Government of Great Britain over her colonies is one of the *lightest, kindest, mildest, and most paternal in the whole world.*'"

XVI

THE DUKE OF KENT AND HIS TRUMPETER

MR. SLICK'S weak point was his vanity. From having risen suddenly in the world, by the unaided efforts of a vigorous, uneducated mind, he very naturally acquired great self-reliance. He undervalued every obstacle, or, what is more probable, over-looked the greater part of those that lay in his way. To a vulgar man like him, totally ignorant of the modes of life, a thousand little usages of society would unavoidably wholly escape his notice, while the selection, collocation, or pronunciation of words were things for which he appeared to have no perception and no ear. Diffidence is begotten by knowledge, presumption by ignorance. The more we know, the more extended the field appears upon which we have entered, and the more insignificant and imperfect our acquisition. The less we know, the less opportunity we have of ascertaining what remains to be learned. His success in his trade, his ignorance, the vulgarity of his early occupations and habits, and his subsequent notoriety as a humorist, all contributed to render him exceedingly vain. His vanity was of two kinds, national and personal. The first he has in common with a vast number of Americans. He calls his country "the greatest nation atween the Poles,"—he boasts "that the Yankees are the most free and enlightened citizens on the face of the airth, and that their institutions are the perfection of human wisdom." He is of his father's opinion, that the battle of Bunker Hill was the greatest battle ever fought; that their naval victories were the most brilliant achievements ever heard of; that New York is superior to London in beauty, and will soon be so in extent; and finally, that one Yankee is equal in all respects to two Englishmen, at least. If the Thames is mentioned, he calls it an insignificant creek, and reminds you that the Mississippi extends inland a greater distance than the space between Nova Scotia and England. If a noble old park tree is pointed out to him, he calls it a pretty little scrub oak, and immediately boasts of the pines of the Rocky Mountains, which he affirms are two hundred feet high. Show him a waterfall, and it is a noisy babbling little cascade compared with Niagara; or a lake, and it is a mere duck pond in comparison with Erie, Superior, Champlain, or Michigan. It has been remarked by most travellers, that this sort of thing is so common in the States, that it may be said to be almost universal. This is not *now* the case. It has prevailed more generally heretofore than at present, but it is now not much more obvious than in the people of any other country. *The necessity for it no longer exists.* That the Americans are proud of having won their independence at the point of the sword, from the most powerful nation in the world, under all the manifold disadvantages of poverty, dispersion, disunion, want of discipline in their soldiers, and experience in their officers, is not to be wondered at. They have reason to be proud of it. It is the greatest achievement of modern times. That they are proud of the consummate skill of their forefathers in framing a constitution the best suited to their position and their wants, and one withal, the most difficult in the world to adjust, not only with proper checks and balances, but with any checks at all,—at a time too when there was no model before them, and all experience against them, is still less to be wondered at. Nor have we any reason to object to the honest pride they exhibit of their noble country, their enlightened and enterprising people, their beautiful cities, their magnificent rivers, their gigantic undertakings. The sudden rise of nations, like the sudden rise of individuals, begets under similar circumstances similar effects. While there was the freshness of novelty about all these things, there was national vanity. It is now an old story—their laurels sit easy on them. They are accustomed to them, and they occupy less of their thoughts, and of course less of their conversation, than formerly. At first, too, strange as it may seem, *there existed a necessity for it.*

Good policy dictated the expediency of cultivating this self-complacency in the people, however much good taste might forbid it. As their constitution was based on self-government, it was indispensable to raise the people in their own estimation, and to make them feel the heavy responsibility that rested upon them, in order that they might qualify themselves for the part they were called upon to act. As they were weak, it was needful to confirm their courage by strengthening their self-reliance. As they were poor, it was proper to elevate their tone of mind, by constantly setting before them their high destiny; and as their Republic was viewed with jealousy and alarm by Europe, it was important to attach the nation to it, in the event of aggression, by extolling it above all others. The first generation, to whom all this was new, has now passed away; the second has nearly disappeared, and with the novelty, the excess of national vanity which it necessarily engendered will cease also. Personal vanity stands on wholly different grounds. There not only is no necessity, but no justification for it whatever. It is always offensive, sometimes even disgusting. Mr. Hopewell, who was in the habit of admonishing the Attaché whenever he thought admonition necessary, took occasion to-day to enlarge on both points. As to the first, he observed, that it was an American failing, and boasting abroad, as he often did, in extravagant terms of his country was a serious injury to it, for it always produced argument, and as those who argue always convince themselves in proportion as they fail to convince others, the only result of such discussions was to induce strangers to search for objections to the United States that they knew not before, and then adopt them for ever. But as for personal boasts, he said, they were beneath contempt.

"Tell you what it is, Minister," said Mr. Slick, "I am not the fool you take me to be. I deny the charge. I don't boast a bit more nor any foreigner, in fact, I don't think I boast at all. Hear old Bull here, every day, talkin' about the low Irish, the poor, mean, proud Scotch, the Yankee fellers, the horrid foreigners, the 'nothin' but a colonist,' and so on. He asks me out to entertain me, and then sings 'Britannia rules the waves.' My old grandmother used to rule a copy book, and I wrote on it. I guess the British rule the waves, and we write victory on it. Then hear that noisy, splutterin' crittur, Bull-Frog. He talks you dead about the Grand Nation, the beautiful France, and the capitol of the world,—Paris. What do I do? why I only say, 'our great, almighty republic is the toploftiest nation atween the Poles.' That aint boastin', nor crackin', nor nothin' of the sort. It's only jist a fact, like—all men must die—or any other truth. Oh, catch me a-boastin'! I know a trick worth two of that. It aint pleasant to be your own trumpeter always, I can tell you. It reminds me," said he (for he could never talk for five minutes without an illustration), "it reminds me of what happened to Queen's father in Nova Scotia, Prince Edward as they called him then.

"Oncet upon a time he was travellin' on the Great Western road, and most of the rivers, those days, had ferry-boats and no bridges. So his trumpeter was sent afore him to 'nounce his comin', with a great French horn, to the ferryman who lived on t'other side of the water. Well, his trumpeter was a Jarman, and didn't speak a word of English. Most all that family was very fond of Jarmans, they settle them everywhere a'most. When he came to the ferry, the magistrates and nobs, and big bugs of the county were all drawn up in state, waitin' for Prince. In those days abusin' and insultin' a Governor, kickin' up shindy in a province, and playin' the devil there, war'nt no recommendation in Downin' street. Colonists hadn't got their eyes open then, and at that time there was no school for the blind. It was Pullet Thompson taught them to read. Poor critturs! they didn't know no better then, so out they all goes to meet King's son, and pay their respects, and when Kissinkirk came to the bank, and they seed him all dressed in green, covered with gold-lace, and splenderiferous cocked-hat on, with lace on it, and a great big, old-fashioned brass French-horn, that was rubbed bright enough to put out eyes, a-hangin' over his shoulder, they took him for the Prince, for they'd never seed nothin' half so fine afore. The bugle they took for gold, 'cause, in course, a Prince wouldn't wear nothin' but gold, and they thought it was his huntin' horn—and his bein' alone they took for state, 'cause he was too big for any one to ride with. So they all off hats at once to old Kissinkirk, the Jarman trumpeter. Lord, when he seed that, he was bungfungered!

"'Thun sie ihren hut an du verdamnter thor,' sais he, which means, in English, 'Put on your hats, you cussed fools.' Well, they was fairly stumpt. They looked fust at him and bowed, and then at each other; and stared vacant; and then he sais agin, 'Mynheers, damn!' for that was the only English word he knew, and then he stampt agin, and sais over in Dutch once more to put on their hats; and then called over as many (crooked) Jarman oaths as would reach across the river if they were stretched out strait. 'What in natur' is that?' sais one; 'Why, high Dutch,' sais an old man; 'I heerd the Waldecker troops at the evakyation of New

York speak it. Don't you know the King's father was a high Dutchman, from Brunswick; in course the Prince can't speak English.' 'Well,' sais the other, 'do you know what it means?' 'In course I do,' sais Loyalist, (and oh if some o' them boys couldn't lie, I don't know who could, that's all; by their own accounts it's a wonder how we ever got independence, for them fellers swore they won every battle that was fought,) 'in course I do,' sais he, 'that is,' sais he, 'I used to did to speak it at Long Island, but that's a long time ago. Yes, I understand a leetle,' sais Loyalist. 'His Highness' excellent Majesty sais,—Man the ferry-boat, and let the magistrates row me over the ferry.—It is a beautiful language, is Dutch.' 'So it is,' sais they, 'if one could only understand it,' and off they goes, and spreads out a great roll of home-spun cloth for him to walk on, and then they form two lines for him to pass through to the boat. Lord! when he comes to the cloth he stops agin, and stamps like a jackass when the flies tease him, and gives the cloth a kick up, and wouldn't walk on it, and sais in high Dutch, in a high Jarman voice too, 'You infarnal fools!—you stupid blockheads!—you cussed jackasses!' and a great deal more of them pretty words, and then walked on. 'Oh dear!' sais they, 'only see how he kicks the cloth; that's cause it's homespun. Oh dear! but what does he say?' sais they. Well, Loyalist felt stumpt; he knew some screw was loose with the Prince by the way he shook his fist, but what he couldn't tell; but as he had begun he had to go knee deep into it, and push on. 'He sais, he hopes he may die this blessed minit if he wont tell his father, the old King, when he returns to home, how well you have behaved,' sais he, 'and that it's a pity to soil such beautiful cloth.' 'Oh!' sais they, 'was that it?' we was afraid somethin' or another had gone wrong; come, let's give three cheers for the Prince's Most Excellent Majesty,' and they made the woods and the river ring agin. Oh, how mad Kissenkirk was! he expected the Prince would tie him up and give him five hundred lashes for his impedence in representin' of him. Oh! he was ready to bust with rage and vexation. He darsn't strike any one, or he would have given 'em a slap with the horn in a moment, he was so wrathy. So what does he do as they was holdin' the boat, but ups trumpet and blew a blast in the Custos' ear, all of a sudden, that left him hard of hearin' on that side for a month; and he sais in high Dutch, 'Tunder and blitzen! Take that, you old fool; I wish I could blow you into the river.' Well, they rowed him over the river, and then formed agin two lines, and Kissenkirk passed up atween 'em as sulky as a bear; and then he put his hand in his pocket, and took out somethin', and held it out to Custos, who dropt right down on his knee in a minit, and received it, and it was a fourpenny bit. Then Kissinkirk waved his hand to them to be off quick-stick, and muttered agin somethin' which Loyalist said was 'Go across agin and wait for my sarvants,' which they did. 'Oh!' sais the magistrates to Custos, as they was a-goin' back agin 'how could you take pay, squire? How could you receive money from Prince? Our county is disgraced for ever. You have made us feel as mean as Ingians.' 'I wouldn't have taken it if it had been worth anythin',' sais Custos, 'but didn't you see his delicacy; he knowed that too, as well as I did, so he offered me a fourpenny bit, as much as to say, 'You are above all pay, but accept the smallest thing possible, as a keepsake from King's son.' 'Those were his very words,' sais loyalist; I'll swear to 'em, the very identical ones.' 'I thought so,' sais Custos, looking big. 'I hope I know what is due to his Majesty's Royal Highness, and what is due to me, also, as Custos of this county.' And he drew himself up stately, and said nothin', and looked as wise as the owl who had been studyin' a speech for five years, and intended to speak it when he got it by heart. Jist then down comes Prince and all his party, galloppin' like mad to the ferry, for he used to ride always as if old Nick was at his heels; jist like a streak of lightnin'. So up goes the Custos to prince, quite free and easy, without so much as touchin' his hat, or givin' him the time o' day. 'What the plague kept you so long?' sais he; 'your master has been waitin' for you this half-hour. Come, bear a hand, the Prince is all alone over there.' It was some time afore Prince made out what he meant; but when he did, if he didn't let go it's a pity. He almost upsot the boat, he larfed so obstroperous. One squall o' larfin' was hardly over afore another come on. Oh, it was a tempestical time, you may depend; and when he'd got over one fit of it, he'd say, 'Only think of them takin' old Kissinkirk for me!' and he'd larf agin ready to split. Kissinkirk was frightened to death; he didn't know how Prince would take it, or what he would do, for he was an awful strict officer; but when he seed him larf so he knowed all was right. Poor old Kissinkirk! the last time I seed him was to Windsor. He lived in a farm-house there, on charity. He'd larnt a little English, though not much. It was him told me the story; and when he wound it up, he sais, 'It tante always sho shafe, Mishter Shlick, to be your own drumpeter;' and I'll tell you what, Minister, I am of the same opinion with the old bugler. It is *not* always safe to be one's own trumpeter, and that's a fact."

XVII

REPEAL

EVER since we have been in London we have taken "The Times" and "The Morning Chronicle," so as to have before us both sides of every question. This morning, these papers were, as usual, laid on the breakfast table; and Mr. Slick, after glancing at their contents, turned to Mr. Hopewell, and said, "Minister, what's your opinion of O'Connell's proceedings? What do you think of him?"

"I think differently from most men, Sam," he said; "I neither join in the unqualified praise of his friends, nor in the wholesale abuse of his enemies, for there is much to approve and much to censure in him. He has done, perhaps, as much good and as much harm to Ireland as her best friend or her worst enemy. I am an old man now, daily treading on the confines of the grave, and not knowing the moment the ground may sink under me and precipitate me into it. I look, therefore, on all human things with calmness and impartiality, and besides being an American and a Republican, I have no direct interest in the man's success or failure, farther than they may affect the happiness of the great human family. Looking at the struggle, therefore, as from an eminence, a mere spectator, I can see the errors of both sides, as clearly as a bystander does those of two competitors at a game of chess. My eyesight, however, is dim, and I find I cannot trust to the report of others. Party spirit runs so high in Ireland, it is difficult to ascertain the truth of anything. Facts are sometimes invented, often distorted, and always magnified. No man either thinks kindly or speaks temperately of another, but a deadly animosity has superseded Christian charity in that unhappy land. We must not trust to the opinions of others, therefore, but endeavour to form our own. Now, he is charged with being a Roman Catholic. The answer to this is, he has a right to be one if he chooses—as much right as I have to be a Churchman; that if I differ from him on some points, I concur with him in more, and only grieve we cannot agree in all; and that whatever objections I have to his Church, I have a thousand times more respect for it than I have for a thousand dissenting political sects, that disfigure and degrade the Christian world. Then they say, 'Oh, yes, but he is a bigoted Papist!' Well, if they have nothing worse than this to allege against him, it don't amount to much. Bigotry means an unusual devotion, and an extraordinary attachment to one's church. I don't see how a sincere and zealous man can be otherwise than bigoted. It would be well if he were imitated in this respect by Protestants. Instead of joining schismatics and sectarians, a little more bigoted attachment to our excellent Mother Church would be safer and more respectable for them, and more conducive to the interests of true religion. But the great charge is he is an Agitator; now I don't like agitation even in a good cause. It is easy to open flood-gates, but always difficult, and sometimes impossible, to close them again. No; I do not like agitation. It is a fearful word. But if ever there was a man justified in resorting to it, which I doubt, it was O'Connell. A Romish Catholic by birth, and, if you will have it, a bigoted one by education, he saw his countrymen labouring under disabilities on account of their faith,—what could be more natural for him than to suppose that he was serving both God and his country, by freeing his Church from its distinctive and degrading badge, and elevating Irishmen to a political equality with Englishmen. The blessings of the priesthood, and the gratitude of the people, hailed him wherever he went; and when he attained the victory, and wrested the concession from him who wrested the sceptre from Napoleon, he earned the title, which he has since worn, of 'the Liberator.' What a noble and elevated position he then stood in! But, Sam, agitation is progressive. The impetus of his onward course was too great to suffer him to rest, and the 'Liberator' has sunk again into the Agitator, without the sanctity of the cause to justify, or the approval of mankind to reward him. Had he then paused for a moment, even for a moment, when he gained emancipation, and looked around him, what a prospect lay before him which ever way he turned, for diffusing peace and happiness over Ireland. Having secured an equality of political rights to his countrymen, and elevated the position of the peasantry,—had he then endeavoured to secure the rights of the landlord, and revive the sympathy between them and their tenants, which agitation had extinguished;—had he, by suppressing crime and outrage, rendered it safe for absentees to return, or for capital to flow into his impoverished country,—had he looked into the future for images of domestic comfort and tranquillity to delight the imagination, instead of resorting to the dark vistas of the past for scenes of oppression and violence to. inflame the passions of his countrymen,—had he held out the right hand of fellowship to his Protestant brethren, and invited and induced them to live in the unity of love and the bonds of peace with their Romish neighbours, his second victory would have surpassed the first, and the stern Liberator would have been again crowned amid the benedictions of all, as 'the Father' of his country. But, alas! agitation has no tranquil eddies to repose in; it rides on the billow and the tempest, and lives but on the troubled waters of the deep.

"Instead of this happy condition, what is now the state of Ireland? The landlord flies in alarm from a home that is no longer safe from the midnight marauder. The capitalist refuses to open his purse to develop the resources of a country, that is threatened with a civil war. Men of different creeds pass each other with looks of defiance, and with that stern silence that marks the fixed resolve, to 'do or die.' The Government, instead of being able to ameliorate the condition of the poor, is engaged in garrisoning its forts, supplying its arsenals, and preparing for war; while the poor deluded people are drawn away from their peaceful and honest pursuits, to assemble in large bodies, that they may be inflamed by seditious speeches, and derive fresh confidence from the strength or impunity of numbers.

"May God of his infinite goodness have mercy on the author of all these evils, and so purify his heart from the mistaken motives that now urge him onwards in his unhappy course, that he may turn and repent him of his evil way, while return is yet practicable, and repentance not too late

"Now, what is all this excitement to lead to? A Repeal of the Union? what is that? Is it independence, or is it merely a demand for a dependant local legislature? If it is independence, look into futurity, and behold the state of Ireland at the end of a few years. You see that the Protestants of the North have driven out all of the opposite faith, and that the Catholics, on their part, have exiled or exterminated all the heretics from the South. You behold a Chinese wall of separation running across the island, and two independent, petty, separate States, holding but little intercourse, and hating each other with an intensity only to be equalled by tribes of savages. And how is this unhappy condition to be attained? By a cruel, a wicked, and a merciless civil war, for no war is so bloody as a domestic one, especially where religion, terrified at its horrors, flies from the country in alarm, and the banner of the Cross is torn from the altar to be desecrated in the battlefield. Sam, I have seen one, may my eyes never behold another. No tongue can tell, no pen describe, no imagination conceive its horrors. Even now, after the lapse of half a century, I shudder at the recollection of it. If it be not independence that is sought, but a local legislature, then Ireland descends from an integral part of the empire into a colony, and the social position of the people is deteriorated. Our friend, the Squire, who, at this moment, is what O'Connell desires to be, a colonist, is labouring incessantly to confirm and strengthen the connexion of the possessions abroad with England, to break down all distinctions, to procure for his countrymen equal rights and privileges, and either to abolish that word 'English,' and substitute 'British,' or to obliterate the term 'Colonial,' and extend the generic term of English to all. He is demanding a closer and more intimate connexion, and instead of excluding Colonists from Parliament, is anxious for them to be represented there. In so doing he evinces both his patriotism and his loyalty. O'Connell, on the contrary, is struggling to revive the distinction of races, to awaken the hostility of separate creeds, to dissolve the Political Union. If he effects his purpose, he merely *weakens England*, but he *ruins Ireland*. This line of conduct may originate in his bigotry, and probably it does, but vanity, temper, and the rent, are nevertheless to be found at the bottom of this boiling cauldron of agitation.

"Oh! that some Father Matthew would arise, some pious priest, some holy bishop, some worthy man, (for they have many excellent clergymen, learned prelates, and great and good men in their Church,) and staff in hand, like a pilgrim of old, preach up good will to man, peace on earth, and Unity of Spirit. Even yet the struggle might be avoided, if the good would act wisely, and the wise act firmly. Even now O'Connell, if he would adopt this course, and substitute conciliation for agitation, (for hitherto conciliation has been all on the other side,) would soon have the gratification to see his country prosperous and happy. While those who now admire his talents, though they deprecate his conduct, would gladly unite in acknowledging the merits, and heaping honours on the 'Pacificator of all Ireland.' No, my friends, so far from desiring to see the Union dissolved, as a philanthropist and a Christian, and as a politician, I say, 'Esto Perpetua.'"

XVIII

THE HORSE STEALER, OR ALL TRADES HAVE TRICKS BUT OUR OWN

AFTER dinner to-day the conversation turned upon the treaties existing between England and the United States, and I expressed my regret that in all, the Americans had a decided advantage.

"Well, I won't say we hante," said Mr. Slick. "The truth is, we *do* understand diplomacy, that's a fact. Treaties, you see, are bargains, and a feller would be a fool to make a bad bargain, and if there aint no rael cheatin' in it, why a man has a right to make as good a one as he can. We got the best of the Boundary Line, that's a fact, but then Webster aint a crittur that looks as if the yeast was left out of him by mistake, he aint quite as soft as dough, and he aint onderbaked nother. Well, the tariff is a good job for us too, so is the fishery story, and the Oregon will be all right in the eend too. We write our clauses so they bind; your diplomatists write them so you can drive a stage coach and six through 'em, and not touch the hobs on either side. Our socdolagers is too deep for any on 'em. So polite, makes such soft-sawder speeches, or talks so big; hints at a great American market, advantages of peace, difficulty of keepin' our folks from goin' to war; boast of our old home, same kindred and language, magnanimity and good faith of England; calls compensation for losses only a little affair of money, knows how to word a sentence so it will read like a riddle, if you alter a stop, grand hand at an excuse, gives an answer that means nothing, dodge and come up t'other side, or dive so deep you can't follow him. Yes, we have the best of the treaty business, that's a fact. Lord! how I have often laughed at that story of Felix Foyle and the horse-stealer! Did I ever tell you that contrivance of his to do the Governor of Canada?"

"No," I replied, "I never heard of it." He then related the story, with as much glee as if the moral delinquency of the act was excusable in a case of such ingenuity.

"It beats all," he said. "Felix Foyle lived in the back part of the State of New York, and carried on a smart chance of business in the provision line. Beef, and pork, and flour was his staples, and he did a great stroke in 'em. Perhaps he did to the tune of four hundred thousand dollars a-year, more or less. Well, in course, in such a trade as that, he had to employ a good many folks, as clerks, and salters, and agents, and what not, and among them was his book-keeper, Sossipater Cuddy. Sossipater (or Sassy, as folks used to call him, for he was rather high in the instep, and was Sassy by name and Sassy by natur' too,)—well, Sassy was a cute man, a good judge of cattle, a grand hand at a bargain, and a'most an excellent scholar at figures. He was ginerally allowed to be a first-rate business man. Only to give you an idee, now, of that smartness, how ready and up to the notch he was at all times, I must jist stop fust, and tell you the story of the cigar.

"In some of our towns we don't allow smokin' in the streets, though in most on 'em we do, and where it is agin law it is two dollars fine in a gineral way. Well, Sassy went down to Bosten to do a little chore of business there, where this law was, only he didn't know it. So, as soon as he gets off the coach, he outs with his case, take a cigar, lights it, and walks on smokin' like a furnace flue. No sooner said than done. Up steps constable, and sais, 'I'll trouble you for two dollars for smokin' agin law in the streets.' Sassy was as quick as wink on him. 'Smokin'!' sais he, 'I warn't a-smokin'.' 'Oh, my!' sais constable, 'how you talk, man. I won't say you lie, 'cause it aint polite, but it's very like the way I talk when I lie. Didn't I see you with my own eyes?' 'No,' sais Sassy, 'you didn't. It don't do always to believe your own eyes, they can't be depended on more nor other people's. I never trust mine, I can tell you. I own I had a cigar in my mouth, but it was because I like the flavor of the tobacco, but not to smoke. I take it it don't convene with the dignity of a free and enlightened citizen of our almighty nation to break the law, seein' that he makes the law himself, and is his own sovereign, and his own subject too. No, I warn't smokin', and if you don't believe me, try this cigar yourself, and see if it aint so. It hante got no fire in it.' Well, constable takes the cigar, puts it into his mug, and draws away at it, and out comes the smoke like anythin'.

"'I'll trouble *you* for two dollars, Mr. High Sheriff devil,' sais Sassy, 'for smokin' in the streets; do you undercenstand, my old 'coon?' Well, constable was all taken aback, he was finely bit. 'Stranger,' sais he, 'where was you raised?' 'To Canady line,' sais Sassy. 'Well,' sais he, 'your a credit to your broghtens up. Well, let the net drop, for we are about even I guess. Lets liquor;' and he took him into a bar and treated him to a mint julep. It was ginerally considered a great bite that, and I must say I don't think it was bad—do you? But to get back to where I started from. Sassy, as I was a-sayin', was the book-keeper of old Felix Foyle. The old gentleman sot great store by him, and couldn't do without him, on no account, he was so ready like, and always on hand. But Sassy thought he could do without *him*, tho'. So, one fine day, he absgotilated with four thousand dollars in his pocket, of Felix's, and cut dirt for Canady as hard as he could clip. Felix Foyle was actilly in a most beautiful frizzle of a fix. He knew who he had to deal with, and that he might as well follow a fox a'most as Sassy, he was so everlastin' cunnin', and that the British wouldn't give up a debtor to us, but only felons; so he thought the fust loss was the best, and was about givin' it up as a bad job, when an idee struck him, and oft he started in chase with steam on. Felix was the clear grit when his dander was up, and he never slept night or day till he reached Canady, too; got on the trail of Sassy, and came up to where he was airthed at Niagara. When he arrived it was about noon, so as he enters the tavern he sees Sassy standin' with his face to the fire and his back to the door, and what does he do but slip into the meal-room and hide himself till night. Jist as it was dark in comes old Bambrick, the inn-keeper, with a light in his hand, and Felix slips behind him, and shuts too the door, and tells him the whole story from beginnin' to eend; how Sassy had sarved him; and lists the old fellow in his sarvice, and off they set to a magistrate and get out a warrant, and then they goes to the deputy sheriff and gets Sassy arrested. Sassy was so taken aback he was hardly able to speak for the matter of a minit or so, for he never expected Felix would follow him into Canady at all, seem' that if he oncet reached British side he was safe. But he soon come too agin, so he ups and bullies 'Pray, sir,' sais he, 'what do you mean by this?' 'Nothin' above partikelar,' sais Felix, quite cool, 'only I guess I want the pleasure of your company back, that's all,' and then turnin' to the onder sheriff, 'Squire,' sais he, 'will you take a turn or two in the entry, while Sassy and I settle a little matter of business together,' and out goes Nab. 'Mr. Foyle,' sais Sassy, 'I have no business to settle with you—arrest me, sir, at your peril, and I'll action you in law for false imprisonment.' 'Where's my money?' sais Felix—'where's my four thousand dollars?' 'What do I know about your money?' sais Sassy. 'Well,' sais Felix, 'it is your business to know, and I paid you as my book-keeper to know, and if you don't know you must jist return with me and find out, that's all—so come, let's us be a-movin'. Well, Sassy larfed right out in his face; 'why you cussed fool,' sais he, 'don't you know I can't be taken out o' this colony State, but only for crime, what a rael soft horn you be to have done so much business and not know that?' 'I guess I got a warrant that will take you out tho', sais Felix—'read that,' a-handin' of the paper to him. 'No. I shall swear to that agin, and send it to Governor, and down will come the marchin' order in quick stick. I'm soft I know, but I aint sticky for all that, I ginerally come off clear without leavin' no part behind.' The moment Sassy read the warrant his face fell, and the cold perspiration rose out like rain-drops, and his color went and came, and his knees shook like anythin'. 'Hoss-stealin'!' sais he, aloud to himself—'hoss-stealin'!'—Heavens and airth, what parjury!! Why, Felix,' sais he, 'you know devilish well I never stole your hoss, man; how could you go and swear to such an infarnal lie as that?' 'Why I'm nothin' but "a cussed fool" and a "rael soft horn," you know,' sais Felix, 'as you said jist now, and if I had gone and sworn to the debt, why you'd a kept the money, gone to jail, and swore out, and I'd a-had my trouble for my pains. So you see I swore you stole my hoss, for that's a crime, tho' absquotolative aint, and that will force the British Governor to deliver you up, and when I get you into New York state, why you settle with me for my four thousand dollars, and I will settle with you for stealin' my hoss,' and he put his finger to the tip eend of his nose, and winked and said, 'young folks *think* old folks is fools, but old folks *know* young folks is fools. I warn't born yesterday, and I had my eye-teeth sharpened before your'n were through the gums, I guess—you hante got the Bosten constable to deal with now, I can tell you, but old Felix Foyle himself, and he aint so blind but what he can feel his way along I guess— do you take my meanin', my young 'coon?' 'I'm sold,' sais Sassy, and he sot down, put both elbows on the table, and covered his face with his hands, and fairly cried like a child. 'I'm sold,' sais he. 'Buy your pardon, then,' sais Felix, 'pay down the four thousand dollars and you are a free and enlightened citizen once more.' Sassy got up, unlocked his portmanter, and counted it out all in paper rolls jist as he received it. 'There it is,' sais he, 'and I must say you desarve it; that was a great stroke of your'n.' 'Stop a bit,' sais Felix, seein' more money there, all his savin's for years, 'we aint done yet, I must have 500 dollars for expenses.' 'There, d—n you,' sais Sassy, throwin' another roll at him, 'there it is; are you done yet?' 'No,' sais Felix, 'not yet; now you have done me justice, I must do you the same, and clear your character. Call in that gentleman, the constable, from the entry, and I will go a treat of half a pint of brandy.—'Mr. Officer,' sais Felix,—'here is some mistake, this gentleman has convinced me he was only follerin', as my clerk, a debtor of mine here, and when he transacts his business, will return, havin' left his hoss at the lines, where I can get him if I choose; and I must say I am glad on't for the credit of the nation abroad. Fill your glass, here's a five dollar bill for your fees, and here's to your good health. If you want provision to ship off in the way of trade, I'm Felix Foyle, and shall be happy to accommodate you.'

"Now," said Mr. Slick, "that is what I call a rael clever trick, a great card that, warn't it? He desarves credit, does Felix, it aint every one would a-been up to trap that way, is it?"

"Sam," said his father, rising with great dignity and formality of manner, "was that man, Felix Foyle, ever a military man?"

"No, sir; he never had a commission, even in the militia, as I knows on."

"I thought not," said the Colonel, "no man, that had seen military life, could ever tell a lie, much less take a false oath. That feller, sir, is a villain, and I wish Washington and I had him to the halberts; by the 'tarnal, we'd teach him to disgrace our great name before those benighted colonists. A liar, sir! as Doctor Franklin said, (the great Doctor Franklin, him that burn't up two forts of the British in the revolution war, by bringin' down lightnin' on 'em from Heaven by a wire string)—a liar, sir! Show me a liar, and I'll show you a thief."

"What was he?" said Mr. Hopewell.

"A marchant in the provision line," said the Attaché.

"No, no; I didn't mean that," he replied. "What sect did he belong to?"

"Oh! now I onderstand. Oh! a wet Quaker to be sure, they are the cutest people its ginerally allowed we have in all our nation."

"Ah!" said the Minister, "I was certain he was not brought up in the Church. We teach morals as well as doctrines, and endeavour to make our people exhibit the soundness of the one by the purity of the other. I felt assured, either that he could not be a churchman, or that his parish minister must have grossly and wickedly neglected his duty in not inculcating better principles."

"Yes," said Mr. Slick, with a very significant laugh, "and he warn't a clockmaker, nother."

"I hope not," said his father, gravely,

"I hope not, Sam. Some on 'em," (looking steadily at his son,) "some on 'em are so iley and slippery, they do squeeze between a truth and a lie so, you wonder how it was ever possible for mortal man to go thro', but for the honor of the clockmakers, I hope he warn't one."

"No," said Mr. Slick, "he warn't, I assure you. But you Father, and Minister, and me, are all pretty much tarred with the same stick, I guess— we all think, *all trades have tricks but our own.*"

VOLUME II

VOLUME II

I

THE PLEASURES OF HOPE

TO-DAY we witnessed the interment of Thomas Campbell, the author of "The Pleasures of Hope," in the Poet's Corner in Westminster Abbey. Owing to some mismanagement in the arrangements, a great part of the friends of the deceased did not arrive until the service was nearly half over, which enabled us, who were very early in the Abbey, to obtain a good position within the barriers. Sir Robert Peel, the Duke of Argyle, Lord Brougham, and a great number of noblemen and statesmen, were present to do honour to his remains, while the service was read by Mr. Milman—himself a distinguished poet. For a long time after the ceremony was over, and the crowd had dispersed, we remained in the Abbey examining the monuments, and discoursing of the merits or the fortunes of those whose achievements had entitled them to the honour of being laid with the great and the good of past ages, in this national temple of Fame. Our attention was soon arrested by an exclamation of Mr. Slick.

"Hullo!" said he, "how the plague did this feller get here? Why, Squire, as I'me a livin' sinner, here's a colonist! what crime did he commit that they took so much notice of him? 'Sacred to the memory of William Wragg, Esq., of South Carolina, who, when the American colonies revolted from Great Britain, inflexibly maintained his loyalty to the person and government of his Sovereign, and was therefore compelled to leave his distressed family and ample fortune.' Oh Lord! I thought it must have been some time before the flood, for loyalty in the colonies is at a discount now; its a bad road to preferment, I can tell you. Agitation,

bullyin' governors, shootin' down sogers, and rebellin' is the passport
now-a-days. Them were the boys Durham and Thompson honoured;—
all the loyal old cocks, all them that turned out and fought and saved the
country, got a cold shoulder for their officiousness. But they are curious
people is the English; they are like Deacon Flint,—he never could see
the pint of a good thing till it was too late. Sometimes arter dinner he'd
bust out a larfin' like anything, for all the world as if he was a born fool,
seemin'ly at nothin', and I'd say, 'why, Deacon, what maggot's bit you
now?' 'I was larfin,' he'd say, 'at that joke of your'n this mornin'; I did'nt
take jist then, but I see it now.' 'Me!' sais I, 'why, *what* did I say, it's so long
ago I forget!' 'Why,' sais he, 'don't you mind we was a-talkin' of them two
pirates the jury found not guilty, and the court turned *loose* on the town;
you said it was all right, for they was *loose characters*. Oh! I see it *now*, it
was rael jam that.' 'Oh!' sais I, not overly pleased nother, for a joke, like an
egg, is never no good 'xcept it's fresh laid,—is it?

"Well, the English are like the old Deacon; they don't see a man's merit
till he's dead, and then they wake up all of a sudden and say, 'Oh! we must
honour this feller's skeleton,' and Peel, and Brougham, and all the dons,
go and play pall-bearers to it, stand over his grave, look sentimental, and
attitudenize a few; and when I say to 'em you hadn't ought to have laid
him right a'top of old Dr. Johnson—for he hated Scotchmen so like old
Scratch; if he was to find it out he'd kick strait up on eend, and throw
him off; they won't larf, but give me a look, as much as to say, Westminster
Abbey aint no place to joke in. Jist as if it warn't a most beautiful joke
to see these men, who could have done ever so much for the poet in
his life-time, when it could have done him good—but who never even
so much as held out a finger to him, except in a little matter not worth
havin',—now he is dead, start up all at once and patronize his body
and bones when it can't do him one mossel of good. Oh! they are like
Deacon Flint, they understand when it's too late.

"Poor old Tom Campbell, there was some pleasures of hope that he
never sot down in his book, I know. He hoped—as he had charmed and
delighted the nation, and given 'em another ondyin' name, to add to their
list of poets, to crack and to brag of—he'd a had a recompense at least
in some government appointment that would have cheered and soothed
his old age, and he was disappinted, that's all: and that's the pleasures of
hope, Squire, eh? He hoped that fame, which he had in his life, would

have done him some good in his life—didn't he? Well, he lived on that hope till he died, and that didn't disappint him; for how can a feller say he is disappinted by a thing he has lived on all his days? and that's the Pleasures of Hope.

"He hoped, in course, Peel would be a patron of poets—and so he is, he acts as a pall-bearer, 'cause as soon as the pall is over him, he'd never bother him, nor any other minister no more. Oh! 'Hope told a flatterin' tale;' but all flatterers are liars. Peel has a princely fortune, and a princely patronage, and is a prince of a feller; but there is an old sayin', 'Put not your trust in Princes.' If poor Tom was alive and kickin', I'd tell him who to put his trust in—and that's Bentley. He is the only patron worth havin', that's a fact. He does it so, like a gentleman: 'I have read the poem, Mr. Campbell, you were so kind as to indulge me with the perusal of; if you would permit me to favour the world with a sight of it, I shall have great pleasure in placin' a cheque for two thousand guineas in your banker's hands.'

"Oh that's the patron. The great have nothin' but smiles and bows, Bentley has nothin' but the pewter—that's what I like to drink my beer out of. Secretaries of State are cattle it's pretty hard to catch in a field and put a bridle on, I can tell you. No, they have nothin' but smiles, and it requires to onderstand the language of smiles, for there are all sorts of them, and they all speak a different tongue.

"I have seen five or six of them secretaries, and Spring Rice, to my mind, was the toploftiest boy of 'em all. Oh! he was the boy to smile; he could put his whole team on sometimes if he liked, and run you right off the road. Whenever he smiled very gracious, followed you to the door, and shook you kindly by the hand, and said,—call again, your flint was fixed; you never seed him no more. Kind-hearted crittur, he wanted to spare you the pain of a refusal, and bein' a little coquettish he puts his prettiest smile on as you was never to meet agin, to leave a favourable impression behind him; they all say—call agin: Bentley, never! No *pleasures of hope with him*; he *is* a patron, he don't wait for the pall.

"Peel, sportsman-like, is in at the death; Bentley comes with the nurse, and is in at the birth. There is some use in such a patron as that. Ah! poor Campbell! he was a poet, a good poet, a beautiful poet! He knowed all about the world of imagination, and the realms of fancy; but he didn't know nothin' at at all about this world of our'n, or of the realm of England, or he never would have talked of the 'Pleasures of Hope' for an author. Lord bless you! let a dancin' gal come to the opera, jump six foot high, 'light on one toe, hold up the other so high you can see her stays a'most, and then spin round like a daddy-long legs that's got one foot caught in a taller candle, and go spinnin' round arter that fashion for ten minits, it will touch Peel's heart in a giffy. This spinnin' jinny will be honored by the highest folks in the land, have diamond rings, gold snuffboxes, and pusses of money given her, and gracious knows what.

"Let Gineral Torn Thumb come to London that's two foot nothin', and the Kentucky boy that's eight foot somethin', and see how they will be patronised, and what a sight of honor they will have. Let Van Amburg come with his lion, make him open his jaws, and then put his head down his throat and pull it out, and say, 'What a brave boy am I!' and kings and queens, and princes and nobles will come and see him, and see his lion feed too. Did any on 'em ever come to see Campbell feed? he was a great lion this many a long day. Oh dear! he did'nt know nothin', that's a fact; he thought himself a cut above them folks: it jist showed how much he know'd. Fine sentiments! Lord, who cares for them!

"Do you go to Nova Scotia now, and begin at Cape Sable, and travel all down to Cape Canso,—the whole length of the province, pick out the two best lines from his 'Hope,' and ask every feller you meet, 'did you ever hear these?' and how many will you find that has seen 'em, or heerd tell of 'em? Why a few gals that's sentimental, and a few boys that's a-courtin', spooney-like, that's all.

"But ax 'em this, 'Master, if that house cost five hundred dollars, and a barrel of nails five dollars, what would a good sizeable pig come to?—do you give it up?' Well, he'd come to a bushel of corn. Every man, woman, and child would tell you they heerd the clown say that to the circus, and that they mind they larfed ready to kill themselves. Grinnin' pays better nor rhymin', and ticklin' the ribs with fingers pleases folks more, and makes 'em larf more, than ticklin' their ears with varses—that's a fact.

"I guess, when Campbell writ 'The Mariners of England,'—that will live till the Britisher's sailors get whipped by us so they will be ashamed to sing it—he thought himself great shakes; heavens and airth! he warn't harf so big as Tom Thumb—he was jist nothin'. But let some foreign hussey, whose skin aint clear, and whose character aint clear, and whose debts aint clear, and who hante nothin' clear about her but her voice, let her come and sing that splendid song that puts more ginger into sailors than grog or prize money, or anythin', and Lord! all the old admirals and flag-officers, and yacht-men and others that do onderstand, and all the lords and ladies and princes, that don't onderstand where the springs are in that song, that touch the chords of the heart,—all on 'em will come and worship a'most; and some young Duke or another will fancy he is a young Jupiter, and come down in a shower of gold a'most for her, while the poet has 'The Pleasures of Hope' to feed on. Oh! I envy him, glorious man, I envy him his great reward; it was worth seventy years of 'hope,' was that funeral.

"He was well repaid—Peel held a string of the pall, Brougham came and said 'how damn cold the Abbey is:' the Duke of Argyle, Scotchman-like, rubbed his back agin Roubilliac's statue of his great ancestor, and thought it was a pity he hadn't migrated to Prince Edward's Island; D'Israeli said he was one of the 'Curiosities of Literature;' while Macaulay, who looks for smart things, said, 'Poor fellow, this was always the object of his ambition; it was his 'hope beyond the grave.'"

"Silence, sir," said Mr. Hopewell, with more asperity of manner than I ever observed in him before; "Silence, sir. If you will not respect yourself, respect, at least, the solemnity of the place in which you stand. I never heard such unworthy sentiments before; though they are just what might be expected from a pedlar of clocks. You have no ideas beyond those of dollars and cents, and you value fame as you would a horse, by what it will fetch in ready money. Your observations on the noblemen and gentlemen who have done themselves honor this day, as well as the Poet, by taking a part in this sad ceremony, are both indecent and unjust; while your last remark is absolutely profane. I have every reason to believe, sir, that he had a 'hope beyond the grave.' All his writings bear the stamp of a mind strongly imbued with the pure spirit of religion: he must himself have felt 'the hope beyond the grave' to have described it as he has done; it is a passage of great beauty and sublimity.

'Eternal Hope! when yonder spheres sublime
Pealed their first notes to sound the march of Time,
Thy joyous youth began—but not to fade,—When all the sister
planets have decay'd;
When wrapt in fire the realms of ether glow,

And Heaven's last thunder shakes the world below;
    Thou undismay'd, shalt o'er the ruins smile,
And light, thy torch at Nature's funeral pile.'

"We have both done wrong to-day, my son; you have talked flippantly and irreverently, and I have suffered my temper to be agitated in a very unbecoming manner, and that, too, in consecrated ground, and in the house of the Lord. I am not disposed to remain here just now—let us depart in peace—give me your arm, my son, and we will discourse of other things."

When we returned to our lodgings, Mr. Slick, who felt hurt at the sharp rebuke he had received from Mr. Hopewell, recurred again to the subject.

"That was one of the old man's crotchets to-day, Squire," he said; "he never would have slipt off the handle that way, if that speech of Macaulay's hadn't a-scared him like, for he is as skittish as a two-year-old, at the least sound of such a thing. Why, I have heerd him say himself, the lot of a poet was a hard one, over and over again; and that the world let them fust starve to death, and then built monuments to 'em that cost more money than would have made 'em comfortable all their born days. Many and many a time, when he used to make me say over to him as a boy 'Gray's Elegy,' he'd say, 'Ah! poor man, he was neglected till attention came too late.—When he was old and infirm, and it could do him no good, they made him a professor in some college or another;' and then he'd go over a whole string—Mason, Mickle, Burns, and I don't know who all, for I aint much of a bookster, and don't recollect;—and how often I've heerd him praise our Government for makin' Washington Irvin' an embassador, and say what an example we sot to England, by such a noble spontaneous act as that, in honorin' letters. I feel kinder hurt at the way he took me up, but I'll swear I'me right arter all. In matters and things of this world, I won't give up my opinion to him nor nobody else. Let some old gineral or admiral do something or another that only requires the courage of a bull, and no sense, and they give him a pension, and right off the reel make him a peer. Let some old field-officer's wife, go follerin' the army away back in Indgy further than is safe or right for a woman to go,—git taken pris'ner, give a horrid sight of trouble to the army to git her back, and for this great service to the nation she gits a pension of five hundred pounds a-year. But let some misfortunate devil of an author do—what only one man in a century can, to save his soul alive, write a book that will live—a thing that *does* show the perfection of human mind, and what do they do here?—let his body live on the "Pleasures of Hope" all the days of his life, and his name live afterwards on a cold white marble in Westminster Abbey. They be hanged—the whole bilin' of them—them and their trumpery procession too, and their paltry patronage of standin' by a grave, and sayin', 'Poor Campbell!'

"*Who the devil cares for a monument, that actilly desarves one?* He has built one that will live when that are old Abbey crumbles down, and when all them that thought they was honorin' him are dead and forgotten; his monument was built by his own brains, and his own hands, and the inscription aint writ in Latin nor Greek, nor any other dead language, nother, but in a livin' language, and one too that will never die out now, seem' our great nation uses it—and here it is—

'The Pleasures of Hope, by Thomas Campbell.'"

II

DON'T I LOOK PALE?
OR, THE IRON GOD

MR. SLICK having as usual this morning boasted of the high society he mingled with the preceding evening, and talked with most absurd familiarity, of several distinguished persons, very much to the delight of his father, and the annoyance of Mr. Hopewell, the latter at last interrupted him with some very judicious advice. He told him he had observed the change that had come over him lately with very great regret; that he was altogether in a false position and acting an unnatural and absurd part.

"As a Republican," he said, "it is expected that you should have the simplicity and frankness of manner becoming one, and that your dress should not be that of a courtier, but in keeping with your character. It is well known here that you were not educated at one of our universities, or trained to official life, and that you have risen to it like many others of our countrymen, by strong natural talent. To assume, therefore, the air and dress of a man of fashion is quite absurd, and if persisted in will render you perfectly ridiculous. Any little errors you may make in the modes of life will always be passed over in silence, so long as you are natural; but the moment they are accompanied by affectation, they become targets for the shafts of satire.

"A little artificial manner may be tolerated in a very pretty woman, because great allowance is to be made for female vanity; but in a man it is altogether insufferable. Let your conversation therefore be natural, and as to the fashion of your dress take the good old rule—

'Be not the first by whom the new is tried,
      Nor yet the last to lay the old aside.'

In short be Sam Slick."

"Don't be afeerd, Minister," said Mr. Slick, "I have too much tact for that. I shall keep the channel, and avoid the bars and shallows, I know. I never boast at all. Brag is a good dog, but hold-fast is a better one. I never talk of society I never was in, nor never saw but once, and that by accident. I have too much sense for that; but I *am* actilly in the first circles here, quite at home in 'em, and in speaking of 'em. I am only talkin' of folks I meet every day, see every day, and jaw with every day. I am part and parsel of 'em. Now risin' sudden here aint a bit stranger than men risin' with us. It's done every day, for the door is wide open here; the English aint doomed to stand still and vegitate like cabbages, I can tell you; it's only colonists like Squire there, that are forced to do that. Why, they'll tell you of a noble whose grandfather was this, and another whose grandfather was that small beer; of one who was sired by a man that was born in our old Boston, and another whose great-grandfather was a farmer on Kenebec river, and if the family had remained colonists would have been snakin' logs with an ox-team to the Bangor mills, instead of being a minister for all the colonies, as he was not long ago. No, catch me a crackin' and a braggin' for nothin', and then tell me of it. I'm not a-goin' to ask every feller I meet, 'Don't I look pale?' like Soloman Figg, the tailor to St. John New Brunswick—him they called the 'Iron God.'"

"Oh, oh, Sam!" said Mr. Hopewell, lifting up both hands, "that was very profane; don't tell the story if there's any irreverence in it, any flippancy, any thing, in short, at all unbecoming. That is not a word to be used in vain."

"Oh never fear, Minister, there is nothin' in the story to shock you; if there was, I'm not the boy to tell it to any one, much less to you, sir."

"Very well, very well, tell the story then if it's harmless, but leave that word out when you can, that's a good soul!"

"Soloman Figg was the crittur that give rise to that sayin' all over New Brunswick and Nova Scotia, 'Don't I look pale?' and I calculate it never will die there. Whenever they see an important feller a-struttin' of it by, in tip top dress, tryin' to do a bit of fine, or hear a crittur a-braggin' of great men's acquaintance, they jist puts their finger to their nose, gives a wink to one another, and say, 'Don't I look pale?' Oh, it's grand! But I believe I'll begin at the beginnin', and jist tell you both stories about Soloman Figg.

"Soloman was a tailor, whose tongue ran as fast as his needle, and for sewin and talkin' perhaps there warn't his equal to be found nowhere. His shop was a great rondivoo for folks to talk politics in, and Soloman was an out-and-out Radical. They are ungrateful skunks are English Radicals, and ingratitude shews a bad heart: and in my opinion to say a feller's a Radical, is as much as to say he's everything that's bad. I'll tell you what's observed all over England, that them that make a fortin out of gentlemen, as soon as they shut up shop turn round, and become Radicals and oppose them. Radicalism is like that Dutch word Spitzbube. It's everything bad biled down to an essence. Well, Soloman was a Radical—he was agin the Church, because he had no say in the appointment of the parsons, and couldn't bully them. He was agin lawyers 'cause they took fees from him when they sued him. He was agin judges 'cause they rode their circuits and didn't walk. He was agin the governor 'cause the governor didn't ask him to dine. He was agin the admiral 'cause pursers had ready-made clothes for sailors, and didn't buy them at his shop. He was agin the army 'cause his wife ran off with a sodger—the only good reason he ever had in his life; in short, he was agin every thing and every body.

"Well, Soloman's day came at last, for every dog has his day in this world. Responsible government came, things got turned upside down, and Soloman turned up, and was made a magistrate of. Well, there was a Carolina refugee, one Captain Nestor Biggs, lived near him, an awful feller to swear, most o' those refugees were so, and he feared neither God nor man.

"He was a sneezer of a sinner was Captain Nestor, and always in law for everlastin'. He spent his whole pension in Court, folks said. Nestor went to Soloman and told him to issue a writ agin a man. It was Soloman's first writ, so sais he to himself, 'I'll write fust afore I sue; writin's civil, and then I can charge for letter and writ too, and I'm always civil when I'm paid for it. Mother did right to call me Soloman, didn't she?' Well, he wrote the letter, and the man that got it didn't know what under the sun to make of it. This was the letter—

"'Sir, if you do not return to Captain Nestor Biggs, the Iron God of his, now in your possession, I shall sue you. Pos is the word. Given under my hand, Soloman Figg, one of her most gracious Majesty's Justices of the Peace in and for the County of St. John.'

"Radicals are great hands for all the honors themselves, tho' they won't ginn none to others. 'Well,' sais the man to himself, 'what on airth does this mean?' So off he goes to the church parson to read it for him.

'Dear me,' sais he, 'this is awful; what is this? I by itself, I-r-o-n—Iron, G-o-d—God. Yes, it is Iron God!—Have you got such a graven image?'

"'Me,' sais the man, 'No; I never heard of such a thing.'

"'Dear, dear,' sais the parson, 'I always knew the Captain was a wicked man, a horrid wicked man, but I didn't think he was an idolater. I thought he was too sinful to worship any thing, even an iron idol. What times we live in, let's go to the Captain.'

"Well, off they sot to the Captain, and when he heerd of this graven image, he swore and raved—so the parson put a finger in each ear, and ran round the room, screamin' like a stuck pig. 'I'll tell you what it is, old boy,' says the Captain, a-rippin' out some most awful smashers, 'if you go on kickin' up such a row here, I'll stop your wind for you double-quick, so no mummery, if you please. Come along with me to that scoundrel, Soloman Figg, and I'll make him go down on his knees, and beg pardon. What the devil does he mean by talkin' of iron idols, I want to know.'

"Well, they went into Soloman's house, and Soloman, who was sittin' straddle-legs on a counter, a-sewin' away for dear life, jumps down in a minit, ons shoes and coat, and shows 'em into his office which was jist opposite to his shop. 'Read that, sir,' sais the Captain, lookin' as fierce as a tiger; 'read that, you ever lastin' radical scoundrel! did you write that infamous letter?' Soloman takes it, and reads it all over, and then hands it back, lookin' as wise as an owl. 'Its all right,' sais he. 'Right,' sais the Captain, and he cought hum by the throat. 'What do you mean by my "Iron God," sir? what do you mean by that, you infernal libellin', rebel rascal?' 'I never said it,' said Soloman. 'No, you never said it, but you wrote it.' 'I never wrote it; no, nor I never heerd of it.' 'Look at these words,' said the Captain, 'did you write them?' "Well, well,' sais Soloman, 'they do spell alike, too, don't they; they are the identical same letters G-o-d, dog; I have spelt it backwards, that's all; it's the iron dog, Captain; you know what that is,—don't you, Squire; it is an iron wedge sharpened at one eend, and havin' a ring in it at t'other, It's drove into the butt eend of a log, an' a chain is hooked to the ring, and the cattle drag the log eend-ways by it on the ground; it is called an iron dog.' Oh, how the Captain swore!"

"Well," said the Minister, "never mind repeating his oaths; he must have been an ignorant magistrate indeed not to be able to spell dog."

"He was a Radical magistrate of the Jack Frost school, sir," said Mr. Slick. The Liberals have made magistrates to England not a bit better nor Soloman, I can tell you. Well, they always called him arter that the Iron G—."

"Never mind what they called him," said Mr. Hopewell: "but what is the story of looking pale, for there is a kind of something in that last one that I don't exactly like? There are words in it that shock me; if you could tell the story without them, it is not a bad story; tell us the other part."

"Well, you know, as I was a-sayin', when responsible government came to the Colonies, it was like the Reform bile to England, stirring up the pot, and a-settin' all a-fermentin', set a good deal of scum a floatin' on the top of it. Among the rest, Soloman, being light and frothy, was about as buoyant as any. When the House of Assembly met to Fredericton, up goes Soloman, and writes his name on the book at Government House— Soloman Figg, J.P. Down comes the Sargent with a card, quick as wink, for the Governor's ball that night. Soloman warn't a bad lookin' feller at all; and bein' a tailor, in course he had his clothes well made; and, take him altogether, he was jist a leetle nearer the notch than one half of the members was, for most on 'em was from the country, and looked a nation sight more like Caraboos than legislators; indeed the nobs about Fredericton always call them Caraboos.

"Well, his tongue wagged about the limberest you ever see; his head was turned, so he talked to every one; and at supper he eat and drunk as if he never see vittals afore since he was weaned. He made a great night of it. Our Consul told me he thought he should have died a larfin' to see him: he talked about the skirts of the country, and the fork of the river, and button-hole connections, and linin' his stomach well, and basting the Yankees, and everything but cabbaging. No man ever heerd a tailor use that word, any more than they ever see a Jew eat pork. Oh! he had a reg'lar lark of it, and his tongue ran like a mill-wheel, whirlin' and sputterin' like anythin'. The officers of the —— regiment that was stationed there took him for a member of Assembly, and seem' he was a character, had him up to the mess to dine next day.

"Soloman was as amazed as if he was jist born. 'Heavens and airth!' said he, 'responsible government is a great thin' too, aint it. Here am I to Government House with all the big bugs and their ladies, and upper crust folks, as free and easy as an old glove. To-day I dine with the officers of the —— regiment, the most aristocratic regiment we ever had in the Province. I wish my father had put me into the army; I'd rather wear a red coat than make one any time. One thing is certain, if responsible government lasts long, we shall all rise to be gentlemen, or else all gentlemen must come down to the level of tailors, and no mistake; one coat will fit both. Dinin' at a mess, eh! Well, why not? I can make as good a coat as Buckmaster any day.'

"Well, Soloman was rather darnted at fust by the number of sarvants, and the blaze of uniform coats, and the horrid difficult cookery; but champagne strengthened his eyesight, for every one took wine with him, till he saw so clear he strained his eyes; for they grew weaker and weaker arter the right focus was passed, till he saw things double. Arter dinner they adjourned into the barrack-room of one of the officers, and there they had a game of 'Here comes I, Jack upon hips.'

"The youngsters put Soloman, who had a famous long back, jist at the right distance, and then managed to jump jist so as to come right on him, and they all jumbed on him, and down he'd smash with the weight; then they'd banter him for not bein' game, place him up agin in line, jump on him, and smash him down agin till he could not hold out no longer. Then came hot whisky toddy, and some screechin' songs; and Soloman sung, and the officers went into fits, for he sung such splendid songs; and then his health was drunk, and Soloman made a speech. He said, tho' he had a '*stich*' in the side from laughin', and was '*sewed up*' a'most too much to speak, and was afraid he'd '*rip out*' what he hadn't ought, yet their kindness had '*tied*' him as with '*list*' to them for 'the *remnant*' of his life, and years would never '*sponge*' it out of his heart.

"They roared and cheered him so, a kinder confused him, for he couldn't recollect nothin' arter that, nor how he got to the inn; but the waiter told him four sodgers carried him in on a shutter. Next day, off Soloman started in the steam-boat for St. John. The officers had took him for a member of Assembly, and axed him jist to take a rise out of him.

When they larned the mistake, and that it was ready-made Figg, the tailor, they had been makin' free with, they didn't think it was half so good a joke as it was afore; for they seed one half of the larf was agin them, and only t'other half agin Soloman. They never tell the story now; but Soloman did and still does like a favorite air with variations. As soon as he got back to St. John, he went about to every one he knew, and said, 'Don't I look pale?' 'Why no, I can't say you do.' 'Well, I feel used up enough to look so, I can tell you. I'm ashamed to say I've been horrid dissipated lately. I was at Government House night before last.'

"'You at Government House?' 'Me! to be sure; is there anything strange in that, seeing that the family compact is gone, the Fredericton clique broke up, and 'sponsible governments come? Yes, I was to Government House—it was such an agreeable party; I believe I staid too late, and made too free at supper, for I had a headache next day. Sad dogs them officers of the —— regiment; they are too gay for me. I dined there yesterday at their mess; a glorious day we had of it—free and easy—all gentlemen—no damn starch airs, sticking themselves up for gentlemen, but rael good fellers. I should have gone home arter mess, but there's no gettin' away from such good company. They wouldn't take *no* for an answer; nothin' must serve them but I must go to Captain's room. 'Pon honor, 'twas a charming night. Jack upon hips—whisky speeches, songs and whisky again, till I could hardly reach home. Fine fellers those of the —— regiment, capital fellers; no nonsense about them; had their shell jackets on; a stylish thing them shell jackets, and not so formal as full dress nother. What a nice feller Lord Fetter Lane is; easy excited, a *thimble* full does it, but it makes him as sharp as a *needle*.'

"Then he'd go on till he met another friend; he'd put on a doleful face, and say, 'Don't I look pale?' 'Well, I think you do; what's the matter?' and then he'd up and tell the whole story, till it got to be a by-word. Whenever any one sees a feller now a-doin' big, or or a-talkin' big, they always say, 'Don't I look pale?' as ready-made Figg said.

"Now, Minister, I am not like Soloman, I've not been axed by mistake, I'm not talkin' of what I don't know; so don't be afeerd, every one knows me; tante necessary for me, when I go among the toploftiest of the nation, to run about town the next day, sayin' to every man I meet, 'Don't I look pale?'"

III

THE COLONIAL OFFICE

THE last three days were devoted to visiting the various mad-houses and lunatic asylums in London and its vicinity. In this tour of inspection we were accompanied by Dr. Spun, a distinguished physician of Boston, and an old friend of Mr. Hopewell's. After leaving Bedlam, the Doctor, who was something of a humorist, said there was one on a larger scale which he wished to show us, but declined giving the name until we should arrive at it, as he wished to surprise us.

Our curiosity was, of course, a good deal excited by some vague allusions he made to the condition of the inmates; when he suddenly ordered the carriage to stop, and conducting us to the entrance of a court, said, "Here is a pile of buildings which the nation has devoted to the occupation of those whose minds having been engrossed during a series of years by politics, are supposed to labour under monomania. All these folks," he said, "imagine themselves to be governing the world, and the only cure that has been discovered is, to indulge them in their whim. They are permitted to form a course of policy, which is submitted to a body of persons chosen for the express purpose, who either approve or reject it, according as it appears more or less sane, and who furnish or withhold the means of carrying it out, as they see fit.

"Each man has a department given to him, filled with subordinates, who, though not always the best qualified, are always in their right mind, and who do the working part of the business; the board of delegates, and of superior clerks, while they indulge them in their humor, as far as possible, endeavour to extract the mischievous part from every measure. They are, therefore, generally harmless, and are allowed to go at large, and there have been successive generations of them for centuries. Sometimes they become dangerous, and then the board of delegates pass a vote of 'want of confidence' in them, and they are all removed, and other imbeciles are substituted in their place, when the same course of treatment is pursued."

"Is a cure often effected?" said Mr. Hopewell.

"Not very often;" said the Doctor, "they are considered as the most difficult to cure of any insane people, politics having so much of excitement in them; but now and then you hear of a man being perfectly restored to health, abandoning his ruling passion of politics, and returning to his family, and devoting himself to rural or to literary pursuits, an ornament to society, or a patron to its institutions. Lately, the whole of the inmates became so dangerous, from some annoyances they received, that the whole country was alarmed, and every one of them was removed from the buildings.

"In this Asylum it has been found that harsh treatment only aggravates the disease. Compliance with the whim of patients soothes and calms the mind, and diminishes the nervous excitement. Lord Glencoe, for instance, was here not long since, and imagined he was governing all the colonies. Constant indulgence very soon operated on his brain like a narcotic; he slept nearly all the time, and when he awoke, his attendant, who affected to be first clerk, used to lay before him despatches, which he persuaded him he had written himself, and gravely asked him to sign them: he was very soon permitted to be freed from all restraint. Lord Palmerstaff imagined himself the admiration of all the women in town, he called himself Cupid, spent half the day in bed, and the other half at his toilet; wrote all night about Syria, Boundary line, and such matters; or else walked up and down the room, conning over a speech for Parliament, which he said was to be delivered at the end of the session. Lord Wallgrave fancied he was the devil, and that the Church and the Bench were conspiring against him, and punishing his dearest friends and supporters, so he was all day writing out pardons for felons, orders for opening jails, and retaining prisoners, or devising schemes for abolishing parsons, making one bishop do the work of two, and so on. Lord M——"

Here the words "Downing Street" caught my eye, as designating the place we were in, which I need not say contains the government offices, and among others, the Colonial Office. "This," I said, "is very well for you, Dr. Spun, as an American, to sport as a joke, but it is dangerous ground for me, as a colonist and a loyal man, and therefore, if you please, we will drop the allegory. If you apply your remark to all government offices, in all countries, there may be some truth in it, for I believe all politicians to be more or less either so warped by party feeling, by selfishness, or prejudices, that their minds are not altogether truly balanced; but I must protest against its restriction to the English government alone, as distinguished from others."

"I know nothing about any of their offices, said Mr. Hopewell "but the Colonial office; and that certainly requires re-construction. The interests of the colonies are too vast, too various, and too complicated to be intrusted to any one man, however transcendant his ability, or persevering his industry, or extensive his information may be. Upon the sudden dissolution of a government a new colonial minister is appointed: in most cases he has everything to learn, having never had his attention drawn to this branch of public business, during the previous part of his political life; if this happens unfortunately to be the case, he never can acquire a thorough knowledge of his departments for during the whole of his continuance in office, his attention is distracted by various government measures of a general nature, which require the attention of the whole cabinet. The sole qualification that now exists for this high office is parliamentary influence, talent, and habits of business; but none of them separately, nor all of them collectively, are sufficient. Personal and practical experience, for a series of years, of the people, and the affairs of the colonies, is absolutely indispensable to a successful discharge of duty.

"How many persons who have held this high office were either too indolent to work themselves, or too busy to attend to their duties, or too weak, or too wild in their theories, to be entrusted with such heavy responsibilities? Many, when they acted for themselves, have acted wrong, from these causes; and when they allowed others to act for them have raised a subordinate to be a head of the office whom no other persons in the kingdom or the colonies but themselves would have entrusted with such important matters: it is, therefore, a choice of evils colonists have either to lament a hasty or erroneous decision of a principal or submit to the dictation of an upper clerk, whose talents, or whose acquirements are perhaps much below that of both contending parties, whose interests are to be bound by his decision."

"How would you remedy this evil," I said, for it was a subject in which I felt deeply interested, and one on which I knew he was the most competent man living to offer advice."

"Every board," he said, "must have a head, and according to the structure of the machinery of this government I would still have a Secretary of State for the Colonies; but instead of under secretaries, I would substitute a board of controul, or council, whichever board best suited, of which board he should be *ex officio* President. If it is thought necessary, even in a colony, where a man can both hear, and see, and judge for himself, to surround a governor with a council, how much more necessary is it to afford that assistance to a man who never saw a colony, and, until he accepted office, probably never heard of half of them, or if he has heard of them, is not quite certain even as to their geographic situation. It is natural that this obvious necessity should not have presented itself to a minister before: it is a restraint on power, and therefore not acceptable. He is not willing to trust his governors, and therefore gives them a council; he is then unwilling to trust both, and reserves the right to approve or reject their acts in certain cases. *He* thinks *them* incompetent; but who ever supposed *he* was competent? If the resident governor, aided by the best and wisest heads in a colony, advised, checked, and sounded by local public opinion, is not equal to the task, how can a Lancashire or Devonshire Member of Parliament be? Ask the weak or the vain, or the somnolent ones, whom I need not mention by name, and they will severally tell you it is the easiest thing in the world; we understand the principles, and our under secretaries understand the details; the only difficulty we have is in the ignorance, prejudice, and rascality of colonists themselves. Go and ask the present man, who is the most able, the most intelligent, the most laborious and eloquent one of them all, if there is any difficulty in the task to a person who sedulously strives to understand, and honestly endeavours to remedy colonial difficulties, and hear what he will tell you.

"'How can you ask *me* that question, sir? When did you ever call and find me absent from my post? Read my despatches and you will see whether I work: study them and you will see whether I understand. I may not always judge rightly, but I endeavour always to judge honestly. You inquire whether there is any difficulty in the task. Can you look in my face and ask that question? Look at my care-worn brow, my hectic eye, my attenuated frame, my pallid face, and my premature age, and let them answer you. Sir, the labour is too great, for any one man: the task is Herculean. Ambition may inspire, and fame may reward; but it is death alone that weaves the laurel round the brow of a successful colonial minister.'

"No, my good friend, it cannot be: No one man can do the work. If he attempts it he must do it badly; if he delegates it, it were better left undone: there should be a board of control or council. This board should consist in part of ex-governors and colonial officers of English appointment and in part of retired members of assembly or legislative councillors, or judges, or secretaries, or other similar functionaries, being *native* colonists. All of them should have served in public life a certain number of years, and all should be men who have stood high in public estimation, not as popular men (for that is no test), but for integrity, ability, and knowledge of the world. With such a council, so constituted, and so composed, you would never hear of a Governor dictating the despatches that were to be sent to him, as is generally reported in Canada, with or without foundation, of Poulett Thompson. One of the best governed countries in the world is India; but India is not governed in Downing Street. Before responsible government can be introduced there, it must receive the approbation of practical men, conversant with the country, deeply interested in its welfare, and perfectly competent to judge of its merits. India is safe from experiments; I wish you were equally secure. While your local politicians distract the attention of the public with their personal squabbles, all these important matters are lost sight of, or rather are, carefully kept out of view. The only voice that is now heard is one that is raised to mislead, and not to inform; to complain without truth, to demand without right, and to obstruct without principle. Yes, you want a board of controul. Were this once established, instead of having an office in Downing Street for the Secretary of State for the Colonies which is all you now have, you would possess in reality what you now have nominally,—'a Colonial Office.'"

IV

BARNEY OXMAN AND THE DEVIL

THE manner and conduct of Colonel Slick has been so eccentric, that for several days past I have had some apprehensions that he was not altogether *compos mentis*. His spirits have been exceedingly unequal, being at times much exhilarated, and then subject to a corresponding depression. To-day I asked his son if he knew what had brought him to England, but he was wholly at a loss, and evidently very anxious about him. "I don't know," he said, "what onder the sun fetched him here. I never heerd a word of it till about a week afore he arrived. I then got a letter from him, but you can't make head or tail of it: here it is

"'DEAR SAM,—Guess I'll come and see you for a spell; but keep dark about it. I hante been much from home of late, and a run at grass won't hurt me I reckon. Besides, I have an idea that somethin' may turn up to advantage. At any rate, it's worth looking after. All I want is proof, and then I guess I wouldn't call old Hickory, or Martin Van, no nor Captain Tyler nother, my cousin. My farm troubles me, for a farm and a wife soon run wild if left alone long. Barney Oxman has a considerable of a notion for it, and Barney is a good farmer, and no mistake; but I'm most afeerd he aint the clear grit. Godward, he is very pious, but, manward, he is a little twistical. It was him that wrestled with the evil one at Musquash Creek, when he courted that long-legged heifer, Jerusha Eells. Fast bind, sure find, is my way; and if he gets it, in course he must find security. I have had the rheumatiz lately. Miss Hubbard Hobbs, she that was Nancy Waddle, told me two teaspoonsful of brimstone, in a glass of gin, going to bed, for three nights, hand-runnin', was the onlyest thing in natur' for it. The old catamount was right for oncet in her life, as it cured me of the rheumatiz; but it cured me of gin too. I don't think I could drink it any more for thinkin' of the horrid' brimstone. It was a little the nastiest dose I ever took; still it's worth knowin'. I like simples better nor doctors' means any day. Sal made a hundred dollars by her bees, and three hundred dollars by her silk-worms, this year. It aint so coarse that, is it? But Sal is a good girl, too good for that cussed idle fellow, Jim Munroe. What a fool I was to cut him down that time he got hung by the leg in the moose-trap you sot for him, warn't I? There is nothin' new here, except them almighty villains, the Loco Focos, have carried their man for governor; but this you will see by the papers. The wonder is what I'm going to England for; but that is my business, and not theirn. I can squat low and say nothin' as well as any one. A crittur that goes blartin' out all he knows to every one aunt a man in no sense of the word. If you haven't nothin' above partikelar to do, I should like you to meet me at Liverpool about the 15th of next month that is to be, as I shall feel considerable scary when I first land, seein' that I never was to England afore, and never could cleverly find my way about a large town at no time. If all eventuates right, and turns out well, it will sartinly be the making of the Slick family, stock, lock, and barrel, that's a fact. I most forgot to tell you about old Varginy, sister of your old Clay. I depend my life on that mare. You can't ditto her nowhere. There actilly aint a beast fit to be named on the same day with her in all this county. Well, Varginy got a most monstrous fit of the botts. If she didn't stamp and bite her sides, and sweat all over like Statiee, its a pity. She went most ravin' distracted mad with pain, and I actilly thought I'd a-lost her, she was so bad. Barney Oxman was here at the time, and sais he, I'll cure her, Colonel, if you will leave it to me. Well, sais I—do what you please, only I wish you'd shoot the poor crittur to put her out of pain, for I believe her latter eend has come, that's a fact. Well, what does he do, but goes and gets half a pint of hardwood ashes and pours on to it a pint of vinegar, opens Varginy's mouth, holds on to her tongue, and puts the nose of the bottle in; and I hope I may never live another blessed minit, if it didn't shoot itself right off down her throat. Talk of a beer bottle bustin' its cork, and walkin' out quick stick, why it aint the smallest part of a circumstance to it.

"'It cured her. If it warn't an *active* dose, then physic aint medicine, that's all. It made the botts lose their hold in no time. It was a wonder to behold. I believe it wouldn't be a bad thing for a man in the cholera, for that aint a bit wuss than botts, and nothin' in natur' can stand that dose—I aint sure it wouldn't bust a byler. If I had my way, I'd physic them cussed Loco Focos with it; it would drive the devil out of them, as drownin' did out of the swine that was possessed. I raised my turnips last year in my corn hills at second hoeing; it saved labour, land, and time, and was all clear gain: it warn't a bad notion, was it? The Squash Bank has failed. I was wide awake for them; I knowed it would, so I drawed out all I had there, and kept the balance agin me. I can buy their paper ten cents to the dollar to pay with. I hope you have nothin' in the consarn. I will tell you all other news when we meet. Give my respects to Gineral Wellington, Victoria Queen, Mr. Everett, and all inquiring friends.

Your affectionate Father,
S. SLICK, Lieut.-Col.'"

"There it is," said Mr. Slick. "He has got some crotchet or another in his head, but what, the Lord only knows. To-day, seein' he was considerable up in the stirrups, I axed him plain what it actilly was that fetched him here. He turned right round fierce on me, and eyein' me all over, scorny like, he said, 'The Great Western, Sam, a tight good vessel, Sam—it was that fetched me over; and now you have got your answer, let me give you a piece of advice;—Ax me no questions, and I'll tell you no lies.' And he put on his hat, and walked out of the room."

"Old men," I said, "love to be mysterious. He probably came over to see you, to enjoy the spectacle of his son moving in a society to which he never could have aspired in his most visionary and castle-building days. To conceal this natural feeing, he affects a secret. Depend upon it, it is merely to pique your curiosity."

"It may be so," said Mr. Slick, shaking his head, incredulously; "it may be so, but he aint a man to pretend nothin' is father."

In order to change the conversation, which was too personal to be agreeable, I asked him what that story of wrastling with the evil one was, to which his father hinted in his letter.

"Oh, wrastling with the evil one," says he, "it aint a bad story that; didn't I ever tell you that frolic of 'Barney Oxman and the devil?'

"Well, there lived an old woman some years ago at Musquash Creek, in South Carolina, that had a large fortin', and an only darter. She was a widder, a miser, and a dunker. She was very good, and very cross, as many righteous folks are, and had a loose tongue and a tight puss of her own. All the men that looked at her darter she thought had an eye to her money, and she warn't far out o' the way nother, for it seems as if beauty and money was too much to go together in a general way. Rich gals and handsome gals are seldom good for nothin' else but their cash or their looks. Pears and peaches aint often found on the same tree, I tell you. She lived all alone a'most, with nobody but her darter and her in the house, and some old nigger slaves, in a hut near hand; and she seed no company she could help. The only place they went to, in a gineral way, was meetin', and Jerusha never missed that, for it was the only chance she had sometimes to get out alone.

"Barney had a most beautiful voice, and always went there too, to sing along with the gals; and Barney, hearin' of the fortin of Miss Eells, made up to her as fierce as possible, and sung so sweet, and talked so sweet, and kissed so sweet, that he soon stood number one with the heiress. But then he didn't often get a chance to walk home with her, and when he did, she darsn't let him come in for fear of the old woman: but Barney warn't to be put off that way long. When a gal is in one pastur', and a lover in another, it's a high fence they can't get over, that's a fact.

"'Tell you what,' sais Barney, 'sit up alone in the keepin' room, Rushy dear, arter old mother has gone to bed, put out the light, and I'll slide down on the rope from the trap-door on the roof. Tell her you are exercised in your mind, and want to meditate alone, as the words you have heard this day have reached your heart.'

"Jerusha was frightened to death a'most, but what won't a woman do when a lover is in the way. So that very night she told the old woman she was exercised in her mind, and would wrastle with the spirit.

"'Do, dear,' says her, mother, 'and you won't think of the vanities of dress, and idle company no more. You see how I have given them all up since I made profession, and never so much as speak of them now, no, nor even thinks of 'em.'

"Strange, Squire, aint it? But it's much easier to cheat ourselves than cheat the devil. That old hag was too stingy to buy dress, but persuaded herself it was bein' too good to wear it.

"Well, the house was a flat-roofed house, and had a trap-door in the ceilin', over the keepin' room, and there was a crane on the roof, with a rope to it, to pull up things to spread out to dry there. As soon as the lights were all out, and Barney thought the old woman was asleep, he crawls up on the house, opens the trap-door, and lets himself down by the rope, and he and Jerusha sat down into the hearth in the chimney corner courtin', or as they call it in them diggins 'sniffin' ashes.' When daylight began to shew, he went up the rope hand over hand, hauled it up arter him, closed-to the trap-door, and made himself scarce. Well, all this went on as slick as could be for awhile, but the old woman seed that her daughter looked pale, and as if she hadn't had sleep enough, and there was no gettin' of her up in the mornin'; and when she did she was yawkin' and gapin', and so dull she hadn't a word to say.

"She got very uneasy about it at last and used to get up in the night sometimes and call her darter, and make her go off to bed, and oncet or twice came plaguy near catching of them. So what does Barney do, but takes two niggers with him when he goes arter that, and leaves them on the roof, and fastens a large basket to the rope, and tells them if they feel the rope pulled to hoist away for dear life, but not to speak a word for the world. Well, one night the old woman came to the door as usual, and sais, 'Jerusha,' sais she, 'what on airth ails you, to make you sit up all night that way; do come to bed that's a dear.' 'Presently, marm,' sais she, 'I am wrastling with the evil one, now; I'll come presently.' 'Dear, dear,' sais she, 'you have wrastled long enough with him to have throwed him by this time. If you can't throw him now, give it up, or he may throw you.' 'Presently, marm,' sais her darter. 'It's always the same tune,' sais her mother, going off grumbling;—'it's always presently, presently;—what has got into the gal to act so. Oh, dear! what a pertracted time she has on it. She has been sorely exercised poor girl.'

"As soon as she had gone, Barney larfed so he had to put his arm round her waist to steady him on the bench, in a way that didn't look onlike rompin', and when he went to whisper he larfed so he did nothin' but touch her cheek with his lips, in a way that looked plaguily like kissing, and felt like it too, and she pulled to get away, and they had a most reg'lar wrastle as they sat on the bench, when as luck would have it, over went the bench, and down went both on 'em on the floor with an awful smash, and in bounced the old woman, 'Which is uppermost?' sais she;—'Have you throw'd Satan, or has Satan throw'd you? Speak, Rushy; speak, dear; who's throw'd?' 'I have throw'd him;' sais her darter; 'and I hope I have broke his neck, he acted so.' 'Come to bed, then,' sais she, 'darling, and be thankful; say a prayer backward, and'—jist then the old woman was seized round the waist, hoisted through the trap-door to the roof, and from there to the top of the crane, where the basket stopped, and the first thing she know'd she was away up ever so far in the air, swingin' in a large basket, and no soul near her.

"Barney and his niggers cut stick double quick, crept into the bushes, and went all round to the road in front of the house, just as day was breakin'. The old woman was then singin' out for dear life, kickin', and squealin', and cryin', and prayin' all in one, properly frightened. Down runs Barney as hard as he could clip, lookin' as innocent as if he'd never heerd nothin' of it, and pertendin' to be horrid frightened, offers his services, climbs up, releases the old woman, and gets blessed and thanked, and thanked and blessed till he was tired of it. 'Oh!' says the old woman, 'Mr. Oxman, the moment Jerusba throw'd the evil one, the house shook like an airthquake, and as I entered the room he seized me, put me into his basket, and flew off with me. Oh, I shall never forget his fiery eye-balls, and the horrid smell of brimstone he had!'

"'Had he a cloven foot, and a long tail?' sais Barney. 'I couldn't see in the dark,' sais she, 'but his claws were awful sharp; oh, how they dug into my ribs! it e'en a'most took the flesh off,—oh, dear! Lord have mercy on us! I hope he is laid in the Red Sea, now.' 'Tell you what it is aunty,' sais Barney, 'that's an awful story, keep it secret for your life; folks might say the house was harnted,—that you was possessed, and that Jerushy was in league with the evil one. Don't so much as lisp a syllable of it to a livin' sinner breathin'; keep the secret and I will help you.'

"The hint took, the old woman had no wish to be burnt or drown'd for a witch, *and the moment a feller has a woman's secret he is that woman's master.* He was invited there, stayed there, and married there; but the old woman never know'd who 'the evil one' was, and always thought till her dyin' day it was old Scratch himself. Arter her death they didn't keep it secret no longer; and many a good laugh has there been at the story of Barney Oxman and the Devil."

V

REPUDIATION

DURING the last week I went into Gloucestershire, for the purpose of visiting an old and much valued friend who resides near Cirencester. In the car there were two gentlemen, both of whom were strangers to me, but we soon entered into conversation. One of them, upon ascertaining where I was from, made many anxious inquiries as to the probability of the Repudiating States ever repaying the money that had been lent to them by this country. He said he had been a great sufferer himself, but what he regretted much more than his own loss was, that he had been instrumental in inducing several of his friends to invest largely in that sort of stock. I told him I was unable to answer the question, though I thought the prospect rather gloomy; that if, however, he was desirous of procuring accurate information, I could easily obtain it for him, as the celebrated Mr. Slick, and a very distinguished American clergyman, were now in London, to whom I would apply on the subject.

"Mr Slick!" he said, with much surprise, "is there, then, really such a person as Sam Slick; I always thought it a fictitious character, although the man is drawn so naturally, I have never been able to divest myself of some doubts as to his reality."

"There is," I said, "*such a man as Mr. Slick*, and such a man as *Mr. Hopewell*, although those are not their real names; I know the persons well. The author has drawn them from life. *Most* of the anecdotes in those books called 'The Clockmaker,' and 'Attaché,' are real ones. The travelling parts of them are fictitious, and introduced merely as threads to string the conversations on, while the reasoning and humorous parts are only such as both those persons are daily in the habit of uttering, or would have uttered if the topics were started in their presence. *Both are real characters*; both have sat for their likeness, and those who know the originals as I do, are struck with the fidelity of the portraits.

"I have often been asked the question before," I said, "if there really was such a man as 'Sam Slick,' and the author assures me that that circumstance, which has frequently occurred to him also, he considers the greatest compliment that can be paid to his work, and that it is one of the reasons why there have been so many continuations of it."

He then asked my opinion as to the ballot; and I ridiculed it in no measured terms, as every man of experience does on both sides of the water; expressed a hope that it might never be introduced into England, to the character and feelings of whose inhabitants it was so much opposed; and bestowed on its abettors in this country some very strong epithets, denoting my contempt, both for their principles and their understanding.

At Bath he left us, and when the train proceeded, the other gentleman asked me if I knew who he was with whom I had been conversing, and on my replying in the negative, he said he took it for granted I did not, or I would have been more guarded in my language, and that he was delighted I had not known him, otherwise he would have lost a lesson which he hoped would do him good.

"That man, sir," said he, "is one of the great advocates of the ballot here; and with the leaders of the party, has invested large sums of money in these State stocks of which he was inquiring. They thought their money must be safe in a Country that had vote by ballot for that they conceived to be a remedy for all evils. In my opinion, vote by ballot, or rather universal suffrage, another of his favourite hobbies, is one of the reasons why they have lost it. He is one of those persons to whom you are indebted for the Republicanism lately introduced into your Colonial constitutions.

"At the time Lord Durham visited Canada, the United States were swarming with labourers, cutting canals, constructing railways, opening coal mines, building towns, and forming roads. In everything was life and motion; for English capital was flowing rapidly thither under one delusion or another for investment, and had given an unnatural stimulus to every branch of industry, and every scheme of speculation; while in Canada, which was in a healthy and sound condition, all these things were in no greater progress than the ordinary wants of the country required or the ordinary means of the people could afford.

"The moment these visionary and insane reformers saw this contrast, instead of deploring as all good and sensible men did, a delirious excitement that could not but soon exhaust itself, and produce a long period of inanition and weakness they seized upon it as a proof of their favourite scheme. 'Behold,' they said, 'the difference between a country that has universal suffrage and vote by ballot, responsible government and annual elections, and a British colony with a cumbrous English constitution. One is all life, the other all torpor. One enjoys a rapid circulation that reaches to every extremity, the other suffers under a feeble pulsation barely sufficient to support life. Read in this a lesson on free institutions, and doubt who can.'

"Having talked this nonsense for a long time, they began at last, like all credulous and weak people, to believe it themselves, and invested their money, for which they had no other but their favorite security, vote by ballot. How much is the security worth?—It is worth a thousand arguments, and will be comprehended, even by those who cannot appreciate the wit or feel the force of the reasoning of Sydney Smith. But I believe we part at this station. Goodbye! Sir. I am happy to have had the pleasure of making your acquaintance." On my return to London, I took occasion one evening, when Mr. Slick and Mr. Hopewell were present, to relate this anecdote; and, turning to the former, asked him what prospect he thought there was of these "repudiated debts" being paid. To my surprise he did not answer, and I at once perceived he was in a "brown study." Though he had not heard what I said, however, he found there was a cessation of talk, and turning to me with an absent air, and twirling his moustache between his forefinger and thumb, he said, "Can you tell me what a (jager) yaw-g-her is?"

I said, "it is a German word, and signifies a hunter. In the revolutionary war there was a regiment called Jagers."

"Ah," said he, "it's a beautiful dress they wear—very becoming—very rich. Me and the socdolager dined with one o' the royal dukes lately, and he had several in attendance as servants—devilish handsome fellows they are too—. I'me sorry I made that mistake, tho'—how much they look like officers and gentlemen—cussed awkward that em-yaugher—eh!—I don't know whether it's worth larnin' arter all—hem!"—and was again abstracted.

Mr. Hopewell looked at him with great concern, drew a long sigh, and shook his head, as if much distressed at his behaviour.

I renewed my enquiry, and put the same question to the Minister.

"Squire," he said, mournfully, "that is a painful subject either to contemplate or to talk upon. What they ought to do as honest men, there can be no doubt; what they will do, is less certain. I have read the correspondence between one of our citizens and Sydney Smith. Those letters of Mr. Smith, or rather Smith I should say—for he is too celebrated a man for the appellation of "Mr."—will do more good in America than a fleet, or an ambassador, or even reprisals. We cannot stand ridicule—we are sensitively alive to European opinion, and these letters admit of but one answer—and that is, *payment*. An American is wrong in thinking of resorting to the pen. Repudiation cannot be justified—no, not even palliated. It is not insolvency, or misfortune, or temporary embarrassment, that is pleaded—it is a refusal to pay, and a refusal to pay a just debt, in public or private life, is—mince it as you will—*dishonest*. If the aged and infirm, the widow and the orphan, recover their just debts, and are restored once more to the comfort they have lost, they must never forget they are indebted to Sydney Smith for it.

"It is the first plunge that shocks the nerves. Men who have so little honour as to repudiate a debt, have altogether too little to retract their words and be honest. But if by repudiating, they lose more than the amount they withhold, a sordid motive may induce them to do that which a sense of right is unable to effect. Smith has put those States on their trial in Europe. If they do not pay, their credit and their character are gone for ever. If they do pay, but not till then, I will furnish them with the only extenuation their conduct is susceptible of?"

"And pray what is that?" I said.

He replied, "I would reason this way; it is unfair to condemn the American people, as a nation, for the acts of a few States, or to punish a whole country for the fraudulent conduct of a part of the people. Every honest and right-minded man in our country deplores and condemns this act, as much as every person of the same description does in Europe. When we speak of American or English honor, we speak of the same thing; but when we speak of the honor of the American people, and of the English people, we speak of two different things, because the word people is not used in the same sense; in one case it is understood in a restricted form, and in the other in its most extensive signification. When we speak, of the honor of an European, we don't mean the honor of a chimney-sweep or street or cabman, or coal-heaver, or hodman, or such persons; but of those that are responsible for the acts of the people as a government. When we speak of the honor of an American citizen, we speak of every individual, high or low, rich or poor, because, as all have the franchise, all are responsible for public acts. Take the same class with us that the word's applied to in England, and if the honor of that class is not equal to its corresponding one in Great Britain, I think I may say it will at least bear a very favorable comparison with it. The question of payment, or non-payment, in the repudiating States has been put to every male in those States over the age of twenty-one years, and repudiation has been the result.

Put the question of the payment of the national debt to every adult in Great Britain, and let reformers inflame their minds and excite their cupidity, as they always do on such occasions, and what would be the result?—I fear the holders of the old Three per Cents would find repudiation a word as well understood in Europe as it is in America. The almost universal suffrage in Canada is the cause of the ungenerous, ungrateful, and insatiable conduct of their reformers: all good men there acknowledge their degradation, and deplore it: but, alas, they cannot help it. Mankind are much the same everywhere; the masses are alike at least, ignorant, prejudiced, needy, and not over scrupulous. It is our misfortune then, rather than our fault; you will observe I am not justifying repudiation, far from it; but let us know where the fault lies, before we inflict censure— *It lies in our Institutions and not in our people*; it is worth all they have lost in England to know this, it is a valuable political lesson. Let them beware how they extend their franchise, or increase the democratic privileges.

"The Reform Bill has lowered the character of the House of Commons in exact proportion as it has opened it to the representatives of the lower orders. Another Reform Bill will lower the character of the people; it will then only require universal suffrage, and vote by ballot, to precipitate both the altar and the throne into the cold and bottomless abyss of democracy, and in the froth and worthless scum that will float on the surface will be seen among the fragments of their institutions, 'English repudiation.'"

"Give me your hand, Minister;" said Mr. Slick: "Oh, you did that beautiful! Heavens and airth!—"

"Stop, Sam," said Mr. Hopewell "Swear not by Heaven, for it is *his* throne, nor by the earth, for it is *his* footstool."

"Well, then, lawful heart! land of Goshen! airth and seas! or, oh Solomon! take any one that will suit you; I wish you would lay down preachin' and take to politics, as Everitt did."

"I could not do it," he replied, "if I would; and I would not do it if I could."

"Well, I wish you had never taken up the trade of preachin'."

"Trade, Sam! do you call it a trade?"

"Well, art."

"Do you call it an art?"

"Well, call it what you like, I wish you had never been bred a preacher."

"I have no such wish; I do not, at the close of my life, desire to exclaim with Wolsey, 'Had I served my God with half the zeal I have served my king, he would not now have deserted me in my old age.'"

"You hante got a king, and nobody sarves a president, for he is nothin' but one of us, so you needn't be skeered, but I do wish you'd a-taken to politics. Good gracious, why can't Stephenson or Everitt talk as you do; why don't they put the nail in the right place, and strike it right strait on the head? The way you put that repudiation is jist the identical thing. Bowin' gallus polite, and sayin'—'Debt is all right, you ought to have it,—a high tone of feelin'—very sorry—force of circumstances—political institutions—universal suffrage—happy country, England—honor all in my eye—good bye!' How much better that is than justifyin', or bullyin' or sayin' they are just as bad themselves, and only make matters wus; I call that now true policy."

"If you call that true policy, I am sorry for you," he replied; "because it is evident you are ignorant of a very important truth."

"What is that Minister?"

"'*That honesty is always the best policy.*' Had this great moral lesson been more universally known, you never would have heard of '*Repudiation*'"

VI

THE BACKLOG, OR COOLNESS

As we sat chatting together late last night, the danger of a fire at sea was talked of, the loss of the Kent Indiaman, and the remarkable coolness of Col. M'Grigor on that occasion was discussed, and various anecdotes related of calmness, presence of mind, and coolness, under every possible form of peril.

"There is a good deal of embellishment in all these stories," said Mr. Slick. "There is always a fact to build a story on, or a peg to hang it on, and this makes it probable; so that the story and its fictions get so mixed up, you can't tell at last what is truth and what is fancy. A good story is never spiled in the tellin', except by a crittur that don't know how to tell it. Battles, shipwrecks, highway robberies, blowed-up steamers, vessels a-fire, and so on, lay a foundation as facts. Some people are saved,—that's another fact to build on;—some captain, or passenger, or woman hante fainted, and that's enough to make a grand affair of it. You can't hardly believe none of them, that's the truth. Now, I'll tell you a story that happen'd in a farm-house near to father's, to Slickville, jist a common scene of common life, and no about it, that does jist go for to shew what I call coolness:—

"Our nearest neighbour was Squire Peleg Sanford; well, the old squire and all his family was all of them the most awful passionate folks that ever lived, when they chose, and then they could keep in their temper, and be as cool at other times as cucumbers. One night, old uncle Peleg, as he was called, told his son Gucom, a boy of fourteen years old, to go and bring in a backlog for the fire. A backlog, you know, Squire, in a wood fire, is always the biggest stick that one can find or carry. It takes a stout junk of a boy to lift one.

"Well, as soon as Gucom goes to fetch the log, the old Squire drags forward the coals, and fixes the fire so as to leave a bed for it, and stands by ready to fit it into its place. Presently in comes Gucom with a little cat stick, no bigger than his leg, and throws it on. Uncle Peleg got so mad, he never said a word, but just seized his ridin' whip, and gave him a'most an awful wippin'. He tanned his hide properly for him, you may depend. 'Now,' sais he, 'go, sir, and bring in a proper backlog.'

"Gucom was clear grit as well as the old man, for he was a chip of the old block, and no mistake; so out he goes without so much as sayin' a word, but instead of goin' to the wood pile, he walks off altogether, and staid away eight years, till he was one-and-twenty, and his own master. Well, as soon as he was a man grown, and lawfully on his own book, he took it into his head one day he'd go to home and see his old father and mother agin, and shew them he was alive and kickin', for they didn't know whether he was dead or not, never havin' heard of or from him one blessed word all that time. When he arrived to the old house, daylight was down, and lights lit, and as he passed the keepin'-room winder, he looked in and there was old Squire sittin' in the same chair he was eight years afore, when he ordered in the back log, and gave him such an onmarciful whippin'. So what does Gucom do, but stops at the wood pile, and picks up a most hugaceous log, (for he had grow'd to be a'most a thunderin' big feller then) and openin' the door he marches in and lays it down on the hearth, and then lookin' up, sais he, 'Father, I've brought you in the backlog.'

"Uncle Peleg was struck up all of a heap; he couldn't believe his eyes, that that great six-footer was the boy he had cow-hided, and he couldn't believe his ears when he heard him call him father; a man from the grave wouldn't have surprised him more,—he was quite onfakilized, and be-dumbed for a minute. But he came too right off, and was iced down to freezin' point in no time.

"'What did you say?' sais he.

"'That I have brought you in the backlog, sir, you sent me out for.'

"'Well, then, you've been a d——'d long time a-fetchin' it,' sais he; 'that's all I can say. Draw the coals forrard, put it on, and then go to bed.'

"Now, that's a fact, Squire; I know'd the parties myself,—that's what I do call *coolness*—and no mistake!"

VII

MARRIAGE

TO-DAY, as we passed St. James church, we found the streets in the neighbourhood almost obstructed by an immense concourse of fashionable carriages. "Ah!" said Mr. Slick, "here is a splice in high life to-day. I wish to goodness I could scrouge in and see the gal. Them nobility women are so horrid handsum, they take the shine off all creation a'most. I'll bet a goose and trimmins she looks like an angel, poor thing! I'd like to see her, and somehow I wouldn't like to see her, nother. I like to look at beauty always, my heart yarns towards it; and I do love women, the dear critturs, that's a fact. There is no musick to my ear like the rustlin' of petticoats: but then I pity one o' these high bred gals, that's made a show of that way, and decked out in first chop style, for all the world to stare at afore she is offered up as a sacrifice to gild some old coronet with her money, or enlarge some landed estate by addin' her'n on to it. Half the time it aint the joinin' of two hearts, but the joinin' of two pusses, and a wife is chose like a hoss, not for her looks, but for what she will fetch. It's the greatest wonder in the world them kind o' marriages turn out as well as they do, all thin's considered. I can't account for it no way but one, and that is, that love that grows up slow will last longer than love that's born full grown. The fust is love, the last is passion. Fashion rules all here.

"These Londoners are about as consaited folks of their own ways as you'll find onder the sun a'most. They are always a-jawin' about good taste, and bad taste, and correct taste, and all that sort o' thin'. Fellers that eat and drink so like the devil as they do, it's no wonder that word 'taste' is for everlastin' in their mouth. Now to my mind, atween you and me

and the post, for I darsn't say so here to company, they'd stare so if I did,
but atween you and me, I don't think leadin' a girl out to a church chock
full of company, to be stared at, like a prize ox, by all the young bucks and
the old does about town, to criticise, satirize, and jokerise on, or make
prophecies on, a-pityin' the poor feller that's caught such an almighty
tartar, or a-feelin' for the poor gal that's got such an awful dissipated feller;
or rakin' up old stories to new-frame 'em as pictures to amuse folks with,
(for envy of a good match always gets to pityin' 'em, as if it liked 'em, and
was sorry for 'em,) and then to lead her off to a dejuney a la fussier; to hear
her health drunk in wine, and to hear a whisper atween a man-woman
and a woman-man, not intended to be heerd, except on purpose; and then
posted off to some old mansion or another in the country; and all along
the road to be the standin' joke of post-boys, footmen, and ladies' maids,
and all them kind o' cattle; and then to be yoked together alone with her
lover in that horrid large, lonely, dismal house, shut up by rain all the time,
and imprisoned long enough to git shockin' tired of each other; and then
to read her fate on the wall in portraits of a long line of ancestral brides,
who came there bloomin', and gay, and young like her, and in a little while
grew fat and old, or skinny and thin, or deaf, or blind, (women never get
dumb,) and who sickened and pined and died, and went the way of all
flesh; and she shudders all over, when she thinks in a few years some other
bride will look at her pictur' and say, 'What a queer looking woman that is!
how unbecomin' her hair is done up!' and then, pi'ntin' to her bustle, say
to her bridesmaid in a whisper, with a scorny look, 'Do you suppose that
mountain was a bustle, or was she a Hottentot Venus, grandpa' married?'
and bridesmaid will say, 'Dreadful looking woman! and she squints too, I
think;' then to come back to town to run into t'other extreme, and never
to be together agin, but always in company, havin' a great horror of that
long, lone, tiresome honey-moon month in the country;—all this aint to
my mind, now, jist the best taste in the world nother. I don't know what
you may think, but that's my humble opinion, now that's a fact. We make
everlastin' short work of it sometimes. It reminds me of old uncle Peleg
I was a-tellin' you of last night, who acted so cool about the backlog. He
was a magistrate to Slickville, was Squire Peleg; and by our law, Justices
of the peace can splice folks as well as Ministers can. So, one day Slocum
Outhouse, called there to the Squire's with Deliverance Cook. They was
well acquainted with the Squire, for they was neighbours of his, but they

was awful afeerd of him, he was such a crotchical, snappish, peevish, odd, old feller. So after they sot down in the room old Peleg sais, 'You must excuse my talkin' to-day, friend Outhouse, for,' sais he, 'I'm so almighty busy a-writin'; but the women-folks will be in bime bye; the'r jist gone to meetin'.' 'Well,' sais Slocum, 'we won't detain you a minit, Squire; me and Deliverance come to make declaration of marriage, and have it registered.' 'Oh! goin' to be married,' sais he; 'eh? that's right, marry in haste and repent at leisure. Very fond of each other now; quarrel like the devil by and bye. Hem! what cussed fools some folks is;' and he never sais another word, but wrote and wrote on, and never looked up, and there they sot and sot, Slocum and poor Deliverance, a-lookin' like a pair of fools; they know'd they couldn't move him to go one inch faster than he chose, and that he would have his own way at any rate; so they looked at each other and shook their heads, and then looked down and played with their thumbs, and then they scratched their pates and put one leg over t'other, and then shifted it back agin, and then they looked out o' the winder, and counted all the poles in the fence, and all the hens in the yard, and watched a man a-ploughin' in a field, goin' first up and then down the ridge; then Slocum coughed, and then Deliverance coughed, so as to attract old Squire's attention, and make him 'tend to their business; but no, nothin' would do: he wrote, and he wrote, and he wrote, and he never stopped, nor looked up, nor looked round, nor said a word. Then Deliverance looked over at the Squire, made faces, and nodded and motioned to Outhouse to go to him, but he frowned and shook his head, as much as to say, I darsn't do it, dear, I wish you would.

"At last she got narvous, and began to cry out of clear sheer spite, for she was good stuff, rael steel, put an edge on a knife a'most; and that got Slocum's dander up,—so he ups off of his seat, and spunks up to the old Squire, and sais he, 'Squire, tell you what, we came here to get married; if you are a-goin' for to do the job well and good, if you aint say so, and we will go to someone else.' 'What job,' sais old Peleg, a-lookin' up as innocent as you please. 'Why, marry us,' sais Slocum. 'Marry you!' sais he, 'why d—n you, you was married an hour and a-half ago, man. What are you a-talkin' about? I thought you was a goin' to spend the night here, or else had repented of your bargain;' and he sot back in his chair and larfed ready to kill himself. 'What the devil have you been waitin' for all this time?' sais he; 'don't you know that makin' declaration, as you did is all that's required?—but come, let's take a glass of grog.—Here's to your good health, Mr. Slo*cum*, or *Slow-go*, as you ought to be called, and the same to you, Deliverance. What a nice name you've got, too, for a bride;' and he larfed agin till they both joined in it, and larfed, too, like anythin'; for larfin' is catchin', you can't help it some times, even suppose you are vexed,

"'Yes,' sais he, 'long life and as much happiness to you both as you can cleverly disgest;' and then he shook hands with the bride, and whispered to her, and she coloured up, and looked horrid pleased, and sais, 'Now, Squire, posi*tively*, you ought to be ashamed, that's a fact.'

"Now," said Mr. Slick, "a feller that aint a fool, like Slocum, and don't know when he *is* married, can get the knot tied without fuss or loss of time with us, can't he?—Yes, I don't like a show affair like this. To my mind, a quiet, private marriage, like that at Uncle Peleg's is jist about the right thing."

"Sam," said Mr. Hopewell, "I am surprised to hear you talk that way. As to the preference of a quiet marriage over one of these public displays, I quite agree with you. But you are under a great mistake in supposing that you dare not express that opinion in England, for every right-minded person here will agree with you. *Any opinion that cannot be expressed here must be a wrong one, indeed; the judgment, the feeling, and the taste of society is so good!* But still the ceremony should always be performed in the church, and as I was saying, I'm surprised to hear you approve of such an affair as that at Squire Peleg's office. Making marriage a mere contract, to be executed like any other secular obligation before the civil magistrate, is one of the most ingenious contrivances of the devil to loosen moral obligations that I know of at all.

"When I tell you the Whigs were great advocates for it here, I am sure I need not give you its character in stronger language. Their advent to office depended on all those opposed to the church; every thing, therefore, that weakened its influence or loosened its connexion with the state, was sure to obtain their strenuous assistance. Transferring this ceremony from the church to the secular power was one of their popular kites; and to show you how little it was required by those who demanded it, or how little it was valued when obtained, except in a political point of view, I need only observe that the number of magisterial marriages is on the decrease in England, and not on the increase.

"The women of England, much to their honour, object to this mode of marriage. Intending to fulfil their own obligations, and feeling an awful responsibility, they desire to register them at the altar, and to implore the blessing of the Church on the new career of life into which they are about to enter, and at the same time they indulge the rational and well-founded hope that the vows so solemnly and publicly made to them before God and man will be more strictly observed in proportion as they are more deeply considered, and more solemnly proclaimed. There are not many things that suggest more important considerations than that connexion which is so lightly talked of, so inconsiderately entered into, and so little appreciated as—Marriage."

VIII

PAYING AND RETURNING VISITS

"WHICH way are you a-goin', Squire?" said Mr. Slick, who saw me preparing to go out this morning.

"I am going," I said, "to call on an old schoolfellow that is now living in London. I have not seen him since we sat on the same benches at school, and have been unable to ascertain his address until this moment."

"Could he have ascertained your address?"

"Oh, yes, easily; all the Nova Scotians in town know it; most of the Canada merchants, and a very large circle of acquaintance. Many others who did not know so well where to inquire as he does, have found it."

"Let me see," he replied, "how long have we been here? Four months.— Let him be, then; he aint worth knowin', that feller,—he hante a heart as big as a pea. Oh! Squire, you don't know 'cause you hante travelled none; but I do, 'cause I've been every where a'most, and I'll tell you somethin' you hante experienced yet. Aint there a good many folks to Halifax, whose faces you know, but whose names you don't, and others whose mugs and names you know, but you don't parsonally know them? Certainly. Well, then, s'pose you are in London, or Paris, or Canton, or Petersburg, and you suddenly come across one o' these critturs, that you pass every day without lookin' at or thinkin' of, nor knowin' or carin' to know when you are to home.—What's the first thing both of you'd do, do you suppose? Why run right up to each other, out paws and shake hands, till all is blue again. Both of you ax a bushel of questions, and those questions all lead one way,—to Nova Scotia, to Halifax, to the road to Windsor;—then you try to stay together, or travel together, and if either of you get sick, tend each other, or get into scrapes, fight for each other.—Why? because you are countrymen,—countymen,— townsmen,—because you see home wrote in each other's face as plain as any thing; because each of you is in t'other's eyes a part of that home, a part that when you are in your own country you don't valy much; because you have both nearer and dearer parts, but still you have a kind of nateral attraction to each other, as a piece of home; and then that awakens all the kindly feelin's of the heart, and makes it as sensitive and tender as a skinned eel. But, oh, dear me! if this piece of home happens to be an old schoolfeller, don't it awaken idees not only of home, but idees long since forgotten of old times? *Memory acts on thought like sudden heat on a dormant fly, it wakes it from the dead, puts new life into it, and it stretches out its wings and buzzes round as if it had never slept.* When you see him, don't the old schoolmaster rise up before you as nateral as if it was only yesterday and the school-room, and the noisy, larkin', happy holidays, and you boys let out racin', yelpin' hollerin', and whoopin' like mad with pleasure, and the playground and the game at bass in the fields, or hurly on the long pond on the ice, or campin' out a-night at Chester lakes to fish—catchin' no trout, gettin' wet thro' and thro' with rain like a drown'd rat,—eat up body and bones by black flies and muschetoes, returnin' tired to death, and callin' it a party of pleasure; or riggin' out in pumps for dancin' schools, and the little fust loves for the pretty little gals there, when the heart was romantic and looked away ahead into an avenue of years, and seed you and your little tiny partner at the head of it, driven in a tandem sleigh of your own, and a grand house to live in, and she your partner through life; or else you in the grove back o' the school, away up in a beech tree, settin' straddle-legged on a limb with a jack-knife in your hand cuttin' into it the two fust letters of her name—F. L., fust love; never dreamin' the bark would grow over them in time on the tree, and the world, the flesh, and the devil rub them out of the heart in arter years also. Then comes robbin' orchards and fetchin' home nasty puckery apples to eat, as sour as Greek, that stealin' made sweet; or gettin' out o' winders at night, goin' down to old Ross's, orderin' a supper, and pocketin' your fust whole bottle o' wine—oh! that fust whole bottle christened the man, and you woke up sober next mornin', and got the fust taste o' the world,—sour in the mouth—sour in the stomach—sour in the temper, and sour all over;—yes, that's the world. Oh, Lord! don't them and a thousand more things rush right into your mind, like a crowd into a theatre seein' which can get in fust. Don't it carry you back afore sad realities, blasted hopes, and false hearts had chilled your affections.

"Oh, dear! you don't know, 'cause in course you hante travelled none, and can't know, but I do. Lord! meetin' a crittur away from home that way, has actilly made me pipe my eye afore now. Now a feller that don't feel this, that was to school with you, and don't yarn towards you, that is a-sojournin' here and knows *you* are here, and don't run full clip to you and say, 'Oh how glad I am to see you! Come and see me as often as you can;—can't I do anything for you, as I know town better nor you do? Is there anything I can shew you? Oh! how glad I've been to see your name in the papers, hear folks praise your books,—to find you've got on in the world. Well, I am glad of it for your sake—for the sake o' the school and old Nova Scotia, and then how's so and so? Does A drink as hard as ever? is B as busy a-skinnin' a sixpence? and C as fond of horse racing? They tell me D is the most distinguished man in New Brunswick, and so on—eh? What are you a-doin' to-day, come and dine with me?—engaged; to-morrow?—engaged; next day?—engaged. Well, name a day—engaged every day for a fortnight.—The devil you are;—at this rate I shan't see you at all. Well, mind you are engaged to me for your Sunday dinner every Sunday you are in town, and as much oftener as you can. I'll drop in every mornin' as I go to my office about breakfast time and give you a hail—I have an appointment now. Good bye! old feller, devilish glad to see you;' and then returnin' afore he gets to the door, and pattin' you on the shoulders, affectionate like, he'd say with a grave face,—'Good heavens! how many sad recollections you call up! How many of our old schoolfellows are called to their long account!—eh? Well, I am right glad to see *you* agin safe and sound, wind and limb, at any rate—good bye!'

"Yes, Squire, every pleasure has its pain, for pain and pleasure are like the Siamese twins. They have a nateral cord of union, and are inseparable. Pain is a leetle, jist a leetle smaller than t'other, is more narvous, and, in course, twice as sensitive; you can't feel pleasure without feelin' pain, but that aint the worst of it nother; for git on t'other side of 'em, and you'll find you can often feel pain without as much as touchin' pleasure with the tip eend of your finger. Yes, the pleasure of seein' you brings up to that crittur that pang of pain that shoots through the heart. 'How many of our old school-fellers are called to their long accounts!'

"How nateral that was! for, Squire, of all that we knew when young, how few are raelly left to us! The sea has swallowed some, and the grave has closed over others; the battle-field has had its share, and disease has marked out them that is to follow

"Ah me! *we remember with pleasure*, we *think* with *pain*. But this crittur— heavens and airth! what's the sea, the grave, the battle-field, or disease, in comparison of him? Them's nateral things; but here's a feller without a heart; it has been starved to death by the neglect of the affections.

"Oh! Squire, if you'd a-travelled alone in distant countries as I have, you'd a-knowed its a great relief in a foreign land to meet one from home, and open the flood-gate, and let these thoughts and feelin's out; for when they are pent up they aint healthy, and breed home-sickness, and that's an awful feelin'; *and the poorer a country is folks come from, the more they are subject to this complaint.* How does he know you aint home-sick, for that aint confined to no age? How does he know there never was a man in the world met with so much kindness in London as you have, and from entire strangers too, and that you don't need him or his attentions? How does he know I am with you, that can talk a man dead? He don't know, and he don't care. Now, as he hante been near you, and you here four months, he aint worth a cuss; he aint nateral and a crittur that aint nateral aint worth nothing. Cut him as dead as a skunk; say as Crockett did, 'you may go to h—l and I'll go to Texas.' If I was you I wouldn't tell that story, it tante no credit to Nova Scotia; and your countrymen won't thank you a bit for it, I can tell you.

"Oh! Squire, I am 'most afraid sometimes there aint no sich thing as rael friendship in the world. I am a good natered crittur, and always was, and would go to old Nick to sarve a friend. Father used to say I was like a saw horse, my arms was always open, and I'd find in the eend I'de be sawed up myself for my pains. Faith! if I'm in trouble or keeled up with sickness, every feller has an excuse: one's goin' to marry a wife, another to buy a yoke of oxen, and a third sais it will cost him sixpence. Doin' a man a favor is no way to make a friend: the moment you lay him under an obligation you've sold him. An obligation is a horrid heavy thing to carry. As soon as he buckles it on and walks a little way he sais, 'Well, this is a-most a devil of a heavy pack to carry; I'm e'en a'most tired to death.

I'll sit down and rest;' so down he pops and laments his hard fortin. Then he ups and tries it again, and arter joggin' on a space, sais, 'Plague take the strap, how it cuts into the shoulder, don't it? I must stop agin and fix it.' Then he takes a fresh departur', and grumbles and growls as he goes on like a bear with a sore head, and sais, 'Oh! my sakes, am I to carry this infarnal bundle all my life long? Why it will kill me, its so everlastin' almighty heavy, that's a fact. I must stop to drink, for I am 'nation thirsty.' Well, he slips it off, and lays down and takes a drink, and then gets up and stretches himself, and sais, 'Well, I feel a great deal better, and lighter too, without that 'tarnal knapsack. I'll be shot if I'll take it up agin, see if I do; so there now!' and he jist gives it a kick into the brook and walks on without it, a free man, whistlin' as he goes that are old psalm tune, 'O! be joyful, all ye lands!'

"Nothin' is so heavy to carry as gratitude. Few men have strength enough to bear the weight long, I can tell you. The only way that I know to make a feller your friend is to kick him. Jist walk into the street, look out a good countenanced crittur that you think you'd like, seize him by the scruff of the neck, hold him out to arm's-length, and kick him into a jelly a'most, and when you've done, turn him round, stare him in the face, look puzzled like, and say, 'I beg your pardon, I am very sorry, but I took you for so and so; I'll make you any compensation in the world; I feel quite streaked, I do indeed.' 'I'll tell you what it is, *my friend*,' he'll say—he'll call you friend at oncet,—'tell you what, my friend, another time, when you assault a man, be sure that you get hold of the right one. A mistake of this kind is no joke, I assure you.' 'My *dear friend*,' sais you,—for you'll call him dear friend at oncet,—'you can't feel more ugly about it than I do; I'm grieved to death.'

"You and him will be sworn friends arterwards for ever and a day, see if you aint; he has been kicked into an intimacy; an obligation sells one out of it. We may like those we have injured or that have injured us, 'cause it is something we can forgive or forget. We can't like those that have done us a favor, for it is a thing we never forgive. *Now, what are ceremonials but ice-houses that keep affections cold, when the blood is at a high temperature.* Returnin' calls by leavin' cards; what sense is there in that? It consumes good card-board, and wastes valuable time. Doctors are the only people that understand payin' and returnin' visits. I shall never forget a story brother Josiah, the Doctor, told me oncet about the medical way of visitin'. I was a-goin' oncet from Charleston to Baltimore, and sais Josiah, 'Sam,' sais he, 'when do you go?' 'To-morrow,' sais I, 'at eight.' 'I'll go with you,' he sais; 'I want to make a mornin' call there.' 'A mornin' call,' sais I; 'it's a plaguy long way to go for that, and considerable costly, too, unless it's a gal you want to see, and that alters the case. Are you so soft in the horn as to go all that distance jist to leave a card?' 'Sam,' he sais, 'do you recollect when we was to night-school to old Minister, his explainin' what ellipsis was?' 'No, I never heerd of it afore, is it a medicine?' 'Medicine? what a fool you be!' 'Well, what the plague is it then,' sais I, 'is it French?' 'Why, Sam, do you recollect one single blessed thing you ever larnt to school?' 'Yes, I do,' sais I, 'I larnt that a man who calls his brother a fool is apt to git knocked down, in the first place, and is in danger of somethin' worse hereafter, a plaguy sight stronger nor your doctor's stuff.' 'Don't you recollect ellipsis?' sais he; 'it somethin' to be onderstood but not expressed.' 'Well, I think I do mind it, now you mention it,' sais I. 'Well,' sais he, 'doctors' visits are ellipsis visits; there is a great deal onderstood, but not expressed. I'll tell you how it is: I've got business at the bank at Baltimore. Well, I go there, do my business up all tight and snug, and then go call on Doctor Flagg. Flagg sais, 'How are you, Slick? when did you come, eh? glad to see you, old fellow. Come with me, I have a most interestin' case; it's a lady; she gobbles her food like a hen-turkey, and has got the dispepsy. I don't like to talk to her about chawin' her food fine, and bolt for I'm afeerd of offendin' her so I give her medicine to do the work of her teeth.' 'Oh!' sais I, 'I take'—and I goes with him to see her; he tells me her treatment afore her, jist as if he had never mentioned it, and as grave as if he was in airnest. 'Excellent' I say, nothin' could be better; that infusion of quassia chips is somet new in practice, that I take to be a discovery of your own.' He sais, 'Yes; I rather pride myself on it.' 'You have reason,' I say—'I think, madam,' sais I, 'there is some plethora here. I would recommend you to comminuate your food into a more attenuated shape, for the peristallic action is weak.'—We return, and he slips a twenty-dollar bill into my hands; as we go out the front door, he winks and sais, 'Do you stay to-morrow, Slick, I have another case.'—'No, thank you, I'm off at daylight.'

"When he comes to Charleston I *return* the visit, *my* patients fee *him*, and travellin' costs neither of us a cent. Its done by ellipses, it aint all put down in writin', or expressed in words, but its onderstood.

"No, Squire, *friendship is selfishness half the time*. If your skunk of a blue-nose friend could a-made anythin' out o' you, he'd a-called on you the day arter you arrived. Depend upon it that crittur onderstands ellipses, and its the principle he acts on in *making* and *returning visits*."

IX

THE CANADIAN EXILE—PART I

YESTERDAY we visited the Polytechnic, and on our return through Regent Street I met a person whose face, although I did not recognise it, reminded me so strongly of some one I had seen before, that my attention was strongly attracted towards him by the resemblance The moment he saw me he paused, and taking a second look at me, advanced and offered me his hand.

"It is many years since we met, Mr. Poker," he said. "I observe you do not recollect me, few of my old friends do, I am so altered. I am Major Furlong."

"My dear Major," I said, "how do you do? I am delighted to see you again; pray how is all your family, and especially my dear young friend, Miss Furlong?"

A dark shadow passed suddenly across his face, he evaded the question and said he was glad to see me looking so well; and then inquiring my address, said he would take an early opportunity of calling to see me.

I am a blunderer, and always have been. Every man knows, or ought to know, that after a long interval of absence he should be cautious in asking questions about particular individuals of a family, lest death should have invaded the circle in the meantime, and made a victim of the object of his inquiry. It was evident that I had opened a wound not yet healed, and instead of giving pleasure had inflicted pain. A stumbling horse is incurable, a blundering man, I fear, is equally so. One thing is certain, I will never hereafter inquire for any one's health in particular, but after the family generally. I now understand the delicate circumspection of Mr.

Slick's phraseology, who invariably either asks, "How is all to home to-day?" or "How is all to home in a gineral way, and yourself in particular, to day?" I will be cautious for the future. But to return to my narrative, for as I grow older I find my episodes grow longer. I said we should dine at home that day, at our lodgings, 202, Piccadilly, (I insert the number, gentle reader, because I recommend Mr. Weeks, of 202, to your particular patronage,) and that Mr. Hopewell and myself would be most happy to see him at seven, if he would favour us with his company. "Weeks," I said, "is a capital purveyor. I can promise you an excellent bottle of wine, and you will meet 'Mr. Slick.'" Neither the good wine, of which I knew him to be an excellent judge, nor the humour of "the clockmaker," which, eight years before, he so fully appreciated and so loudly applauded, appeared to have any attractions for him; he said he should be most happy to come, and took his leave. Happy!—how mechanically we use words! how little we feel what we say when we use phrases which fashion has prescribed, instead of uttering our thoughts in our own way, or clothing them in their natural apparel! Happy!! Poor man, he will never again know happiness, until he reaches that place "Where the wicked cease from troubling, and the weary are at rest."

"Who the plague is that horrid solemncoly man?" said Mr. Slick when I rejoined him; "he looks as if he had lost his last shillin', and as it was the only survivin' one out of twenty, which made the round sum of the family, he was afeerd he should not get another. Who the plague is he? London aint no place for a man to be in who is out of the tin, I can tell you."

"He is Major Furlong, of the —— regiment," I said. "When I first became acquainted with him, eight years ago, he was stationed at Halifax, Nova Scotia; he was one of the most agreeable men I ever met, and was a general favorite with his brother officers and the people of *the west end of the town*. He was a married man, and had two daughters, grown up, and two sons at school."

"He was married, was he?" said Mr. Slick. "Well, we find, in our sarvice when a feller is fool enough to accommodate himself with a wife it is time for the country to disaccomodate itself of him. I don't know how it is in your sarvice, seein' that when I was to Nova Scotia I was only a clockmaker, and, in course, didn't dine at mess; but I know how 'tis in our'n. We find now and then the wives of officers of marchin' regiments, the very delightful critturs, not always the most charmin' women in the world arter all. A little money and no beauty, or a little beauty and no money, or a little interest and nothin' else, are the usual attractions to idle or speculatin' men who want to drive a tandem or to sport a belle. Nor is every married man by any means either the most sensible or the most agreeable of his corps neither. Sensible he cannot be, or he would not have married. The gaudy tinsel of military life soon tarnishes, and when poverty shows thro' it like a pictur'-frame when the gildin' is worn off, it sours the temper too much to let 'em be agreeable. Young subalterns should never be sent on detachments to country quarters in our great Republic. This duty should be done either by sargints or old Field officers. A sargint cannot marry without obtainin' permission and is therefore safe; and if an old officer takes to drinkin' at their out-o'-the-way posts, in Maine or Florida, as he probably will, and kill himself in his attempts to kill time, the regiment will be more efficient, by being commanded by younger and smarter men. To die in the sarvice of one's country is a glorious thing, but to die of a wife and ten children, don't excite no pity, and don't airn no praise, I'll be shot if it does. To expose a young man to the snares and spring of match-makin' mothers, and the charms of idle uneducated young gals in country quarters, is as bad as erectin' barracks on marshy grounds that are subject to fever and ague. It renders the corps unfit for duty. To be idle is to be in danger, and to be idle in danger is sure and certain ruin. Officers stationed at these outposts have nothing to do but to admire and be admired—to sport and to flirt. They fish every day, and are fished for every evenin', and are, in course, as we say in the mackarel line, too often 'book'd in.' If the fish is more valuable than the bait, what must the bait be, where so little value is placed on the fish? This is the reason that we hear of so many solemncoly instances of blasted prospects, of unhappy homes, of discontented, or dissipated husbands, and reckless or broken-hearted wives. Indeed, marriage in the army should be aginst the regulations of the service. A man can't serve two mistresses— his country and his wife. It spiles a good soldier to make a bad husband; but it changes a woman wuss, for it convarts her, by changing Holton ice and snows for Alabama's heats and fevers, into a sort of Egyptian mummy. She dries as much, but she don't keep so well. Lord! how I pity an officer's wife, that's been dragged about from pillar to post that way. In a few years her skin is as yaller as an orange, or as brown as mahogany.

She looks all eyes and mouth, as if she could take her food whole, and as thin and light in the body as a night-hawk. She gets mannish too, from bein' among men so much, and her talk gets a sportin' turn, instead of talk of the feminine gender. She tells stories of hosses, and dogs, and huntin', and camps, and our young fellers, as she calls the boy officers, and their sprees. She sees what she hadn't ought to see, and hears what she hadn't ought to hear, and knows what oughtn't to know, and sometimes talks what she hadn't ought to talk. It e'en a jist sp'iles her the long bun. And the children—poor little wretches!—what a school a barracks is for them! What beautiful new oaths the boys larn, and splendid leetle bits and scraps of wickedness they pick up from the sodgers and sodger boys; and the leetle gals, what nice leetle stories they hear; and what pretty leetle tricks they larn from camp women, and their leetle gals! And if there aint nothin' but the pay, what an everlastin' job it is to alter frocks, and razee coats, and coax down stockin's for them. A gold epaulette on the shoulder, and a few coppers in the pocket, makes poverty farment till it gets awful sour; and silk gowns and lace collars, and muslin dresses and feathers, for parties abroad, and short allowance for the table to home, makes gentility not very gentle sometimes. When the gals grows up, its wuss. There is nobody to walk with, or ride with, or drive with, or sing with, or dance with, but young officers. Well, it aint jist easy for poor marm, who is up to snuff, to work it so that they jist do enough of all this to marry; and yet not enough talkin' to get talked of themselves—to get a new name afore they have sp'ilt their old one, and jist walk the chalks exactly. And then, what's wuss than all, its a roost here, and, a roost there, and a-wanderin' about everywhere; but there aint *no home*—no leetle flower garden—no leetle orchard—no leetle brook—no leetle lambs— no leetle birds—no pretty leetle rooms, with pretty leetle nick-knackery on 'em; but an empty barrack room; cold, cheerless lodgin's, that aint in a nice street; or an awful door, and awful bad inn. Here to-day, and gone to-morrow—to know folks but to forget 'em—to love folks but to part from 'em—to come without pleasure, to leave without pain; and, at last—for a last will come to every story,—no home. Yes! there is a home too, and I hadn't ought to forget it, tho' it is a small one.

"Jist outside the ramparts, in a nice little quiet nook, there is a little grass mound, the matter of five or six feet long, and two feet wide or so, with a little slab at one eend, and a round stone at t'other eend; and wild roses grow on it, and some little birds build there and sing, and there aint no more trouble then. Father's house was the *fust home*—but that was a gay, cheerful, noisy one; this is a quiet, silent, but very safe and secure one. It is *the last home!!* No, sir! matrimony in the army should be made a capital offence, and a soldier that marries, like a man who desarts his post, should be brought to a court-martial, and made an immediate example of, for the benefit of the sarvice. Is that the case in your regiments?"

"I should think not," I said; "but I do not know enough of the army to say whether the effects are similar or not; but, as far as my little experience goes, I should say the picture is overdrawn, even as regards your own. If it be true, however, Mrs. Furlong was a delightful exception; she was as amiable as she was beautiful, and had a highly cultivated and a remarkably well regulated mind. I had not the good fortune to make their acquaintance when they first arrived, and in a few months after we became known to each other, the regiment was ordered to Canada, where I lost sight of them. I had heard, indeed, that he had sold out of the army, purchased an estate near Prescott, and settled on it with his family. Soon after that the rebellion broke out, and I was informed that his buildings had been destroyed by the reformers, but I never learned the particulars. This was all that I could recall to my mind, and to this I attributed his great alteration of manner and appearance." Punctually at seven the Major arrived for dinner. The conversation never rose into cheerfulness by a reference to indifferent subjects, nor sunk into melancholy by allusions to his private affairs, but it was impossible not to see that this even tenour was upheld by a great exertion of moral courage. During the evening Mr. Hopewell, who only knew that he was a half-pay officer that had settled in Canada, unfortunately interrogated him as to the rebellion, and the share he had taken, if any, in suppressing it, when he told us the melancholy story related in the following chapter.

X

THE CANADIAN EXILE—PART II

"YOU are aware, Mr. Poker," said Major Furlong, "that shortly after I had the pleasure of making your acquaintance at Halifax, my regiment was ordered to Canada; I was stationed in the Upper province, the fertility and beauty of which far exceeded any accounts I had ever heard of it. Our next tour of duty was to be in the West Indies. My poor Amelia shuddered at the thought of the climate, and suggested to me, as our family was getting to be too expensive to remove so often, to terminate our erratic life by settling in Canada. A very favourable opportunity occurring soon after, I sold out of the army, purchased a large tract of land, erected a very pretty cottage, and all necessary farm buildings, and provided myself with as many cattle of the best description as the meadow-land would warrant me in keeping. In a short time I was very comfortably settled, and my wife and daughters were contented and happy. We had not only all the necessaries and comforts of life about us, but many of the luxuries, and I congratulated myself upon having turned my sword into a ploughshare. This state of things, however, was not doomed to last long. So many unwise concessions had been recently made by the Colonial Office to local demagogues, that they became emboldened in their demands, and the speeches of Roebuck and Hume, in Parliament, and a treasonable letter of the latter, which had been widely circulated through the country, fanned the flame of discontent until it broke out into open rebellion. They gave themselves the very appropriate title of 'Patriots,' Reformers,' and 'Liberals'—names that are always assumed when the deception and delusion of the lower orders is to be attempted. They were desperate men, as such people generally are, destitute of property, of character, or of principle, and as such found a warm sympathy in the scum of the American population, the refuse of the other colonies, and the agitators in England. A redress of grievances was their watchword, but fire and murder were their weapons, and plunder their real object. The feeble Government of the Whigs had left us to our own resources—we had to arm in our own defence, and a body of my neighbours, forming themselves into a volunteer corps, requested me to take the command. The duties we had to perform were of the most harassing nature, and the hardships we endured in that inclement season of the year baffle all description and exceed all belief. I soon became a marked man—my life was threatened, my cattle were destroyed, and my family frequently shot at. At last the Reformers seized the opportunity of my absence from home with the volunteers, to set fire to my house, and as the family escaped from the flames to shoot at them as they severally appeared in the light of the fire. My eldest daughter was killed in attempting to escape, the rest reached the woods, with the slight covering they could hastily put on in their flight, where they spent the night in the deep snow, and were rescued in the morning, nearly exhausted with fatigue and terror, and severely frostbitten.

"During all this trying period, my first care was to provide for my houseless, helpless family; I removed them to another and more tranquil part of the country, and then resumed my command. By the exertions and firmness of M'Nab and the bravery and loyalty of the British part of the population, the rebellion was at last put down, and I returned to my desolate home. But, alas! my means were exhausted—I had to mortgage my property to raise the necessary funds to rebuild my house and re-stock my farm, and, from a state of affluence, I found myself suddenly reduced to the condition of a poor man. I felt that my services and my losses, in my country's cause, gave me a claim upon the Government and I solicited a small country office, then vacant, to recruit my finances.

"Judge of my surprise, when I was told that I was of different politics from the local administration which had recently been formed from disaffected party; that I was a loyalist; that the rebels must be pacified— that the well-understood wishes of the people must be considered, a large portion of whom were opposed to Tories, Churchmen, and Loyalists; that the rebels were to be pardoned, conciliated, and promoted; and that I had not the necessary qualifications for office, inasmuch as I was a gentleman, had been in arms against the people, upheld British connexion, and was a monarchist. This I could have borne. It was a sad reverse of fortune, it is true; my means were greatly reduced, my feelings deeply wounded, and my pride as a man and an Englishman severely mortified. I knew, however, I was in no way the cause of this calamity, and that I still had the fortitude of a soldier and the hope of Christian. But, alas! the sufferings my poor wife endured, when driven, at the dead of night, to seek shelter in the snowdrifts from her merciless pursuers, had thrown her into a decline, and day by day I had the sad and melancholy spectacle before my eyes of this dear and amiable woman, sinking into the grave with a ruined constitution and a broken heart. Nor was I suffered to remain unmolested myself, even when the rebellion had ceased. Murder, arson, and ruin had not yet glutted the vengeance of these remorseless Reformers. I constantly received threatening letters; men in disguise were still occasionally seen lurking about my premises, and three several times I was shot at by these assassins. Death at last put an end to the terrors and sufferings of poor Amelia, and I laid her beside her murdered daughter. Having sold my property, I left the country with the little remnant of my fortune, and sought refuge in my native land with my remaining daughter and two sons. Good heavens! had I taken your advice, which still rings in my ears, I should have escaped this misery. 'Don't settle in Canada,' you said, 'it is a border country; you are exposed to sympathisers without, and to patriots within, below you is treason, and above you is Durhamism. Years and Whigs must pass away, and Toryism and British feeling return, before tranquillity will be restored in that unhappy country. Remarkable prophecy! wonderfully fulfilled! Oh! had I taken your advice, and gone among Turks and infidels, obedience to the laws would have, at all events, insured protection; and defending the government, if it had not been followed by reward, would at least not have incurred displeasure and disgrace. But, alas! I had been bred a soldier, and been taught to respect the British flag, and, unhappily, sought a home in a colony too distant for a British army to protect or British honour to reach. My poor dear sainted wife—my poor murdered daughter may—."

Here, overcome by his feelings, he covered his face with his hands, and was dreadfully and fearfully agitated. At last, springing suddenly up in a manner that brought us all to our feet, he exhibited that wildness of eye peculiar to insanity, and seizing me with wonderful muscular energy by the arm he pointed to the corner of the room, and screamed out, "There! there! do you see it?—look, look!—it is all on fire!—do you hear those cursed rifles?—that's Mary in the light there!" and then raising his voice to a fearful pitch, called out, "Run! for God's sake; run, Mary, to the shade, or they'll shoot you!—make for the woods!—don't stop to look behind!—run, dear, run!"—and then suddenly lowering his tone to a harsh whisper, which still grates in my ears as I write, he continued, "There! look at the corner of that barn—do you see that Reformer standing in the edge of the light?—look at him!—see him!—good Heavens! he is taking aim with his rifle!—she's lost, by G—d!" and then shouting out again "Run, Mary!—run to the shade;" and again whispering "Do you hear that? He has fired—that's only the scream of fright—he missed her—run! run!" He shouted again, "one minute more, and you are safe—keep to the right;" and then pressing my arm with his hand like a vice, he said, "They have given him another rifle—he is aiming again—he has shot her!—by Heavens, she's killed!" and springing forward, he fell on the floor at full length in a violent convulsion fit, the blood gushing from his nose and mouth in a dreadful manner.

"This is an awful scene!" said Mr. Hopewell after the Major had been undressed, and put to bed, and tranquillity in some measure restored again. "This is a fearful scene. I wonder how much of this poor man's story is correct, or how much is owing to the insanity under which he is evidently labouring.—I fear the tale is too true. I have heard much that confirms it. What a fearful load of responsibility rests on the English Government of that day, that exposed the loyal colonists to all these horrors; and then regarded their fidelity and valour, their losses and their sufferings, with indifference,—almost bordering on contempt. It was not always thus. After the American Revolution, the British gave pensions to the provincial officers, and compensation to those who had suffered for their loyalty. Fidelity was then appreciated, and honoured. But times have sadly changed. When I heard of the wild theories Lord Durham propounded, and the strange mixture of absolutism and democracy pre scribed by the quackery of Thompson, I felt that nothing but the advent of the Tories would ever remedy the evils they were entailing on the colonies. Removed they never can be, but they can be greatly palliated: and a favourable change has already come over the face of things. A man is no longer ashamed to avow himself loyal; nor will his attachment to his Queen and country be any longer, I hope, disqualification for office. I trust the time has now arrived, when we shall never again hear of—*A Canadian Exile!*"

XI

WATERING PLACES

MR. HOPEWELL having gone into the country for a few weeks, to visit some American families, the Attaché and myself went to Brighton, Leamington, Cheltenham, and some minor watering-places, for the purpose of comparing them with each other; as also with Saratoga and other American towns of a similar kind. "As a stranger, Mr. Slick, and a man of small means," I said, "I rather like a place like Cheltenham, The country around is very beautiful, the air good; living very cheap, amusement enough provided, especially for one so easily amused as myself. And then there is less of that chilly and repulsive English reserve than you find elsewhere."

"Well," said. Mr. Slick, "I like 'em, and I don't like 'em; kinder sort o' so, and kinder sort of not so, but more not so nor so. For a lark, such as you and me has had, why, it's well enough; and it aint bad as a place for seein' character; but I wouldn't like to live here, some how, all the year round. They have but four objects in view here, and them they are for everlastin' a-chasin' arter—health or wealth—life or a wife. It would be fun enough in studyin' the folks, as I have amused myself many a day in doin', only them horrid solemncoly-lookin' people that are struck with death, and yet not dead—totterin', shakin', tremblin', crawlin', and wheelin' about, with their legs and feet gone, wheezin', coffin', puffin' and blowin', with their bellowses gone—feelin', leadin', stumblin' and tumblin', with their eyes gone,—or trumpet-eared, roarin', borein', callin', and bawlin', with their hearin' gone,—don't let you think of nothin' else. These, and a thousand more tricks, death plays here, in givin' notice to quit, makes me feel as if I might be drafted myself some fine day into the everlastin' corps of veteran invalids, and have to put on the uniform, and go the rounds with the awkward squad. Oh, dear! for a feller like me, that's always travelled all my life as hard as ever I could lick, or a horse like old Clay could carry me, for to come at the eend of the journey to wind up the last stage, with a leetle four-wheeled waggon, and a man to drag me on the side-path! What a skary kind o' thought it is, aint it? Oh, dear! it's sot one o' my feet asleep already, only a-thinkin' of it—it has, upon my soul! Let's walk to the seat over there, where I can sit, and kick my heel, for posi*tive*ly, my legs is gittin' numb. I wonder whether palsy is ketchin? The sick and the well here ought to have a great caucus meetin', and come to an onderstandin'. Them that's healthy should say to t'others, 'Come now, old fellows, let's make a fair division of these places. If you are sick, choose your ground, and you shall have it. Do you want sea-air? Well, there is Brighton, you shall have it; it's a horrid stupid place, and just fit for you, and will do your business for you in a month.—Do you want inland air? Well, there is Leamington or Cheltenham—take your choice. Leamington, is it? Well then, you shall have it; and you may take Herne Bay and Bath into the bargain; for we want to be liberal, and act kindly to you, seein' you aint well. Now there's four places for you—mind you stick to 'em. If you go anywhere else, you shall be transported for life, as sure as rates. Birds of a feather flock together. All you sick folks go there, and tell your aches and pains, and receipts, and quack medicines to each other. It's a great comfort to a sick man to have some feller to tell his nasty, dirty, short stories about his stomach to; and no one will listen to you but another sick man, 'cause when you are done, he's a-goin' to up and let you have his interestin' history. Folks that's well, in gineral always vote it a bore, and absquotolate—they won't listen, that's a fact. They jist look up to the sky, as soon as you begin,—I suffer dreadfully with bile,—and say,—Oh! it's goin' to rain, do go in, as you have been takin' calomel;—and they open a door, shove you into the entry, and race right off as hard as they can clip. Who the devil wants to hear about bile? Well, then, as you must have somebody to amuse you, we will give you into the bargain a parcel of old East Indgy officers, that aint ill and aint well; ripe enough to begin to decay, and most likely are a little too far gone in places. They wont keep good long; it's likely old Scratch will take 'em sudden some night; so you shall have these fellows. They lie so like the devil they'll make you stare, that's a fact. If you only promise to let them get on an elephant arter dinner, they'll let you tell about your rumatics, what you're rubbed in, and took in, how 'cute the pain is, and you may grin and make faces to 'em till you are tired; and tell 'em how you didn't sleep; and how shockin' active you was once upon a time when you was young; and describe all about your pills, plaisters, and blisters, and everythin'. Well, then, pay 'em for listenin', for it desarves it, by mountin' them for a tiger hunt, and they'll beguile away pain, I know, they will tell such horrid thumpers. Or you can have a boar hunt, or a great sarpent hunt, or Suttees, or anythin'. Three lines for a fact, and three volumes for the romance. Airth and seas! how they lie! There are two things every feller leaves in the East, his liver and his truth. Few horses can trot as fast as they can invent; yes, you may have these old 'coons, and then when you are tied by the leg and can't stir, it will amuse you to see them old sinners lookin' onder gals' bonnets, chuckin' chambermaids onder the chin, and winkin' impedent to the shop-woman, not 'cause it pleases women, for it don't—young heifers can't abide old fellers—but 'cause it pleases themselves to fancy they are young. Never play cards with them, for if they lose they are horrid cross and everlastin' sarsy, and you have to swaller it all, for it's cowardly to kick a feller that's got the gout; and if they win they make too much noise a-larfin, they are so pleased.'

"'Now there is your four waterin' places for you; stick to 'em, don't go ramblin' about to every place in the kingdom, a'most, and sp'ile 'em all. We well folks will stick to our own, and let you be; and you ill folks must stick to your'n, and you may get well, or hop the twig, or do what you like; and we'll keep well, or hop the broomstick, or do anythin' we like. But let's dissolve partnership, and divide the stock at any rate. Let January be January, and let May be May. But let's get a divorce, for we don't agree over and above well.'

"Strange! Squire, but extremes meet. When society gets too stiff and starch, as it is in England, it has to onbind, slack up, and get back to natur'. Now these waterin' places are the relaxin' places. They are damp enough to take the starch all out. Resarve is thrown off. It's bazaar day here all the time; pretty little articles to be sold at high prices. *Fashion keeps the stalls, and fools are the purchasers.* You may suit yourself with a wife here if you are in want of such a piece of furniture; or if you can't suit yourself, you may get one, at any rate. You can be paired, if you don't get matched, and some folks thinks if critturs have the same action, that's all that's wanted in matin' beasts. Suitin' is difficult. Matrimony is either heaven or hell. It's happiness or misery; so be careful. But there is plenty of critturs such as they be in market here. If you are rich and want a poor gal to spend your cash here, she is ready and willin'—flash edicated, clap-trap accomplishments—extravagant as old Nick—idees above her station—won't stand haglin' long about your looks, she don't care for 'em; she wants the carriage, the —, the town house, the park, and *the tin*. If you are poor, or got an estate that's dipt up to the chin, and want the one thing needful, there's an heiress.—She is of age now—don't care a snap of her finger for her guardian—would like a title, but must be married, and so will take you, if you get yourself up well. She likes a handsum man.

"Everythin' here is managed to bring folks together. The shop must be made attractive now, or there is no custom. Look at that chap a-comin' along. He is a popular preacher. The turf, club, and ball managers have bribed him; for he preaches agin horse-racin', and dancin', and dress, and musick, and parties, and gaieties, with all his might and main; calls the course the Devil's common, and the assembly-room Old Nick's levee. Well, he preaches so violent, and raves so like mad agin' em, it sets all the young folks crazy to go arter this forbidden fruit, right off the reel, and induces old folks to fetch their gals where such good doctrine is taught. There is no trick of modern times equal to it. It's actilly the makin' of the town. Then it jist suits all old gals that have given up the flash line and gay line, as their lines got no bites to their hooks all the time they fished with them, and have taken the serious line, and are anglin' arter good men, pious men, and stupid men, that fancy bein' stupid is bein' righteous. So all these vinegar cruits get on the side-board together, cut out red flannel for the poor, and caps for old women, and baby-clothes for little children; and who go with the good man in their angel visits to the needy, till they praise each other's goodness so, they think two such lumps of goodness, if j'ined, would make a'most a beautiful large almighty lump of it, and they marry. Ah! here comes t'other feller. There is the popular doctor. What a dear man *he* is!—the old like him and the young like him; the good like him, and the not so gooder like him; the well like him and the ill like him, and everybody likes him. *He never lost a patient yet*. Lots of 'em have died, but then they came there on purpose to die: they were done for in London, and sent to him to put out of pain; but he never lost one, since he was knee-high to a goose. He onderstands delicate young gals' complaints most beautiful that aint well, and are brought here for the waters. He knows nothin' is the matter of em but the 'visitin' fever;' but he don't let on to nobody, and don't pretend know; so he tells Ma' she must not thwart her dear gal: she is narvous, and won't bear contradiction—she must be amused, and have her own way. He prescribes a dose every other night of two pills, made of one grain of flour, two grains of sugar, and five drops of water, a-goin' to bed; and—that it's so prepared she can't take cold arter it, for there aint one bit of horrid mercury in it. Then he whispers to Miss 'dancin' is good exercise; spirits must be kept up by company. All nater is cheerful; why shouldn't young gals be? Canary birds and young ladies were never made for cages; tho' fools make cages for them sometimes.' The gal is delighted and better, and the mother is contented and happy. They both recommend the doctor, who charges cussed high, and so he ought: he made a cure, and he is paid with great pleasure. There is another lady, a widder, ill, that sends for him. He sees what she wants with half an eye, he is so used to symptoms. She wants gossip. 'Who is Mr. Adam?' sais she. 'Is he of the family of old Adam, or of the new family of Adam, that lives to Manchester?' 'Oh, yes the family is older than sin, and as rich too,' sais be. 'Who is that lady he walked with yesterday?' 'Oh! *she* is married,' sais doctor. Widder is better directly. 'The sight of you, *dear* doctor, has done me good; it has revived my spirits: do call agin.' 'It's all on the narves, my dear widder,' sais he. 'Take two of these bread and sugar pills, you will be all right in a day or two; and, before goin' into company, take a table spoonful of this mixture. It's a new exilaratin' sedative' (which means it's a dram of parfumed spirits). 'Oh! you will feel as charmin' as you look.' Widder takes the mixture that evenin', and is so brilliant in her talk, and so sparklin' in her eyes, old Adam is in love with her, and is in a fair way to have his flint fixed by this innocent Eve of a widder. No sooner out of Widder's house than a *good lady* sends for him. He laments the gaiety of the town—it's useless for him to contend against the current: he can only lament. How can invalids stand constant excitement? Tells a dreadful tale of distress of a poor orphan family, (not foundlin's, and he groans to think there should be such a word as a foundlin'; for doctors aint sent for to announce their arrival to town, but only ugly old nurses,) but children of pious Christian parents. He will introduce the Rev. Mr. Abel, of the next parish, a worthy young man (capital living, and great expectations): he will shew you where the family is. 'Is his wife with him?' 'Oh, Lord love you! he is not married, or engaged either!' The *good* lady is *better* already. 'Good bye! dear doctor; pray come soon agin and see me.'

"He is a cautious man—a prudent man—a 'cute man, he always writes the rich man's London Physician, and approves of all he has done. That doctor sends him more dyin' men, next train, to give the last bleedin' to. It don't do to send your patients to a crittur that ondervalues you, it tante safe. It might hurt you to have a feller goin' out of the world thinkin' you had killed him, and a-roarin' at you like mad, and callin' you every name he could lay his tongue to, it's enough to ruin practice. Doctor, therefore, is punctilious and gentleman-like he aint parsonal, he praises every London doctor individually and separately and only d—ns 'em all in a lump. There is a picnic, if you like. That will give you a chance to see the gals, and to flirt. There's an old ruin to visit and to sketch, and there's that big castle; there's the library and the fruit shop, and I don't know what all: there's everything a'most all the time, and what's better, new-comers every day. I can't say all this jist exactly comes up to the notch for me. It may suit you, Squire, all this, but it don't altogether suit my taste, for, in the fust place, it tante always fust chop society there. I don't see the people of high life here jist as much as I am used to in my circles, unless they're sick, and then they don't want to see me, and I don't want to see them. And in the next place I can't shake hands along with death all the time without gettin' the cold shivers. I don't mind old fellers goin' off the hook a bit, 'cause it's in the course of natur'. Arter a crittur can't enjoy his money, it's time he took himself off, and left it to some one that can; and I don't mind your dissipated chaps, who have brought it on 'emselves, for it sarves 'em right, and I don't pity 'em one mossel. That old sodger officer, now, with claret-coloured cheeks, who the plague cares about him? he aint no good for war, he is so short winded and gouty; and aint no good for peace, he quarrels so all day. Now if he'd step off, some young feller would jist step in, that's all. And there's that old nabob there. Look at the curry powder and muligatony soup a-peepin' through his skin. That feller exchanged his liver for gold. Well, it's no consarn of mine. I wish him joy of his bargain, that's all, and that I had his rupees when he is done with 'em. The worms will have a tough job of him, I guess, he's so dried with spices and cayenne. It tante that I am afeerd to face death, though, for I aint, but I don't like it, that's all. I don't like assyfittety, but

I aint afeerd on it—Fear! Lord! a man that goes to Missarsippi like me, and can run an Alligator steamer right head on to a Sawyer, high pressure engine, valve sawdered down, three hundred passengers on board, and every soul in danger, aint a coward. It takes a *man*, Squire, I tell you. No, I aint afeerd, and I aint spooney nother; and though I don't like to see 'em, it don't sp'ile my sleep none, that's a fact. But there is folks here, that a feller wouldn't be the sixteenth part of a man if he didn't feel for with all *his* heart and soul. Look over there now, on that bench. Do you see that most beautiful gal there?—aint she lovely? How lily fair she is, and what a delicate color she has on her cheek; that aint too healthy and coarse, but interestin' and in good taste, not strong contrasts of red and white like a milk maid, but jist touched by nature's own artist's brush, blended, runnin' one into the other, so you can't tell where one eends and t'other begins! And then her hair, how full and rich, and graceful them auburn locks be! aint they? That smile too! it's kinder melancholy sweet, and plays round the mouth, sort of subdued like moonlight. But the eye, how mild and brilliant, and intelligent and good, it is! Now that's what I call an angel, that. Well, as sure as you and I are a talkin', she is goin' to heaven afore long. I know that gal, and I actilly love her—I do indeed. I don't mean as to courtin' of her, for she wouldn't have the like of me on no account. She is too good for me or any other feller that's knocked about the world as I have. *Angels didn't visit the airth arter sin got in*, and one o' my spicy stories, or flash oaths, would kill her dead. She is more fitter to worship p'raps than love; but I love her, for she is so lovely, so good, so mild, so innocent, so clever. Oh what a dear she is.

"Now, that gal is a-goin to die as sure as the world; she is in a consumption, and that does flatter so soft, and tantalizes so cruel, its dreadful. It pulls down to and sots up to-morrow. It comes with smiles and hopes, and graces, but all the time it's insinuatin' itself, and it feeds on the inside till it's all holler like, and then to hide its murder, it paints, and rouges, and sets off the outside so handsum, no soul would believe it was at work. 'Vice imitates vartue,' Minister sais, but consumption imitates health, I tell you, and no mistake. Oh! when, death comes that way, it comes in its worst disguise, to my eye, of all its masks, and veils, and hoods, and concealments, it has. Yes, she'll die! and then look at the lady alongside of her. Handsum woman too that, even now, tho' she is considerable older. Well, that's her mother—aint she to be pitied, poor crittur? Oh! how anxious she watches that leetle pet of her heart. One day she is sure she is better, and tells her so, and the gal thinks so too, and they are both happy. Next day mother sees somethin' that knocks away all her hope, but she don't breathe it to no one livin'; keeps up all day before sick one, cheerful-like, but goes to bed at night and cries her soul out a'most, hopin' and fearin', submittin' and rebellin', prayin' and despairin', weepin' and rejoicin', and goin' from one extreme to t'other till natur' gets wearied and falls asleep. Oh! what a life is the poor mother's, what a death is the poor darter's! I don't know whether I pity that gal or not; sometimes I think I do, and then I think I pity myself, selfish like, that such a pure spirit should leave the airth, for it's sartin she is goin' to a better world; a world better fitted for her too, and havin' bein's in it more like herself than we be. But, poor mother! there is no mistake about her; I do pity her from the bottom of my heart. What hopes cut off! what affections torn down! fruit, branch, and all, bone of her bone, flesh of her flesh, a piece and parcel of herself; all her care gone, all her wishes closed for ever, all her fears come true and sartin (and its a great matter to lose anythin' we have had trouble with, or anxiety about, for we get accustomed to trouble and anxiety, and miss it when it's gone). Then there's the world to come, for the mind to go a-wanderin', and a-spekilatin' in a great sea without shores or stars; we have *a compass*—that we have *faith in*! but still it's a fearful voyage. And then there is the world we live in, and objects we know, to think of; there is the crawlin' worm and the horrid toad, and the shockin' earwig, and vile corruption; and every storm that comes we think that those we loved and lost, are exposed to its fury. 'Oh! it's dreadful. I guess them wounds aint never quite cured. *Limbs that are cut off still leave their feelin' behind—the foot pains arter the leg is gone.* Dreams come too, and *dreams are always with the dead, as if they were livin'.* It tante often we dream of the dead as dead, but as livin' bein's, for we can't realize death. Then mornin' dawns, and we start up in bed, and find it is only a dream, and larn that death is a fact, and not fancy. *Few men know what woman suffers, but it's only God above that knows the sufferin's of a mother.*

"It tante every one sees all this, but I see it all as plain as preachin'; I most wish sometimes I didn't. I know the human heart full better than is good for me, I'm a-thinkin'. Let a man or woman come and talk to me, or let me watch their sayins' and doin's a few minutes, and I'll tell you all about 'em right off as easy as big print. I can read 'em like a book, and mind I tell you, there's many a shockin' bad book in very elegant gold bindin', full of what aint fit to be read; and there's many a rael good work in very mean sheepskin covers. The most beautiful ones is women's. In a gineral way mind I tell you the paper is pure white, and what's wrote in it is good penmanship and good dictionary. I love 'em—no man ever loved dear innocent gals as I do, 'cause I know how dear and innocent they be—but man—oh! there is many a black, dirty, nasty horrid sheet in his'n. Yes, I know human natur' too much for my own good, I am afeerd, sometimes. *Such is life in a Waterin' Place, Squire. I don't like it. The ill make me ill, and the gay don't make me gay—that's a fact. I like a place that is pleasant of itself but not a place where pleasure is a business, and where that pleasure is to be looked for among the dyin' and the dead. No, I don't like a Waterin' Place!"*

XII

THE EARL OF TUNBRIDGE

"SQUIRE," said Mr. Slick, "I am afeerd father is a little wrong in the head. He goes away by himself and stays all the mornin', and when he returns refuses to tell me where he has been, and if I go for to press him, he gets as mad as a hatter. He has spent a shockin' sight of money here. But that aint the worst of it nother, he seems to have lost his onderstandin' too. He mutters to himself by the hour, and then suddenly springs up and struts about the room as proud as a peacock, and sings out—'Clear the way for the Lord!' Sometimes I've thought the Irvinites had got hold of him, and sometimes that he is mesmerised, and then I'm afeerd some woman or another has got an eye on him to marry him. He aint quite himself that's sartin. The devil take the legation, I say! I wish in my soul I had stayed to Nova Scotia a-vendin' of clocks, and then this poor, dear old man wouldn't have gone mad as he has. He came to me this mornin', lookin' quite wild, and lockin' the door arter him, sot down and stared me in the face for the matter of five minutes without speakin' a blessed word, and then bust out a-larfin like anythin'.

"'Sam,' sais he, 'I wish you'd marry.'

"'Marry,' sais I, 'why what on airth do I want of a wife, father?'

"'I have my reasons, sir,' sais he, 'and that's enough.'

"'Well,' sais I, 'I have my reasons, sir, agin it, and that's enough. I won't.'

"'You won't, sir?'

"'No, sir, I won't.'

"'Then I discard you, Sam. You are no longer a son of mine. Begone, sir!'

"'Father,' sais I, and I bust out a cryin', for I couldn't hold in no longer. 'Father,' sais I, 'dear father, what ails you,—what makes you act so like a ravin' distracted bed bug? I do believe in my soul you are possess't. Now do tell me, that's a dear, what makes you want me to marry?'

"'Sam,' sais be, 'what brought me here, now jist tell me that, will you?'

"'Ay, father,' sais I, 'what did bring you here, for that's what I want to know?'

"'Guess, Sam,' sais he.

"'Well,' sais I, 'to see me I s'pose a-movin' in high life.'

"'No.'

"'Well, to establish a trade in beef onder the new tariff.'

"'No.'

"'Well, in lard-ile, for that's a great business now.'

"'No, its none o' these things, so guess agin.'

"'Well,' sais I, 'Father, I'm most afeerd, tho' I don't like to hint it; but I'm most afeerd you are a-goin' to spekilate in matrimony, seein' that you are a widower now these five years past.'

"'Sam,' sais he, 'you are a born fool,' and then risin' up quite dignified, 'do you think, sir, I have taken leave of my senses?'

"'Well,' sais I, 'dear father, I'm most thinkin' you have, and that's a fact.'

"'So you think I'm mad, do you, sir?'

"'Well, not 'xactly,' sais I, 'but raelly now, I don't think you are quite right in your mind.'

"'You scoundrel, you,' sais he, 'do you know who I am?'

"'Yes, sir,' sais I, 'you are father, at least mother told me so.'

"'Well, sir, she told you right, *I am* your father, and a pretty ondutiful son I have, too; but I don't mean that, do you know *who* I am?'

"'Yes, sir, Lieut.-Col. Slick, of Slickville, the Bunker Hill hero.'

"'I am, sir,' sais he, a-drawin' himself up, 'and most the only one now livin' that seed that great and glorious battle, but do you know *what* I am?'

"'Yes, sir, dear old father gone as mad as a march hare.'

"'You almighty villain,' sais he, 'who are you; do you know that?'

"'Your son,' sais I.

"'Yes, but *who* are *you?*"

"'I am Sam Slick, the Clockmaker,' sais I, 'at least what is left of me.'

"'You are no such a thing,' sais he, 'I'll tell you *who* I am, and *what* you are. Get up you miserable skunk, and take off your hat, clear the way for the Lord. I am the Earl of Tunbridge, and you are Lord Van Shleek, my eldest son. Go down on your knees, sir, and do homage to your father the Right Honorable the Earl of Tunbridge.'

"'Oh, father, father,' sais I, 'my heart is broke, I wish I was dead, only to think that you should carry on this way, and so far away from home, too, and before entire strangers. What on airth put that are crotchet into your head?'

"'Providence, Sam, and the instinct of our Sal. In lookin' over our family papers, of father and his father, she found we are descendants of General Van Shleek, that come over with King William the Dutchman, when he conquered England, and was created Airl of Tunbridge, as a reward for his heroic deeds. Well, in course, the Van Shleeks came over from Holland and settled near him, and my grandfather was a son of the first Lord's third brother, and bein' poor, emigrated to America. Well, in time the Peerage got dormant for want of an heir, and we bein' in America, and our name gettin' altered into Slick, that everlastin' tyrant George the Third, gave away the estate to a favourite. This, sir, is as clear as preachin', and I have come over to claim my rights. Do you onderstand that, sir? you degenerate son of a race of heroes! What made my veins b'ile over at Bunker Hill? The blood of the Van Shleeks!—What made me charge the British at Peach Orchard, and Mud Creek?—The blood of the Van Shleeks! What made me a hero and a gentleman?—The nobility that was in me! I feel it, sir, I feel it here,' puttin' his hand on his side, 'I feel it here, beatin' at my heart now, old as I am, like a tattoo on a drum. I am the rael Airl of Tunbridge.'

"'Oh, dear, dear,' sais I, 'was the like of this ever heerd tell of afore?'

"'Heerd of afore,' sais he, 'to be sure it has been. America was settled by younger sons, and in time all the great estates have come to 'em, but they have been passed or cheated. Webster, sir, owns Battle Abbey, and is intarmined to have it, and he is a man that knows the law and can plead his own case. There can't be no manner of doubt our great author Cooper is the rael Airl of Shafteshury. A friend of mine here, who knows all about estates and titles, told me so himself, and says for five pounds he could put him on the right track; and he is a man can be depended on, for he has helped many a feller to his rights. You'd be astonished if you know'd how many of our folks are noblemen, or related to 'em very near. How can it be otherwise in natur'? How did they come by the same name if they warn't? The matter of five pounds, my friend sais, will do a good deal some times, provided it's done secret. In all these things, mum's the word;—no blartin'—no cacklin' afore layin' the egg, but as silent as the grave. Airl of Tunbridge! it don't sound bad, does it?'

"'Well,' sais I, 'father,' for I found opposite wouldn't do no longer;— 'well,' sais I, 'father it might be so in your case arter all.'

"'Might be so!' sais he; 'I tell you it is so.'

"'Well, I hope so,' sais I, 'but I feel overcome with the news, s'posin' we go to bed now, and we will talk it over tomorrow.'

"'Well,' sais he, 'if you can sleep arter this, go to bed, but Sam, for heaven's sake, sleep with General Wellington, and talk him over; I don't care a d—n for the Airl of Tunbridge, I want to change it. I want the title to be Bunker Hill, as he is of Waterloo. We are two old veteran heroes, and ought to be two great nobs together. Sleep with him, Sam, for heaven's sake. And now,' sais he, risin', and takin' the candle, 'open the door, sir, and clear the way for the Lord.'

"Oh, dear! dear! I am almost crazed myself, Squire, aint it shockin'? He was evidently very much distressed, I had never seen him so much moved before, and therefore endeavoured to soothe him as well as I could."

"Stranger things than that have happened," I said, "Mr. Slick. It is possible your father may be right, after all, although the proof to substantiate his claim may be unattainable. It is not probable, certainly, but it is by no means impossible."

"Then you think there may be something in it, do you?"

"Unquestionably there may be, but I do not think there is."

"But you think there may be—eh?"

"Certainly, there may be."

After a long pause, he said, "I don't think so either, Squire; I believe it's only his ravin'; but if there was," striking his fist on the table with great energy, "by the 'tarnal I'd spend every cent I have in the world, to have my rights. No there is nothin' in it, but if there was, I'd have it if I died for it. Airl of Tunbridge! well it aint so coarse, is it? I wonder if the estate would come back too, for to my mind a title without the rael grit, aint worth much,—is it? Airl of Tunbridge!—heavens and airth! if I had it, wouldn't I make your fortin, that's all; I hope I may be shot if I'd forget old friends. Lord! I'd make you Governor-Gineral to Canady, for you are jist the boy that's fit for it,—or Lord Nova Scotia; for why shouldn't colonists come in for their share of good things as well as these d—ned monopolists here, or anythin' you pleased a'most. Airl of Tunbridge!—Oh, it's all nonsense, it can't be true! The old man was always mad upon somethin' or another, and now he is mad on this p'int. I must try to drive it out of his head, that is, if it hante no bottom; but if it has, I'm jist the boy to hang on to it, till I get it, that a fact. Well, there may be somethin' in it, as you say, arter all. I'll tell you what, there's no harm in inquirin', at any rate. I'll look into the story of the 'Airl of Tunbridge.'"

XIII

ENGLISH GENTLEMEN

As we were sitting on one of the benches in the park at Richmond to-day, a liveried servant passed us, with an air of self possession and importance that indicated the easy dependance of his condition, and the rank or affluence of his master.

"That," said Mr. Slick, "is what I call a rael English gentleman now. He lives in a grand house, is well clad, well fed; lots of lush to drink, devilish little to do, and no care about corn laws, free trade, blowed-up bankers, run-away lawyers, smashed down tenants, nor nothin'. The mistress is kind to him, 'cause he is the son of her old nurse; and the master is kind to him 'cause his father and grand-father lived with *his* father and grand-father; and the boys are kind to him, 'cause he always takes their part; and the maids are kind to him, 'cause he is a plaguy handsome, free and easy feller, (and women always like handsum men, and impedent men, though they vow they don't); and the butler likes him, 'cause he can drink like a gentleman and never get drunk. His master has to attend certain hours in the House of Lords: he has to attend certain hours in his master's house. There aint much difference, is there? His master loses his place if the Ministry goes out; but he holds on to his'n all the same. Which has the best of that? His master takes the tour of Europe, so does he. His master makes all the arrangements and pays all the expenses; he don't do either. Which is master or servant here? His young master falls in love with an Italian opera gal, who expects enormous presents from him; he falls in love with the bar-maid, who expects a kiss from him. One is loved for his money, the other for his good looks. Who is the best off? When his master returns, he has larned where the Alps is, and which side of them Rome is; so has he. Who is the most improved? Whenever it rains his master sighs for the sunny sky of Italy, and quotes Rogers and Byron. He d—ns the climate of England in the vernacular tongue, relies on his own authority, and at all events is original. The only difference is, his master calls the castle my house, he calls it our castle: his master says my park, and he says our park. It is more dignified to use the plural: kings always do; it's a royal phrase, and he has the advantage here. He is the fust commoner of England too. The sarvants' hall is the House of Commons. It has its rights and privileges, and is plaguy jealous of them too. Let his master give any of them an order out of his line, and see how soon he votes it a breach of privilege. Let him order the coachman, as the horses are seldom used, to put them to the roller and roll the lawn. 'I can't do it, sir; I couldn't stand it, I should never hear the last of it; I should be called the rollin' coachman.' The master laughs; he knows prerogative is dangerous ground, that an Englishman values Magna Charta, and sais, 'Very well, tell farmer Hodge to do it.' If a vine that hides part of the gable of a coach-house, busts its bondage, and falls trailin' on the ground, he sais, 'John, you have nothin' to do, it wouldn't hurt you, when you see such a thing as this loose, to nail it up. You see I often do such things myself, I am not above it.' 'Ah! it may do for *you*, sir; *you can* do it if you like, but *I* can't; I should lose caste, I should be called the gardener's coachman.' 'Well, well! you are a blockhead; never mind.'

"Look at the lady's maid; she is twice as handsum as her mistress, because she worked when she was young, had plenty of exercise and simple diet, and kept early hours, and is full of health and spirits; she dresses twice as fine, has twice as many airs, uses twice as hard words, and is twice as proud too. And what has *she* to do? Her mistress is one of the maids in waitin' on the Queen; she is maid in waitin' on her mistress. Who has to mind her p's and q's most, I wonder? Her mistress don't often speak till she is spoken to to the palace; she speaks when she pleases. Her mistress flatters delicately; she does the same if she chooses, and if not she don't take the trouble. Her mistress is expected to be affable to her equals, considerate and kind to her inferiors, and humane and charitable to the poor. All sorts of things are expected of and from her. But she can skrimage with her equals, be sarsy to her inferiors, and scorny to the poor if she likes, it is not her duty to do all these things, tho' it is her mistress's, and she stands on her rights. Her mistress's interest at court is solicited where she can do but little at last; the world overvalys it amazin'ly. Her interest with her mistress is axed for, where she can do a great deal. There is no mistake about that. Her mistress, when on duty, sais yes or no, as a matter of course. She can't go wrong if she follows the fugle-man. There must be but one opinion at the palace. The decision of a Queen, like that of a Pope, don't admit of no nonconcurrin'. But she can do as she pleases, and is equally sartin of success. She cries up her mistress's new dress, her looks, her enticin' appearance, her perfect elegance. She is agreeable, and a present rewards the honest thoughts of her simple heart. She disapproves the colour, the texture, the becomin'ness of the last new dress. It don't suit her complexion, it don't set well, it don't shew off the figure, it's not fit for her lady. She says she raelly thinks so, and she is seldom mistaken. The dress is condemned and given to her: she is safe any way.—Happy gal! remain as you be, till the butt eend of time: it's better to have a mistress than a master. Take a fool's advice for oncet, and never marry; whoever gits you will have his hands full in the halter-breakin', I know; who the devil could give you a mouth, keep you from shyin' or kickin', or rearm', or boltin'? A mistress has a light bridle-hand, don't curb up too short, and can manage you easy: but a man—Lord a massy! you'd throw him the fust' spring and kick you give, and break his neck, I know.—Oh! these are the gentlemen and ladies of England; these are the people for whom the upper and lower orders were born—one to find money and the other to work for 'em. Next to bein' the duke, I'd sooner be coachman to a gentleman that sports a four in-hand than anythin I know of to England: four spankin', sneezin', hosses that knows how to pick up miles and throw 'em behind 'em in style—g'long you skunks, and turn out your toes pretty—whist—that's the ticket;—streak it off like 'iled lightning, my fox-tails: skrew it up tight, lock down the safety valve, and clap all steam on, my busters; don't touch the ground, jist skim it like hawks, and leave no trail; go a-head handsum, my old clays:—yes! the sarvants are the "Gentlemen of England," they live like fightin' cocks, and yet you hear them infarnal rascals—the radicals, callin' these indulgent masters—tyrants endeavourin' to make these happy crittus hate the hand that feeds them, tellin' these pampered gentlemen they are robbed of their rights, and how happy they'd all be if they lost their places and only had vote by ballot and univarsal suffrage. What everlastin' d—'d rascals they must be!"

"Sam," said Mr. Hopewell, "I am surprised at you. I am shocked to hear you talk that way; how often must I reprove you for swearing?"

"Well, it's enough to make a feller swear, to find critturs fools enough, rogues enough, and wicked enough, to cut apart nateral ties, to preach family treason, ill-will and hatred among men."

"Nothing is so bad, Sam," he replied, "as to justify swearing. Before we attempt to reform others we had better reform ourselves; a profane man is a poor preacher of morality."

"I know it is a foolish practice, Minister," said Mr. Slick, "and I've ginn it over this good while. I've never swore scarcely since I heard that story of the Governor to Nova Scotia. One of their Governors was a military man, a fine, kind hearted, generous old veteran as ever was, but he swore, every few words he said, like anythin' not profane-like or cross, but jist a handy sort of good-humoured oath. He kinder couldn't help it.

"One day on board the steam-boat a crossin' the harbour to Dartmouth, I heerd the Squire here say to him, 'We ought to have another church to Halifax, Sir Thomas,' sais he, 'somewhere in the neighbourhood of Government House. St. Paul's is not half large enough for the congregation.' 'So I think,' sais the Governor, and I told the Bishop so, but the Bishop sais to me,— 'I know that d—ned well, Sir Thomas, but where the devil is the money to come from? If I could find the means, by G—d you should soon have a church.'

"He never could tell a story without puttin' an oath into every one's mouth, whether it was a bishop or any one else. But oath or no oath, he was a good old man that, and he was liked by every man in the province except by them its no great credit to be praised by."

"Your apologies, Sam," he said, "seldom mend the matter. Reproving you makes you offend more; it is like interrupting a man in speaking who wanders from his point, or who is arguing wrong, only lose time, for he speaks longer than he otherwise would. I won't reprove therefore, but I ask your forbearance as a favor. Yes, I agree with you as to servants here,— I like the relative condition of master and servant in this country. There is something to an American or a colonist quite touching in it,—it is a sort of patriarchal tie. But alas! I fear it is not what it was,—as you say, the poison diffused through the country by reformers and radicals has done its work: it has weakened the attachment of the servant to his master; it has created mutual distrust, and dissolved in a great measure what I may call the family tie between them. Enfeebled and diluted, however, as the feeling is in general, it is still so different from what exists among us, that there is no one thing whatever that has come under my observation that has given me so much gratification as the relation of master and servant,—the kindness and paternal regard of the one, and the affectionate and respectful attachment of the other. I do not say in all cases, because it is going out; it is not to be found among the mushroom rich—the cotton lords—the *novi homines, et hoc genus omne;*—but among the nobility and the old gentry, and some families of the middle classes, it is still to be found in a form that cannot be contemplated by a philanthropist without great satisfaction. In many cases the servants have been born on the estates, and their forefathers have held the same situation in the family of their master's ancestors as they do.

"Their interests, their traditions, their feelings, and sympathies, are identified with those of the 'house.' They participate in their master's honors—they are jealous in supporting his rank, as if it was in part their own, and they feel that their advancement is connected with his promotion. They form a class—from that class they do not expect or desire to be removed. Their hopes and affections, therefore, are blended with those of their employers. With us it is always a temporary engagement—hope looks beyond it—and economy furnishes the means of extrication. It is like a builder's contract,—he furnishes you with certain work—you pay a certain stipulated price; when the engagement is fulfilled, you have nothing further to say to each other. There is no favor conferred on either side.

"Punctuality, and not thanks are expected. It is a cold and mercenary bargain, in which there is a constant struggle; on one side to repress the advance of familiarity, and on the other to resist the encroachments of pride. The market price only is given by the master, and of course the least service returned, that is compatible with the terms of the bargain. The supply does not equal the demand, and the quality of the article does not correspond with the price. Those who have been servants seldom look back with complacency on their former masters. They feel no gratitude to them for having furnished them with the means of succeeding in the world, but they regard them with dislike, because they are possessed of a secret which they would have to be forgotten by all,—that they once were household servants.

"As our population becomes more dense, this peculiarity will disappear, and the relation will naturally more nearly resemble that which exists in Europe. There has already been a decided improvement within the last twenty years from this cause. Yes! I like the relative condition of master and servant here amazingly—the kindness, mildness, indulgence and exactness of the master—the cheerfulness, respectfulness, punctuality, and regard of the servant—the strength, the durability, and the nature of the connexion. As I said before, there is a patriarchal feeling about it that touches me. I love them both."

"Well, so do I too," said Mr. Slick, "it's a great comfort is a good help that onderstands his work and does it, and aint above it. I must say I don't like to see a crittur sit down when I'm at dinner, and read the paper, like a Varmonter we had oncet. When father asked him to change a plate.—'Squire,' sais he, 'I came as a help, not as a sarvant; if you want one o' them, get a Britisher, or a nigger. I reckon I am a free and enlightened citizen, as good as you be. Sarvants are critturs that don't grow in our backwoods, and if you take me for one you are mistaken in this, child, that's all. If you want me to work, I'll work; if you want me to wait on you, you'll wait for me a long time fust, I calkelate.' No, Squire, we hante got no sarvants, we've only got helps. The British have got sarvants, and then they are a 'nation sight better than helps, tho' they are a little proud and sarsy sometimes, but I don't wonder, for they are actilly *the Gentlemen of England*, that's a fact."

XIV

ENGLISH NIGGERS

"YES," said Mr. Slick, Pursuing the same subject of conversation. "I like the English sarvant. Sarvice is a trade here, and a house help sarves an apprenticeship to it, is master of his work, and onderstands his business. He don't feel kinder degraded by it, and aint therefore above it. Nothin' aint so bad as a crittur bein' above his business. He is a part of his master here. Among other folks' sarvants he takes his master's title. See these two fellers meet now, and hear them—'Ah, Lothian! how are you?' 'All right; how are you, Douro? It's an age since I saw you.' Aint that droll now? A cotton spinner's sarvant is a snob to these folks. He aint a man of fashion. They don't know him—he uses a tallow candle, and drinks beer; he aint a fit associate for one who uses a wax, and drinks wine. They have their rank and *position* in socie*ty* as well as their masters, them fellers; and to my mind they are the best off of the two, for they have no care. Yes, they are far above our helps, I must say; but their misfortunate niggers here, are a long chalk below our slaves to the south, and the cotton-manufacturers are a thousand times harder task-masters than our cotton planters, that's a fact."

"Negroes!" I said in some astonishment; "why, surely you are aware *we* have emancipated our negroes. *We* have no slaves."

"Come, Squire," said he, "now don't git your back up with me; but for goodness gracious sake, never say we. It would make folks snicker here to hear you say that. It's as bad as a sarvant sayin' 'our castle'—'our park'— 'our pictur' gallery,' and so on. What right have you to, say 'We?' You aint an Englishman, and old Bull won't thank you for your familiarity,

I know. You had better say, 'Our army,' tho' you have nothin' to do with it; or 'our navy,' tho' you form no part of it; or 'our House of Lords,' and you can't boast one Lord; or 'our House of Commons,' and you hante a single blessed member there; or 'our authors,'—well, p'raps you may say that, because you are an exception: but the only reason you warn't shot, was, that you was the fust colonial bird that flew across the Atlantic, and you was saved as a curiosity, and will be stuffed some day or another, and stuck up in a museum. The next one will be pinked, for fear he should cross the breed.—'Our!' heavens and airth! I wonder you hante too much pride to say that; it's too sarvanty for the like o' you. How can you call yourself a part of an empire, in the government of which you have no voice? from whose honours you are excluded, from whose sarvice you are shut out? by whom you are looked on as a consumer of iron and cotton goods, as a hewer of wood for the timber market, a curer of fish to freight their vessels—as worth havin', because you afford a station for an admiral, a place for a governor, a command for a gineral; because, like the stone steps to a hall door, you enable others to rise, but never move yourselves. 'Our!' It makes me curl inwardly to hear you use that word 'Our.' I'll tell you what a colonial 'Our' is. I'll tell you what awaits you: in the process of a few years, after your death, all your family will probably sink into the class of labourers. Some on 'em may struggle on for a while, and maintain the position you have; but it won't be long. Down, down, down they must go; rise they never can. It is as impossible for a colonist to rise above the surface, as for a stone to float on a river. Every one knows this but yourself, and that is the reason gentlemen will not go and live among you. They lose caste—they descend on the scale of life—they cease to be Romans. Din this for ever in the ears of British statesmen: tell them to make you Englishmen, or to give you a Royal Prince for a King, and make you a new people. But that to be made fun of by the Yankees, to be looked down upon by the English, and to be despised by yourselves, is a condition that you only desarve as long as you tolerate it. No, don't use that word 'Our' till you are entitled to it. Be formal, and ever-lastin' polite. Say 'your' empire, 'your' army, &c.; and never strut under borrowed feathers, and say 'our,' till you can point to your own members in both houses of Parliament—your own countrymen filin' such posts in the imperial sarvice as they are qualified for by their talents, or entitled to in right of the population they represent; and if anybody is struck up of a heap by your sayin' 'yours' instead of 'ours,' tell them the reason; say—that was a lesson I learnt from Sam Slick, the clock-maker; and one thing is sartin, to give the devil his due, that feller was 'no fool,' at any rate. But to git back to what we was a-talkin' of. We have two kinds of niggers in the States—free niggers and slaves. In the north they are all free, in the south all in bondage. Now the free nigger may be a member of Congress, but he can't get there; he may be President, but he guesses he can't; and he reckons right. He may marry Tyler's darter, but she won't have him; he may be embassador to the Court of St. James's, Victoria, if he could be only appointed; or he may command the army or the navy if they'd only let him—that's his condition. The slave is a slave, and that's his condition. Now the English have two sorts of niggers—American colonists, who are free white niggers; and manufacturers' labourers at home, and they are white slave niggers. A white colonist, like our free black nigger, may be a member of Parliament, but he can't get there; he may *be* a governor, but he guesses he can't, and he guesses right; he may marry an English nobleman's darter, if she'd only have him; he may be an embassador to our court at Washington, if he could be only appointed; he may command the army or the fleet, if he had the commission; and that's his condition.—A colonist and a free nigger don't differ in anythin' but color: both have naked rights but they have no power given 'em to clothe those rights, and that's the naked truth.

"Your blockheads of Liberals to Canada, are for ever yelpin' about 'sponsible government; if it was all they think it is, what would be the good of it? Now, I'll tell you the remedy. Don't repeal the Union, lay down your life fust, but have a closer union. Let 'em form a Colonial council board to London, and appoint some colonists to it, that they may feel they have some voice in the government of the empire. Let 'em raise provincial regiments and officer them with natives, that you may have somethin' to do with the army. Let 'em have some man devoted to Colony offices, that you may have somethin' to do with the navy. All you've got in that line, is a miserable little cutter, paid by yourselves, commanded by one of yourselves, Captain Darby: and he has sot a proper pattern to your navy. He has seized more Yankee vessels in the last seven years for breakin' the fish treaty than all the admirals and all the squadrons on the American coast has, put together twice over. He and his vessel costs you a few hundred a-year; them fleets durin' that time has cost more nor all Halifax would sell for to-morrow, if put up to vandu. He desarves a feather in his cap from your Government, which he won't get, and a tar-jacket covered with feathers from us, which he is very likely to get. Yes, have some man-o'-war there with colony officers like him, then say 'our navy,' if you like. Remove the restrictions on colonial clergy, so that if they desarve promotion in the church to Britain, they needn't be shut out among big bogs, black logs, and thick fogs, for ever and ever; and then it tante the Church of England, but 'our church.' If there is a feller everlastin' strong in a colony, don't make it his interest to wrastle with a Governor; but send him to another province, and make him one himself. Let 'em have a Member to Parliament, and he will be a safety valve to let off steam. It's then 'our Parliament.' Open the door to youngsters, and let 'em see stars, ribbons, garters, coronets, and all a-hangin' up agin the wall, and when their mouths water, and they lick their chops as if they'd like a taste of them, then say,—'Now d—n you, go a-head, and win 'em, and if you win the race you shall have 'em, and if you lose, turn to, import some gentlemen and improve the breed, and mind your trainin', and try agin; all you got to do, is to win.' Go a-head, I'll bet on you, if you try. Let 'death or victory' be your colony motto—Westminster Abbey or the House of Lords. Go a-head, my young coons, wake snakes, and walk your chalks, streak it off like 'iled lightenin', and whoever gets in first, wins. Yes, that's the remedy. But now they have no chance.

"Now, as to the manufacturin' slave, let's look at the poor devil, for I pity him, and I despise and hate his double-faced, iron-hearted, radical, villanous, low-bred, tyrant of a master as I do a rattlesnake. Oh! he is different from all the Sarvants in England; all other sarvants are well off—most too well off if anythin', for they are pampered. But these poor critturs! oh! their lot is a hard one—not from the Corn-laws, as their Radical employers tell 'em be cause they have not univarsal suffrage, as demagogues tell 'em—nor because there are Bishops who wear lawn sleeves instead of cotton ones, as the Dissenters tell 'em,—but because there is a law of natur' violated in their case. The hawk, the shark, and the tiger; the bird, the fish, and the beast, even the reasonin' brute, man, each and all feed, nurture, and protect, those they spawn, hatch, or breed. It's a law written in the works of God. They have it in instinct, and find it in reason, and necessity and affection are its roots and foundation. The manufacturer alone obeys no instinct, won't listen to no reason, don't see no necessity, and hante got no affections. He calls together the poor, and gives them artificial powers, unfits them for all other pursuits, works them to their utmost, fobs all the profits of their labour, and when he is too rich and too proud to progress, or when bad spekelations has ruined him, he desarts these unfortunate wretches whom he has created, used up, and ruined, and leaves them to God and their country to provide for. But that aint all nother, he first sots them agin the House of God and his Ministers, (the only Church, too, in the whole world, that is the Church of the poor—the Church of England, the fust duty of which is to provide for the instruction of the poor at the expense of the rich,) and then he sots them agin the farmer, who at last has to feed and provide for them in their day of trouble. What a horrid system! he first starves their bodies, and then p'isens their minds—he ruins them, body and soul. Guess, I needn't tell you, what this gony is?—-he is a Liberal; he is rich, and hates those that are richer; he is proud, and hates those of superior station. His means are beyond his rank; his education and breedin' is below that of the aristocracy. He aint satisfied with his own position, for he is able to vie with his superiors; he is dissatisfied with theirs because he can't come it. He is ashamed to own this, his real motive, he therefore calls in principle to his aid. He is then, from principle, a Reformer, and under that pretty word does all the mischief to society he can.

"Then comes to his aid, for figures of speech, the bread of the poor, the starvin' man's loaf, the widder's mite, the orphan's mouldy crust. If he lowers the price of corn, he lowers wages. If he lowers wages, he curtails his annual outlay; the poor is made poorer, but the unfortunate wretch is too ignorant to know this. He is made richer himself, and he is wide awake. It won't do to say all this, so he ups with his speakin' trumpet, and hails principle agin to convoy him. He is an Anti-Corn-Law leaguer on principle, he is agin agricultural monopoly, the protective system, the landed gentry. He is the friend of the poor. What a super-superior villain he is!—he first cheats and then mocks the poor, and jist ups and asks the blessin' of God on his enterprise by the aid of fanatical, furious, and seditious strollin' preachers. Did you ever hear the like of that, Squire?"

"Never," I said, "but once."

"And when was that?"

"Never mind—go on with your description; you are eloquent to-day."

"No; I won't go on one single blessed step if you don't tell me,—it's some fling at us I know, or you wouldn't hum and haw that way. Now out with it—I'll give you as good as you send, I know. What did you ever know equal to that?"

"I knew your Government maintain lately, that on the high seas the flag of *liberty* should protect a cargo of *slaves*. It just occurred to me, that liberty at the *mast-head*, and slavery in *the hold*, resembled the conduct of the manufacturer, who, while he oppressed the poor, affected to be devoted to their cause."

"I thought so, Squire, but you missed the mark that time, so clap in another ball, and try your hand agin. The Prince de Joinville boarded one o' your gun brigs not long ago (mind you, not a tradin' vessel, but a man-o'-war) and took her pilot out of her to steer his ship. Now if your naval man had a-seized the French officer by the cape of his coat with one hand, and the seat of his breeches with the other, and chucked him head and heels overboard, and taught him the new game of leap *Frog*, as he had ought to have done, you'd a know'd a little better than to ax us to let your folks board our vessels. It don't become you British to talk about right o'sarch arter that. I guess we are even now—aint we? Yes, I pity these poor ignorant devils, the English niggers, I do from my soul. If our slaves are old, or infirm, or ill, their master keeps them, and keeps them kindly too. It is both his interest to take care of their health, and his duty to provide for 'em if ill. He knows his niggers, and they know him. They don't work like a white man. They know they must be fed, whether they work or not. White niggers know they must starve if they don't. Our fellers dance and sing like crickets. Your fellers' hearts is too heavy to sing, and their limbs too tired to dance. A common interest binds our master and slave. There is no tie between the English factor and his tugger. He don't know his men by sight—they don't know him but by name. Our folks are and must be kind. Yours aint, and needn't be. They pretend then, and in that pretence become Powerful, 'cause they have the masses with them. Cunnin' as foxes them critturs, too. They know some one would take up the cause of them niggers, and therefore they put them on a false scent—pretend to fight their battles and, instead of waitin' to be attacked, fall to and attack the poor farmer; while the owners of England, therefore, are a-defendin' of themselves from the onjust charge of oppressin' the poor, these critturs are plunderin' the poor like winky. Ah! Squire, they want protectin'—there should be cruisers sent into those manufacturin' seas. The hulks there are under your own flag—board them—examine them. If the thumb-screws are there, tuck up some of the cotton Lords with their own cotton ropes—that's the ticket, sir; ventilate the ships—see the owners have laid in a good stock of provisions for a long voyage, that the critturs aint too crowded, that they have prayers every Sunday."

"Very good, Sam," said Mr. Hopewell; "your heart's in the right place, Sam. I like to hear you talk that way; and let the chaplain not be the barber or shoe-maker, but a learned, pious, loyal man of the Church of England; let him—"

"Let them," said Mr. Slick, "take care no crittur talks mutinous to them—no chartism—no radicalism—no agitation—no settin' of them agin their real friends, and p'isonin' of their minds. If there is any chaps a-doin' of this, up with them in a minute, and let the boatswain lay three dozen into 'em, in rael wide awake airnest; and while they are in hospital, get some of the cheap bread they talk so much about. (Did you ever see it, Squire? it's as black as if it had dropt into a dye-tub—as coarse as saw-dust—so hard, mould can't grow over it, and so infarnal poor, insects can't eat it.) Yes, send to the Baltic for this elegant cheap bread—this wonderful blessin'—this cure for all evils, and make 'em eat it till their backs is cured. Tell old Joe Sturge to look to home afore he talks of the States; for slave ships aint one mossel wuss than some of the factories under his own nose.

"Ah! Squire, Peel has a long head, Muntz has a long beard, and John Russell has a cussed long tongue; but head, tongue, and beard, put together, aint all that's wanted. There wants a heart to feel, a head to conceive, and a resolution to execute, the protection for these poor people. It aint cheap bread, nor ballot, nor reform, nor chartism, nor free-trade, nor repealin' unions, nor such nonsense, that they want. When a man collects a multitude of human bein's together, and founds a factory, the safety of the country and the interests of humanity require there should be some security taken for the protection of the misfortunate 'English Niggers.'"

XV

INDEPENDENCE

MR. HOPEWELL, who was much struck with the Attaché's remarks in the last chapter, especially those in reference to the colonies, pursued the same subject again to-day.

"Squire," said he, "if Great Britain should withdraw her protection from the North American provinces, as I fear she will at no distant period, would they form a separate nation, or become incorporated with us? This is a serious question, and one that should be well considered. There is a kindness, and yet a perverseness, about English rule in America that is perfectly astonishing. Their liberality is unbounded, and their indulgence unexampled; but there is a total absence of political sagacity, no settled principles of Colonial Government, and no firmness and decision whatever. The result cannot be but most disastrous. They seem to forget that the provinces are parts of a monarchy; and instead of fostering monarchical principles, every step they take tends not only to weaken them, but to manifest a decided preference for republican ones. Demagogues discovering this weakness and vacillation of their rulers, have found by experience, that agitation is always successful; that measures of concession or conciliation are the sure and certain fruits of turbulence; and that, as loyalty can always be depended upon, its claims are sure to be sacrificed to those whose adhesion it is necessary to purchase. To satisfy these democrats, and to gratify their ambition, the upper houses of the Legislature have been rendered a mere nullity; while the popular branches have encroached in such a manner upon the executive, as to render the Governor little more than a choice of being the intriguing head, or the degraded tool of a party. If they succeed in the present struggle in Canada, he will be virtually superseded; the real governor will be the leading demagogue, and the nominal one will have but two duties left to fulfil, namely, to keep a good table for the entertainment of his masters, and to affix his name to such documents as may be prepared and presented for his signature. Rebellion will then have obtained a bloodless victory, and the Colonies will be independent"

"D—n them!" said Colonel Slick; "they don't desarve to be free. Why don't they disguise themselves as Indgins, as we did, and go down to the wharf, board the cutter, and throw the tea into the harbour, as we did? Creation! man, they don't desarve to be free, the cowards! they want to be independent, and they darsn't say so."—And he went out of the room, muttering, "that there never was, and never could be, but one Bunker Hill."

"The loyal, the right-minded British party in the colonies," continued Mr. Hopewell, "are discouraged and disheartened by the countenance and protection shewn to these unprincipled agitators. These are things obvious to all the world, but there are other causes in operation which require local experience and a knowledge of the human mind to appreciate properly. Great Britain is a trading country and values everything by dollars and cents, as much as we do; but there are some things beyond the reach of money. English statesmen flatter themselves that if they abstain from taxing the colonies, if they defend them by their fleets and armies, expend large sums on canals and rail roads, and impose no part of the burden of the national debt upon them, they will necessarily appreciate the advantages of such a happy condition; and, in contrasting it with that of the heavy public exactions in the States, feel that it is both their duty and their interest to be quiet. These are sordid considerations, and worthy of the counting house in which Poulett Thompson learned his first lessons in political economy. Most colonists are native born British subjects, and have, together with British prejudices, British pride also. They feel that they are to the English what the English are to the Chinese, outer barbarians. They observe, with pain and mortification, that much of the little local patronage is reserved for Europeans; that when natives are appointed to office by the Governor, in many cases they have hardly entered upon their duties, when they are superseded by persons sent from this side of the water, so vastly inferior to themselves in point of ability and moral character, that they feel the injury they have sustained is accompanied by an insult to the community. The numerous instances you have mentioned to me in the Customs Department, to which I think you said Nova Scotia paid eight thousand pounds a-year, fully justify this remark, and some other flagrant instances of late in the Post-office, you admit have been keenly felt from one end of your province to the other. While deprived of a part of the little patronage at home, there is no external field for them whatever. It would be a tedious story to enter into details, and tell you how it arises, but so it is, the imperial service is practically closed to them. The remedy just proposed by Sam is the true one. They feel that they are surrounded by their superiors, not in talent or education, but by those who are superior to them in interest. That they present a field for promotion to others, but have none for themselves. As time rolls on in its rapid but noiseless course, they have opportunities offered to them to measure their condition with others. To-day the little unfledged ensign sports among them for the first time, in awkward consciousness, his new regimentals, passes away to other colonies, in his tour of duty, and while the recollection of the rosy boy is yet fresh in their memories, he returns, to their amazement, in command of a regiment. The same circle is again described, and the General commanding the forces receives the congratulations of his early friends. The wheel of fortune again revolves, and the ensign ripens into a governor. Five years of Gubernatorial service in a colony, are reckoned five years of exile among the barbarians, and amount to a claim for further promotion. He is followed by the affectionate regard of those among whom he lived, into his new sphere of duty, and in five years more he informs them he is again advanced to further honours. A colonist naturally asks himself, how is this? When I first knew these men I was toiling on in my present narrow sphere, they stopped and smiled, or pitied my humble labours, and passed on, sure of success; while here I am in the same position, not only without a hope but without a possibility of rising in the world; and yet who and what are they? I have seen them, heard them, conversed with them, studied them, and compared them with ourselves. I find most of us equal in information and abilities, and some infinitely superior to them. Why is this? Their tone and manner pain me too. They are not rude, but their manner is supercilious; they do not intentionally offend, but it would seem as if they could not avoid it. My country is spoken of as their exile, their sojourn as a page of life obliterated, the society as by no means so bad as they had heard, but possessing no attractions for a gentleman, the day of departure is regarded as release from prison; and the hope expressed that this 'Foreign Service,' will be rewarded as it deserves. All that they feel and express on this subject is unhappily too true. *It is no place for a gentleman*; the pestilential blasts of democracy, and the cold and chilly winds from Downing Street, have engendered an atmosphere so uncongenial to a gentleman, that he feels he cannot live here. Yes! it is too true, the race will soon become extinct,

"'Why, then, is the door of promotion not open to me also,' he inquires, 'as it is the only hope left to me. Talk not to me of light taxes, I despise your money; or of the favour of defending me, I can defend myself. I, too, have the ambition to command, as well as the forbearance to obey. Talk of free trade to traders, but of honourable competition in the departments of State, to gentlemen. Open your senate to us, and receive our representatives. Select some of our ablest men for governors of other colonies, and not condemn us to be always governed.' It can be no honour to a people to be a part of your empire, if they are excluded from all honour; even bondsmen sometimes merit and receive their manumission. May not a colonist receive that advancement to which he is entitled by his talents, his public services, or his devotion to your cause? No one doubts your justice; the name of an Englishman is a guarantee for that: but we have not the same confidence in your information as to our condition. Read history and learn! In the late rebellion, Sir John Colbourne commanded two or three regiments of British troops. Wherever they were detached they behaved as British soldiers do upon all occasions, with great gallantry and with great skill. His arrangements were judicious, and up on two or three occasions where he attacked some small bodies of rebels he repulsed or dispersed them. He was acting in the line of his profession, and he performed a duty for which he was paid by his country. He was rewarded with the thanks of Parliament, a peerage, a pension, and a government. A colonist at the same time, raised a body of volunteers from an irregular and undisciplined militia, by the weight of his personal character and influence; and with prodigious exertion and fatigue traversed the upper province, awakened the energies of the people, and drove out of the country both native rebels and foreign sympathizers. *He saved the colony*. He was not acting in the line of his profession, nor discharging a duty for which he was paid by his country. He was rewarded by a reluctant and barren grant of knighthood. Don't misunderstand me—I have no intention whatever of undervaluing the services of that excellent man and distinguished officer, Sir John Colbourne,—he earned and deserved his reward; but what I mean to say, is, the colonist has not had the reward that he earned and deserved—'Ex uno disce omnes.'

"The American Revolution has shown you that colonists can furnish both generals and statesmen; take care and encourage their most anxious desire to furnish them to you, and do not drive them to act against you. Yet then, as now, you thought them incapable of any command; we have had and still have men of the same stamp; our cemeteries suggest the same reflections as your own. The moralist often says:—

'Perhaps in this neglected spot is laid,
Some heart once pregnant with celestial fire;
Hands that the rod of empire might have swayed,
Or waked to ecstasy the living lyre.

'The applause of listening senates to command;
The threats of pain and ruin to despise;
To scatter plenty o'er a smiling land,
And read their history in a nation's eyes.

'Their lot forbad.—'

"Whether the lot of the present generation will also forbid it, you must decide—or circumstances may decide it for you. Yes, Squire, this is an important subject, and one that I have often mentioned to you. Instead of fostering men of talent, and endeavouring to raise an order of superior men in the country, so that in them the aristocratic feeling which is so peculiarly monarchial may take root and flourish; Government has repressed them, sacrificed them to demagogues, and, reduced the salaries of all official men to that degree, that but suited the ravenous envy of democracy. Instead of building up the second branch, and the order that is to furnish and support it, everything has been done to lower and to break it. In proportion as they are diminished, the demagogue rises when he in his turn will find the field too limited, and the reward too small;

and, unrestrained by moral or religious feeling, having no principles to guide, and no honour to influence him, he will draw the sword as he has done, and always will do, when it suits his views, knowing how great the plunder will be if he succeeds, and how certain his pardon will be if he fails. He has literally everything to gain and nothing to loose in his struggle for 'Independence.'

XVI

THE EBB TIDE

TO-DAY Mr. Slick visited me as usual, but I was struck with astonishment at the great alteration in his dress and manner—I scarcely knew him at first, the metomorphos was so great. He had shaved off his moustache and imperial, and from having worn those military appendages so long, the skin they had covered not being equally exposed to the influence of the sun as other parts of his face, looked as white as if it bad been painted. His hair was out of curl, the diamond broach had disappeared from his bosom, the gold chain from his neck, and the brilliant from his finger. His attire was like that of other people, and, with the exception of being better made, not unlike what he had worn in Nova Scotia. In short he looked like himself once more.

"Squire," said he, "do you know who I am?"

"Certainly; who does not know you? for you may well say 'not to know me, argues thyself unknown.'"

"Aye, but do you know *what* I am?"

"An *attaché*," I said.

"Well, I aint, I've given that up—I've resigned—I aint no longer an *attaché*; I'm Sam Slick, the clockmaker, agin—at least what's left of me. I've recovered my eyesight—I can see without glasses now. You and Minister have opened my eyes, and what you couldn't do father has done. Father was madder nor me by a long chalk. I've been a fool, that's a fact. I've bad my head turned but, thank fortin', I've got it straight agin. I should like to see the man now that would pull the wool over my eyes. I've been made a tiger and—"

"Lion you mean, a tiger is a term applied to—"

"Exactly, so it is; I meant a lion. I've been made a lion of, and makin' a lion of a man is plaguy apt to make a fool of a feller, I can tell you. To be asked here, and asked there, and introduced to this one, and introduced to that one, and petted and flattered, and made much of, and have all eyes on you, and wherever you go, hear a whisperin' click with the last letters of your name—ick—lick—Slick—accordin' as you catch a part or a whole of the word; to have fellers listen to you to hear you talk, to see the papers full of your name, and whenever you go or stay or return, to have your motions printed. The celebrated Sam Slick—the popular Mr. Slick—the immortal Clock-maker—that distinguished moralist and humourist—that great judge of human natur', Mr. Slick; or to see your phiz in a winder of a print-shop, or in a wood-cut in a picturesque paper, or an engine on a railroad called arter you; or a yacht, or vessel, or racehorse, called Sam Slick. Well, it's enough to make one a little grain consaited, or to carry his head high, as a feller I oncet knew to Slickville, who was so everlastin' consaited, and cocked his chin up so, he walked right off the eend of a wharf without seein' the water, and was near about drowned, and sp'iled all his bran new clothes. Yes, I've had my head turned a bit, and no mistake, but it hante been long. I know human natur', and read the human heart too easy, to bark long up a wrong tree. I soon twigged the secret. One wanted to see me, whether I was black or white; another wanted to brag that I dined with 'em; a third wanted me as a decoy bird to their table, to entice others to come; a fourth, 'cause they made a p'int of havin' distinguished people at their house; a fifth, 'cause they sot up for patrons of literary men; a sixth, 'cause they wanted colony politics; a seventh, 'cause it give 'em something to talk of. But who wanted me for myself? Sam Slick, a mechanic, a retail travellin' trader, a wooden clockmaker. 'Aye,' sais I, to myself sais I, 'who wants you for yourself, Sam,' sais I; books, and fame, and name out of the question, but jist 'Old Slick, the Yankee Pedlar?' 'D—n the one o' them,' sais I. I couldn't help a-thinkin' of Hotspur Outhouse, son of the clerk to Minister's church to Slickville. He was sure to git in the wind wherever he went, and was rather touchy when he was that way, and a stupid feller too. Well, he was axed everywhere a'most, jist because he had a'most a beautiful voice, and sung like a canary bird. Folks thought it was no party without Hotspur—they made everythin' of him. Well, his voice changed, as it does sometimes in men, and there was an eend of all his everlastin' splendid singin'. No sooner said than done—there was an eend to his invitations too. All at oncet folks found out he was a'most a horrid stupid crittur; wondered what anybody ever could have seed in him to ax him to their houses—such a nasty, cross, quarrelsome good feller. Poor Hotspur! it nearly broke his heart. Well, like Hotspur, who was axed for his singin', I reckon I was axed for the books; but as for me, myself, Sam Slick, why nobody cared a pinch of snuff. The film dropt right off my eyes at oncet—my mind took it all in at a draft, like a glass of lignum vity.—Tell you where the mistake was, Squire, and I only claim a half of it—t'other half belongs to the nobility. It was this: I felt, as a free and enlightened citizen of our great nation, on a footin' of equality with any man here, and so I was. Every noble here looks on a republican as on a footin' with the devil. We didn't start fair, if we was, I aint afeerd of the race, I tell you. I guess they've got some good stories about me to larf at, for in course fashions alters in different places. I've dressed like them, and tried to talk like them, on the principle, that when a feller is in Turkey, he must do as the Turkeys do; or when they go from Canady to Buffalo, do as the Buffaloes do. I have the style of a man of fashion, of the upper crust circles, and can do the thing now as genteel as any on 'em; but in course, in larnin', I put my foot in it sometimes, and splashed a little of the nastiest. It stands to reason, it couldn't be otherwise. I'll tell you what fust sot me a considerin'—I saw Lady —, plague take her name, I forgit it now, but you know who I mean, it's the one that pretends to be so fond of foreigners and tries to talk languages—Gibberish! oh! that's her name. Well, I saw Lady Gibberish go up to one of my countrywomen, as sweet as sugar-candy, and set her a-talkin', jist to git out of her a few Yankee words, and for no other airthly purpose, (for you know we use some words different from what they do here), and then go off, and tell the story, and larf ready to kill herself. 'Thinks,' sais I, 'I'll take the change out of you, marm, for that, see if I don't; I'll give you a story about yourself you'll have to let others tell for you, for you won't like to retail it out yourself I know.'—Well, Lady Gibberish, you know, warn't a noble born; she was a rich citizen's daughter and, in course, horrid proud of nobility, 'cause its new to her, and not nateral; for, in a gineral way, nobles, if they have pride, lock it up safe in their jewel case;—they don't carry it about with them, on their persons; its only bran new made ones do that. Well, then, she is dreadful fond of bein' thought to know languages, and hooks on to rich foreigners like grim death. So thinks I, I'll play you off, I know. Well, my moustache (and he put up his hand involuntarily, to twist the end of it, as he was wont to do, forgetting that it was a 'tale that was told'), my moustache," said he, "that was jist suited my purpose, so I goes to Gineral Bigelow Bangs, of Maine, that was here at the time, and sais I, 'Gineral,' sais I, 'I want to take a rise out of Lady Gibberish; do you know her?' 'Well, I won't say I don't,' sais he. 'Well,' sais I, (and I told him the whole story) 'jist introduce me, that's a good feller, will you, to her, as Baron Von Phunjoker, the everlastin' almighty rich German that has estates all over Germany, and everywhere else a'most.' So up he goes at a great swoira party at 'the Duke's,' and introduces me in great form, and leaves me. Well, you know I've heerd a great deal of Dutch to Albany, where the Germans are as thick as huckleberries, and to Lunenburg, Nova Scotia, which is German all thro' the piece, and I can speak it as easy as kiss my hand; and I've been enough in Germany, too, to know what to talk about. So she began to jabber Jarman gibberish to me, and me to her; and when she axed me about big bugs to the Continent, I said I had been roamin' about the world for years, and had lost sight of 'em of late; and I told her about South Sea, where I had been, and America, and led her on to larf at the Yankees, and so on. Then she took my arm, and led me round to several of her friends, and introduced me as the Baron Von Phunjoker, begged me to call and see her, to make her house my home, and the devil knows what all; and when she seed Gineral Bangs arterwards, she said I was the most delightful man she ever seed in her life,—full of anecdote, and been everywhere, and seen everythin', and that she liked me all all things—the dearest and handsomest man that ever was. The story got wind that the trick had been played, but the Gineral was off to Eastport, and nobody know'd it was me that was Baron Phunjoker. When she see me, she stares hard, as if she had her misgivin's, and was doubty; but I look as innocent as a child, and pass on. Oh! it cut her up awful. When I leave town I shall call and leave a card at her house, 'the Baron Von Phunjoker.' Oh! how the little Yankee woman larfed at the story; she fairly larfed till she wet herself a-cryin'.

"Yes, Squire, in course, I have some times put my foot in it. I s'pose they may have a larf at my expense arter I am gone, but they are welcome to it. I shall have many a larf at them, I know, and a fair exchange aint no robbery. Yes, I guess I am out of place as an attaché, but it has enabled me to see the world, has given me new wrinkles on my horn, and sharpened my eye-teeth a few. I shall return home with poor old father, and, dear old soul, old Minister, and take up the trade of clockmakin' agin. There is a considerable smart chance of doin' business to advantage to China. I have contracted with a house here for thirty thousand wooden clocks, to be delivered at Macao. I shall make a good spec' of it, and no mistake. And well for me it is so too, for you have sp'iled the trade everywhere a'most. Your books have gone everywhere, and been translated everywhere; and who would buy clocks now, when the secret of the trade is out; if you know, I don't. China is the only place open now, and that won't be long, for Mr. Chew-chew will take to readin', bime-by, and then I'm in a basket there too. Another thing has entarmined me to go. Poor dear father has been regularly took in by some sharper or another. What fetched him here was a letter from a swindler, (marked private,) tellin' him to send five pounds and he'd give him tidin's of a fortin and a title. Well, as soon as he got that, he writes agin, and tells him of his title and estates, so plausible, it actilly took me in when I fust heard of it. Then he got him over here, and bled him till he couldn't bleed no longer, and then he absquotilated. The story has got wind, and it makes me so dandry, I shall have to walk into some o' them folks here afore I've done, if I stay. Father is most crazy; sometimes he is for settin' the police to find the feller out, that he may shoot him; and then he says it's every word true, and the man is only absent in s'archin' out record. I'm actilly afraid he'll go mad, he acts, and talks, and frets, and raves, and carries on so. I hope they won't get the story to home to Slickville; I shall never hear the last of it if they do.

"Minister, too, is gettin' oneasy; he sais he is too far away from home, for an old man like him; that his heart yearns arter Slickville; that here he is a-doin' o' nothin',—and that although he couldn't do much there, yet he could try to, and the very attempt would be acceptable to his Heavenly Master. What a brick he is! aint he? it will be one while afore they see his like here agin, in these clearin's, I know.

"Yes, all things have their flood and their ebb. It's ebb tide here now. I have floated up stream smooth and grand; now it's a turn of the tide; if I stay too long I shall ground on the flats, and I'm for up killoch and off; while there is water enough to clear the bars and the shoals.

"Takin' the earliest tide, helps you to go furdest up the river; takin the earliest ebb, makes you return safe. A safe voyage shows a good navigator and a good pilot. I hope on the voyage of life I shall prove myself both; but to do so, it is necessary to keep about the sharpest look out for 'the Ebb Tide.'"

XVII

EXPERIMENTAL PHILOSOPHY

OUR arrangements having been all finished, we set out from London, and proceeded to Liverpool, at which place my friends were to embark for America. For many miles after we left London, but little was said by any of the party. Leaving a town that contained so many objects of attraction as London, was a great trial to Mr. Slick, and the separation of our party, and the termination of our tour, pressed heavily on the spirits of us all, except the Colonel. He became impatient at last at the continued silence, and turning to me, asked me if ever I had been at a Quaker meeting, "because if you haven't," he said, "you had better go there, and you will know what it is to lose the use of your tongue, and that's what I call *experimental philosophy*. Strange country this, Minister, aint it? How shockin' full of people, and hosses, and carriages, and what not, it is. It ought to be an amazin' rich country but I doubt that."

"It's not only a great country, but a good country, Colonel," he replied. "It is as good as it is great, and its greatness, in my opinion, is founded on its goodness. 'Thy prayers and thy alms have come up as a memorial for thee before God.'"

"And do you raelly think, now, Minister," he replied, "that that's the cause they have gone a-head so?"

"I do," he said; "it's with nations as with individuals: sooner or later they are overtaken in their iniquity, or their righteousness meets its reward."

"That's your *experimental philosophy*, then, is it?"

"Call it what name you will, that is my fixed belief."

"The British, then, must have taken to prayin' and alms-givin' only quite lately, or the Lord wouldn't a-suffered them to get such an almighty everlastin' whippin' as we give 'em to Bunkers Hill, or as old Hickory give 'em to New Orleans. Heavens and airth! how we laid it into 'em there: we waited till we seed the whites of their eyes, and then we let 'em have it right and left. They larnt *experimental philosophy* (as the immortal Franklin called it) that time, I know."

"Colonel," said Mr. Hopewell, "for an old man, on the verge of the grave, exulting over a sad and stern necessity like that battle,—for that is the mildest name such a dreadful effusion of human blood can claim,— appears to me but little becoming either your age, your station, or even your profession."

"Well, Minister," he said, "you are right there too; it is foolish, I know, but it was a great deed, and I do feel kinder proud of it, that's a fact; not that I haven't got my own misgivin's sometimes, when I wake up in the night, about its lawfulness; not that I am afraid of ghosts, for d—n me, if I am afraid of any thin' livin' or dead; I don't know fear—I don't know what it is."

"I should think not, Colonel, not even the fear of the Lord."

"Oh! as for that," he said, "that's a hoss of another colour; it's no disgrace to be cowardly there; but as for the lawfulness of that battle, I won't deny I hante got my own *experimental philosophy* about it sometimes. I'd like to argue that over a bottle of elder, some day with you, and hear all the pros and cons, and debtors and creditors, and ins and outs, that I might clear my mind on that score. On the day of that battle, I had white breeches and black gaiters on, and my hands got bloody liftin' up Lieutenant Weatherspoon, a tailor from our town, arter he got a clip on the shoulder from a musket ball. Well, he left the print of one bloody hand on my legs—and some times I see it there now; not that I am afeerd on it, for I'd face man or devil. A Bunker Hill boy is afeerd of nothin'. He knows what *experimental philosophy* is.—Did you ever kill a man, Minister?"

"How can you ask such a question, Colonel Slick?"

"Well, I don't mean no offence, for I don't suppose you did; but I jist want you to answer, to show you the experimental philosophy of the thing."

"Well, sir, I never did."

"Did you ever steal?"

"Never."

"Did you ever bear false witness agin your neighbour?"

"Oh! Colonel Slick, don't go on that way."

"Well, oncet more; did you ever covet your neighbour's wife? tell me that now; nor his servant, nor his maid?—As to maidens, I suppose it's so long ago, you are like myself that way—you don't recollect?—Nor his hoss, nor his ox, nor his rifle, nor anythin' that's his?—Jim Brown, the black preacher, says there aint no asses to Slickville."

"He was under a mistake, Colonel," said Mr. Hopewell. "He was one himself, and if he had searched he would have found others."

"And therefore he leaves 'em out, and puts in the only thing he ever did envy a man, and that's a good rifle."

"Colonel Slick," said Mr. Hopewell, "when I say this style of conversation is distasteful to me, I hope you will see the propriety of not pursuing it any further."

"You don't onderstand me, sir, that's the very thing I'm goin' to explain to you by *experimental philosophy*. Who the devil would go to offend you, sir, intentionally? I'm sure I wouldn't, and you know that as well as I do; and if I seed the man that dare do it, I'd call him out, and shoot him as dead as a herrin'. I'll be cussed if I wouldn't. Don't kick afore you're spurred, that way.—Well, as I was a-sayin', you never broke any of the commandments in all your life—"

"I didn't say that, sir! far be such presumption from me. I never—"

"Well, you may a-bent some o' them considerable, when you was young; but you never fairly broke one, I know."

"Sam," said Mr. Hopewell, with an imploring look, "this is very disagreeable—very."

"Let him be," said his son, "he don't mean no harm—it's only his way. Now, to my mind, a man ought to know by *experimental philosophy* them things; and then, when he talked about stings o' conscience, and remorse, and so on, he'd talk about somethin' he knowed.—You've no more stings o' conscience than a baby has—you don't know what it is. You can preach up the pleasure of bein' good better nor any man I ever seed, because you know that, and nothin' else—its all flowers, and green fields, and purlin' streams, and shady groves, and singin' birds, and sunny spots, and so on with you. You beat all when you git off on that key; but you can't frighten folks out of their seventeen sinses, about Scorpion whips, and vultur's tearin' hearts open, and torments of the wicked here, and the damned hereafter. You can't do it to save your soul alive, 'cause you hante got nothin' to repent of; you don't see the bloody hand on your white breeches—you hante got *experimental philosophy*."

"Sam," said Mr. Hopewell who availed himself of a slight pause in the Colonel's "experimental philosophy," to change the conversation; "Sam, these cars run smoother than ours; the fittings, too, are more complete."

"I think them the perfection of travellin'."

"Now, there was Ralph Maxwell, the pirate," continued the Colonel, "that was tried for forty-two murders, one hundred high-sea robberies, and forty ship burnin's, at New Orleans, condemned and sentenced to be hanged—his hide was bought, on spekilation of the hangman, for two thousand dollars, for razor-straps, bank-note books, ladies' needle-cases, and so on. Well, he was pardoned jist at the last, and people said he paid a good round sum for it; but the hangman kept the money; he said he was ready to deliver his hide, accordin' to barg'in, when he was hanged, and so he was, I do suppose, when he *was* hanged. Well, Ralph was shunned by all fashionable society, in course; no respectable man would let him into his house, unless it was to please the ladies as a sight, and what does Ralph do—why he went about howlin', and yellin', and screamin', like mad, and foamin' at the mouth for three days, and then said he was converted, and took up preachin'. Well, folks said, the greater the sinner, the greater the saint and they follered him in crowds—every door was open to him, and so was every puss, and the women all went mad arter him, for he was a horrid handsum man, and he took the rag off quite. That man had *experimental philosophy*—that is, arter a fashion. He come down as far as our State, and I went to hear him. Oh! he told such beautiful anecdotes of pirates and starn chases, and sea-fights, and runnin' off with splenderiferous women, and of barrels of gold, and hogsheads of silver, and boxes of diamon's, and bags of pearls, that he most turned the young men's heads—they called him the handsum young converted pirate. When a man talks about what he knows, I call it *experimental philosophy*. Now, Minister, he warn't a right man you know—he was a villain, and only took to preachin' to make money, and, therefore, instead of frightenin' folks out of their wits, as he would a-done if he'd been frightened him self, and experienced repentance, he allured 'em a'most; he didn't paint the sin of it, he painted the excitement. I seed at once, with half an eye, where the screw was loose, and it proved right—for as soon as he raised fifty thousand dollars by preachin', he fitted out another pirate vessel, and was sunk fightin' a British man-o' war; but he might have been a great preacher, if his heart had raelly been in the right place, 'cause his *experimental philosophy* was great; and, by the bye, talkin' of experimental puts me in mind of practical philosophy. Lord! I shall never forget old Captain Polly, of Nantucket; did you ever hear of him, Squire? In course he was a captain of a whaler. He was what he called a *practical* man; he left the science to his officers and only sailed her, and managed things, and so on. He was a mighty droll man, and p'raps as great a pilot as ever you see a'most; but navigation, he didn't know at all; so when the officers had their glasses up at twelve o'clock to take the sun he'd say, 'Boy,'—'Yes, sir.' 'Hand up my quadrant,' and the boy'd hand up a large square black bottle full of gin. 'Bear a-hand you young rascal,' he'd say, 'or I shall lose the obsarvation,' and he'd take the bottle with both hands, throw his head back, and turn it butt eend up and t'other eend to his mouth, and pretend to be a-lookin' at the sun; and then, arter his breath give out, he'd take it down and say to officer, 'Have you had a good obsarvation to-day?' 'Yes, sir.' 'So have I,' he'd say, a smackin' of his lips—'a capital one, too.' 'Its twelve o'clock, sir.' 'Very well, make it so.' Lord! no soul could help a larfin', he did it all so grave and sarious; he called it *practical philosophy*."

    "Hullo! what large place is this, Sam?"

    "Birmingham, sir."

    "How long do we stop?"

    "Long enough for refreshment, sir."

    "Come, then, let's take an obsarvation out of the black bottle, like Captain Polly. Let's have a turn at Practical Philosophy; I think we've had enough to-day of *Experimental Philosophy*."

    While Mr. Slick and his father were "taking obsarvations," I walked up and down in front of the saloon with Mr. Hopewell. "What a singular character the Colonel is!" he said; "he is one of the oddest compounds I ever knew. He is as brave and as honorable a man as ever lived, and one of the kindest hearted creatures I ever knew. Unfortunately, he is very weak; and having accidentally been at Bunker Full, has had his head turned, as being an *Attaché* has affected Sam's, only the latter's good sense has enabled him to recover from his folly sooner. I have never been able to make the least impression on that old man. Whenever I speak seriously to him, he swears at me, and says he'll not talk through his nose for me or any Preacher that ever trod shoe leather. He is very profane, and imagines, foolish old man as he is, that it gives him a military air. That he has ever had any compunctuous visitations, I never knew before to-day, and am glad he has given me that advantage. I think the bloody hand will assist me in reclaiming him yet. He has never known a day's confinement in his life, and has never been humbled by sickness. He is, of course, quite impenetrable. I shall not forget the *bloody hand*—it may, with the blessing of God, be sanctified to his use yet. That is an awful story of the pirate, is it not? What can better exemplify the necessity of an Established Church than the entrance of such wicked men into the Temple of the Lord? Alas! my friend, religion in our country, bereft of the care and protection of the State, and left to the charge of uneducated and often unprincipled men, is, I fear, fast descending into little more than what the poor old Colonel would call, in his thoughtless way *'Experimental Philosophy'*."

XVIII

PARTING SCENE

HAVING accompanied Mr. Slick on board of the "Great Western," and seen every preparation made for the reception and comfort of Mr. Hopewell, we returned to the "Liner's Hotel," and ordered an early dinner. It was a sad and melancholy meal. It was not only the last I should partake of with my American party in England, but in all human probability the last at which we should ever be assembled. After dinner Mr. Slick said, "Squire, you have often given me a good deal of advice, free gratis. Did ever I flare up when you was walkin' it into me? Did you ever see me get mad now, when you spoke to me?"

"Never," I said.

"Guess not," he replied. "I reckon I've seed too much of the world for that. Now don't you go for to git your back up, if I say a word to you at partin'. You won't be offended will you?"

"Certainly not," I said; "I shall be glad to hear whatever you have to say."

"Well then," said he, "I don't jist altogether like the way you throw away your chances. It aint every colonist has a chance, I can tell you, for you are all out of sight and out of mind, and looked down upon from every suckin' subaltern in a marchin' regiment, that hante got but two ideas, one for eatin' and drinkin', and t'other for dressin' and smokin', up to a parliament man, that sais, 'Nova Scotia—what's that? is it a town in Canady, or in Botany Bay?' Yes, it aint often a colonist gits a chance, I can tell you, and especially such a smart one as you have. Now jist see what you do. When the Whigs was in office, you jist turned to and said you didn't like them nor their principles, that they warn't fit to govern this great nation, and so on. That was by the way of curryin' favour, I guess. Well, when the Consarvatives come in, sais you, they are neither chalk nor cheese, I don't like their *changing their name*; they are leetle better nor the Whigs, but not half so good as the Tories. Capital way of makin' friends this, of them that's able and willin' to sarve you, aint it? Well then, if some out-and-out old Tory boys like yourself were to come in, I'll bet you a goose and trimmin's that you'd take the same crotchical course agin. 'Oh!' you'd say, 'I like their principles, but I don't approve of their measures; I respect the party, but not those men in power.' I guess you always will find fault to the eend of the chapter. Why the plague don't you hook on to some party-leader or another, and give 'em a touch of soft sawder; if you don't, take my word for it, you will never be nothin' but a despisable colonist as long as you live. Now use your chances, and don't throw 'em away for nothin'. Bylin' men in power is no way to gain good will, I can tell you."

"My good friend," I said, "you mistake my objects. I assure you I want nothing of those in power. I am all old man, I want neither office in the colony nor promotion out of it. Whatever aspiring hopes I may once have entertained in my earlier and happier days, they have now ceased to delude me. I have nothing to ask. I neither desire them to redress a grievance, (for I know of none in the Colonies so bad as what we occasion ourselves) nor to confer a favour. I have but a few years to live, and probably they will be long enough for me to survive the popularity of my works. I am more than rewarded for the labour I have spent on my books, by the gratification I derive from the knowledge of the good they have effected. But pray don't misunderstand me. If I had any objects in view, I would never condescend to flatter men in power to obtain it. I know not a more contemptible creature than a party hack."

"You are right sir," said Colonel Slick, "flatterin' men in power is no way to git on; take 'em by the horns and throw 'em. Dress yourself as an Indigin, and go to the cutter and throw the tea in the harbour as we did, then fortify the bill at night, as we did—wait till you see the whites of the eyes of the British, and give 'em cold lead for breakfast, as we did. That's your sort, old boy," said he, patting me on the back with heavy blows of the palm of his hand, "that's you, my old 'coon, wait till you see the whites of their eyes."

"Squire," said Mr. Hopewell, "there is one man whose approbation I am most desirous you should have, because if you obtain his, the approbation of the public is sure to follow."

"Whose is that, sir?"

"Your own—respect yourself, and others will respect you. The only man in the world whose esteem is worth having, is one's self. This is the use of conscience—educate it well—take care that it is so instructed that its judgment is not warped by prejudice, blinded by superstition, nor flattered by self-conceit. Appeal to it, then, in all cases, and you will find its decision infallible. I like the course and the tone you have adopted in your works, and now that you have explained your motives, I like them also. Respect yourself—I recommend moderation to you though, Squire,—ultra views are always bad. *In medio tutissimus ibis* is a maxim founded on great good sense, for the errors of intemperate parties are so nearly alike, that, in proverbial philosophy, extremes are said to meet. Nor is it advisable so to express yourself as to make enemies needlessly. It is not imperative always to declare the truth, because it is not always imperative to speak. The rule is this—Never say what you think, unless it be absolutely necessary to do so, if you are to give pain; but on no account ever say what you do not think, either to avoid inflicting pain, to give pleasure, or to effect any object whatever. Truth is sacred. This is a sad parting, Squire; if it shall please God to spare my life, I shall still hope to see you on your return to Nova Scotia; if not, accept my thanks and my blessing. But this country, Squire, I shall certainly never see again. It is a great and glorious country,—I love it,—I love its climate, its constitution, and its church. I admire its noble Queen, its venerable peers, its manly and generous people; I love—"

"Well, I don't know," said the Colonel, "it is a great country in one sense, but then it aint in another. It might be great so far as riches go, but then in size it aint bigger than New York State arter all. It's nothin' a'most on the map. In fact, I doubt its bein' so rich as some folks brag on. Tell you what, 'wilful waste makes woeful want.' There's a great many lazy, idle, extravagant women here, that's a fact. The Park is chock full of 'em all the time, ridin' and gallavantin' about, tricked out in silks and satins a-doin' of nothin'. Every day in the week can't be Thanksgivin' day, nor Independence day nother. 'All play and no work will soon fetch a noble to ninepence, and make bread timber short,' I know, some on 'em ought to be kept to home, or else their homes must be bad taken care of. Who the plague looks after their helps when they are off frolickin'? Who does the presarvin', or makes the pies and apple sarce and dough-nuts? Who does the spinnin', and cardin', and bleachin', or mends their husband's shirts or darns their stockin's? Tell you what, old Eve fell into mischief when she had nothin' to do; and I guess some o' them flauntin' birds, if they was follered and well watched, would be found a-scratchin' up other folks' gardens sometimes. If I had one on 'em I'd cut her wings and keep her inside her own palm, I know. Every hen ought to be kept within hearin' of her own rooster, for fear of the foxes, that's a fact. Then look at the sarvants in gold lace, and broadcloth as fine as their master's; why they never do nothin', but help make a show. They don't work, and they couldn't if they would, it would sp'ile their clothes so. What on airth would be the valy of a thousand such critturs on a farm?—Lord! I'd like to stick a pitchfork in one o' them rascal's hands, and set him to load an ox cart—what a proper lookin' fool he'd be, wouldn't he? It can't last—it don't stand to reason and common sense. And then, arter all, they hante got no Indgin corn here, they can't raise it, nor punkin pies, nor quinces, nor silk-worms, nor nothin'. Then as to their farmin'—Lord! only look at five great elephant-lookin' beasts in one plough, with one great lummakin' feller to hold the handle, and another to carry the whip, and a boy to lead, whose boots has more iron on 'em than the horses' hoofs have, all crawlin' as if they was a-goin' to a funeral. What sort of a way is that to do work? It makes me mad to look at 'em. If there is any airthly clumsy fashion of doin' a thing, that's the way they are sure to git here. They are a benighted, obstinate, bull-headed people, the English, that's a fact, and always was.

"At Bunker Hill, if they had only jist gone round the line of level to the right, instead of chargin' up that steep pitch, they'd a-killed every devil of us, as slick as a whistle. We know'd that at the time; and Dr. Warren, that commanded us, sais, 'Boys,' sais he, 'don't throw up entrenchments there, 'cause that's where they ought to come; but jist take the last place in the world they ought to attack, and there you'll be sure to find 'em, for that's English all over.' Faith! he was right; they came jist to the identical spot we wanted 'em to come to, and they got a taste of our breed that day, that didn't sharpen their appetite much, I guess. Cold lead is a supper that aint easy digested, that's a fact.

"Well, at New Orleans, by all accounts, they did jist the same identical thing. They couldn't do anything right, if they was to try. Give me old Slickville yet, I hante seed its ditto here no where.

"And then as for Constitution, what sort of one is that, where O'Connell snaps his finger in their face, and tells 'em, he don't care a cent for 'em. Its all bunkum, Minister, nothin' but bunkum, Squire," said he, turning to me; "I wont say I aint sorry to part with you, 'cause I am. For a colonist I must say you're a very decent man, but I kinder guess it would have been most as well for Sam if he and you had never met. I don't mean no offence, but he has been idle now a considerable long time, and spent a shockin' sight o' money. I only hope you hante sot him agin work, and made him above his business, that's all. It's great cry and little wool, bein' an Attachy, as they call it. It aint a very profitable business, that's a fact, nor no other trade that costs more nor it comes to. Here's your good health, sir, here's hopin' you may one day dress yourself as an Indgin as I did, go in the night to—"

"Bed," said Mr. Hopewell, rising and squeezing me kindly by the hand, and with some difficulty giving utterance to his usual valediction, "Farewell, my son." Mr. Slick accompanied me to the door of my room, and as we parted, said, "Squire, put this little cigar case into your pocket. It is made out of the black birch log you and I sot down upon when we baited our hosses arter we fust sot eyes on each other, on the Cumberland road in Nova Scotia. When you smoke, use that case, please; it will remind you of the fust time you saw 'Sam Slick the Clockmaker,' and the last day you ever spent with 'The Attache.'"

XIX

VALEDICTORY ADDRESS

GENTLE reader, having taken my leave of Mr. Slick, it is now fit I should take my leave of you. But first, let me entreat you to join with me in the wish that the Attaché may arrive safely at home, and live to enjoy the reputation he has acquired. It would be ungracious, indeed, in me not to express the greatest gratitude to him for the many favours he has conferred upon me, and for the numerous benefits I have incidentally derived from his acquaintance. When he offered his services to accompany me to England, to make me well known to the public, and to give me numerous introductions to persons of distinction, that as a colonist I could not otherwise obtain, I could scarcely restrain a smile at the complacent self-sufficiency of his benevolence; but I am bound to say that that he has more than fulfilled his promise. In all cases but two he has exceeded his own anticipations of advancing me. He has not procured for me the situation of Governor-General of Canada, which as an ambitious man, it was natural he should desire, whilst as a friend it was equally natural that he should overlook my entire unfitness for the office; nor has he procured for me a peerage, which, as an American, it is surprising he should prize so highly, or as a man of good, sound judgment and common sense, not perceive to be more likely to cover an humble man, like me, with ridicule than anything else. For both these disappointments, however, he has one common solution,—English monopoly, English arrogance, and English pride on the one hand, and provincial dependence and colonial helotism on the other.

For myself, I am at a loss to know which to feel most grateful for, that which he has done, or that which he has left undone. To have attained all his objects, where success would have neutralized the effect of all, would, indeed, have been unfortunate; but to succeed in all that was desirable, and to fail only where failure was to be preferred, was the height of good fortune. I am happy to say that on the whole he is no less gratified himself, and that he thinks, at least, I have have been of equal service to him. "It tante every one, Squire," he would often say, "that's as lucky as Johnston and me. He had his Boswell, and I have had my Squire; and if you two hante immortalized both us fellers for ever and a day, it's a pity, that's all. Fact is, I have made you known, and you have made me known, and it's some comfort too, aint it, not to be obliged to keep a dog and do your own barkin'. It tante pleasant to be your own trumpeter always as Kissinkirk, the Prince's bugler found, is it?"

It must not be supposed that I have recorded, like Boswell, all Mr. Slick's conversations. I have selected only such parts as suited my object. Neither the "Clockmaker" nor the "Attaché" were ever designed as books of travels, but to pourtray character—to give practical lessons in morals, and politics—to expose hypocrisy—to uphold the connexion between the parent country and the colonies, to develope the resources of the province, and to enforce the just claims of my countrymen—to discountenance agitation—to strengthen the union between Church and State—and to foster and excite a love for our own form of government, and a preference of it over all others. So many objects necessarily required several continuations of the work, and although seven volumes warn me not to trespass too long on the patience of the public, yet many excluded topics make me feel, with regret, that I have been either too diffuse, or too presumptuous. Prolixity was unavoidable from another cause. In order to attain my objects, I found it expedient so to intermingle humour with the several topics, so as to render subjects attractive that in themselves are generally considered as too deep and dry for general reading. All these matters, however, high and difficult as they are to discuss properly, are exhausted and hackneyed enough. But little that is new can now be said upon them. The only attraction they are susceptible of is the novelty of a new dress. That I have succeeded in rendering them popular by clothing them in the natural language, and illustrating them by the humour of a shrewd and droll man like Mr. Slick, their unprecedented circulation on both sides of the Atlantic, leaves me no room to doubt, while I am daily receiving the most gratifying testimony of the beneficial effects they have produced, and are still producing in the colonies, for whose use they were principally designed. Much as I value the popularity of these works, I value their utility much higher, and of the many benefits that have accrued to myself as the author, and they have been most numerous, none have been so grateful as that of knowing that "they have done good." Under these circumstances I cannot but feel in parting with Mr. Slick that I am separating from a most serviceable friend, and as the public have so often expressed their approbation of him both as a Clockmaker and an Attaché, I am not without hopes, gentle reader, that this regret is mutual. He has often pressed upon me, and at parting renewed in a most urgent manner, his request that I would not yet lay aside my pen. He was pleased to say it was both a popular and a useful one, and that as the greater part of my life had been spent in a colony, it could not be better employed than in recording "*Provincial Recollections, or Sketches of Colonial Life.*"

In his opinion the harvest is most abundant, and needs only a reaper accustomed to the work, to garner up its riches. I think so too, but am not so confident of my ability to execute the task as he is, and still less certain of having the health or the leisure requisite for it.

I indulge the hope, however, at some future day, of at least making the attempt, and if other avocations permit me to complete it, I shall then, gentle reader, have the pleasure of again inviting your attention to my native land, by presenting you with "Sketches of Colonial Life."

THE END

THE END

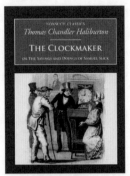

The first series of Sam Slick's 'sayings and doings.' Following his huge success in the pages of *The Novascotian*, Thomas Chandler Haliburton introduced the wry observations and witty opinions of the eponymous Clockmaker to a wider audience with this selection of stories.

ISBN 1 84588 050 1
£10.00
576 pages in 3 volumes

The Romance of the Forest, is the epitome of the Gothic novel: a beautiful, orphaned heiress, a dashing hero, a dissolute, aristocratic villain and a ruined abbey deep in a great forest are combined by the author in a tale of suspense where danger lurks behind every secret trap-door.

ISBN 1 84588 073 0
£6.00
320 pages

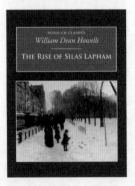

An elegant tale of Boston society and manners, regarded as a subtle classic of its time and written with humour and delicacy. After inheriting his father's business, the eponymous hero moves his family to the sophisticated city of Boston and attempts to break into a world inhabited by wealthy, 'established' families.

ISBN 1 84588 041 2
£6.00
384 pages